DANCING ON THE EDGE
of Moonlight
by

Leandra Simone

Leandra Simone

ISBN: 9781094996578

This is a work of fiction. Names, characters, businesses, places, events and incidents are either the products of the author's imagination or used in a fictitious manner. Any resemblance to actual persons, living or dead, or actual events is purely coincidental.

Front cover image and Book Design by Leland Stein IV

Printed by Amazon, in the United States of America.

First printing edition 2019

IN THE WORDS OF A GREAT PHILOSOPHER:

Love is whatever you want it to be.

Prince

CHAPTER 1

Cara thought for the umpteenth time – how in the hell had her life disintegrated to this - sitting in the fifth row of the practice theatre again instructing Twiddle Dee and Twiddle Dum to re-position the footlights. She might as well have been speaking Chinese, because neither acted as if they understood the words that were coming from her mouth. They continued to giggle and adjust things in every direction except for what she asked.

Her temper was beginning to get the better of her and her tech-niques of counting, breathing and imaging were about to fly out the window. With one last exhale, she again requested the same positioning she had been requesting for the last hour. What good were assistants if they weren't assisting? In truth, they were not her assistants, they belonged to the Creative Director. She was only the Creative Associate. Still, she was the one that did all the stage designs for which the Director took credit.

Again – why was she here?

Oh yeah – out of all her sisters she was the only unmarried, un-attached, childless one. Career oriented, she found herself now as the main provider for their mother.

Raising her voice a little louder than intended, alright a lot louder than appropriate, she slowly reinstructed the non-lis-tening pair. They both immediately stood stock still. Well at least that got their attention. Twiddle Dee – Jeffery or was that Ian, whipped himself around and mumbled something that sounded like he could not work under such circumstances and stomped off. Twiddle Dum, whichever he was, followed suit.

Great, the lights were still not right.

Rising from her seat, gathering all her work paraphernalia, Cara made her way to the stage. Before getting to the first row, all hell broke loose. The Director, who was seldom there, descended onto the stage followed by his twittering assistants. He stopped at center stage. His focus narrowed in on her and he gave a powerful point to the floor in front of him. Apparently that was where she was being summoned. She continued slowly around the aisle and to the side stairs where she gradually made her way up to the stage. There seemed to be a silent hum in the air. Approaching the pre-offered spot, Cara noticed the Twiddles were in a state of pure delight. She supposed she was about to get a read down. It would not be the first nor the last, since everyone she worked with was either a diva or a drama queen. The Director, tapping his foot impatiently, cleared his throat. He adjusted his glasses atop his head and looked to the heavens, or was he looking in the balcony? Everyone else looked up too, except Cara. All this interest in that part of the theater could mean only one thing – Himself was in the house.

'Himself' was an infamous singer/musician/performer. He was known by many things – his name, signs, colors, personas, associations, costumes and a variation of behaviors. Many of his employees called him 'Himself' (behind his back, of course) and it fit because it was very close to Your Highness, Your Majesty, Your Magnificence. Anyone who was all that could easily be condensed into Himself – like no other – just Him. There was also a rumored 'Other'. Supposedly, he was the real person behind the façade of 'Himself', but he was so rarely seen he had breached the mystical and floated into the mythical. It was said he was so aloof, that even the cleaning staff of his residence did not believe he existed. As with all good legends, he was reputed to be courteous, generous and benevolent. How he could be so different from the foul, manipulative control freak of 'Himself' and still be the 'Other' led to suspicions of bipolarism.

Having never had the pleasure of meeting Himself or the Other, or being summoned, or contacted by any of his personal minions in any way, shape, or form in the five years of her employment with his empire, Cara could not muster up the excitement that was currently boiling into a frenzy in her co-workers. Searching for something to say, she was about to begin with 'good afternoon', when the Director jerked to animated life, gave her a scowling look and announced in an Othello stage presence "You're fired!"

The boys behind him gasped. Cara was stunned, but then she believed she misunderstood.

"I beg your pardon?" she questioned.

And now the theatrics really began. The Director advanced to front center stage, passing Cara in the process, and raised his voice as if performing to an audience. "I am tired of your lack of talent, your unprofessionalism and your attitude. You need to pack your shit and get out!"

Cara closed her eyes, took a deep breath and rounded on him with the voracity of a storm. "I know you're not talking to me, you no talented little kiss ass," she hissed, "You have not had an original thought or design since I've been here. You have been using my work and taking all the credit."

"You truly are incompetent and delusional," he sniffed. "If you do not leave now, I will call security."

That last statement brought a thrilling look to his assistants huddled to the side.

"Oh, I'll get out alright and all of you can kiss my big fat black ass," and with that she turned and stomped off the stage.

Cara heard some mumbling behind her, then Jeffrey/Ian-whoever, ran to catch up, "He says to leave your portfolio, its company property."

"The hell I will. You scuttle on back to him and tell him if he wants it, to come and get it."

She walked casually away, but as soon as she turned the first corner, she broke into a run. Arriving at her office she locked the door, took out a flash drive, downloaded her work then wiped her company computer. 'Use that' she thought. Next, she snatched every piece of paper with any type of graphics, layouts or designs and stuffed them into the trash, poured a little acetone nail polish remover on top and lit it with a match. While that was smoldering, she began packing her personal equipment – swatches, pencils, pads, etc. It was then she remembered her self-improvement anger management techniques – wasted. But she did have to admit, she was feeling pretty good. A moment later, the hammering on the door began with a shrill cry of possible smoke. Such dramatics, there was barely a blaze, so she continued packing. The commotion grew louder outside the door. Now she could make out the voices of her ex-coworkers trying to figure out what to do. There was a weak thump, as if someone had thrown themselves on the door, followed by some mewling. At this, she actually stopped and laughed. Apparently security had not been summoned or were very slow in responding because all those big boys could take a door down with little to no effort. To hell with preserving dignity, she cajoled through the door, "You may want to huff and puff and blow the door down." And now it was her turn to giggle.

No sooner had the retort left her lips then there was an astounding crash. The door flew open, rebounded on the wall and swung limply on the shattered doorframe. Cara dropped everything, the items scattering across the floor. Security had arrived.

Brian, at least that was the name on his tag, entered with an extinguisher. The growing crowd attempted to follow but he gave them the 'stop palm' and closed the door which swung haphazardly awry. He walked to the small blaze, shook his head and extinguished it. With the fire gone, Cara lost a lot of her bravado. In fact, the impact of the entire situation suddenly settled upon her. Brian turned to her, "You'll be allowed to finish packing. No more fires. There will be no charges. You have twenty minutes to get done and get out. If you remain on these premises after that, all bets are off." He did an about-face and left, leaving the door open. The crowd had apparently dispersed, there was nothing but silence.

Cara hadn't realized she was trembling. Adrenaline free in the growing silence, she became aware of it and the fact that now her eyes were brimming with tears. She began collecting strewed items. First bending, then eventually getting down on all fours to retrieve things that had rolled under her desk. She was making slow progress, probably because tears were blurring her vision, when she heard a low wolf whistle behind her.

"That is one big fat ass! The things I could do with that!"

Tears or not, Cara immediately snapped back to reality/insanity. She turned abruptly, sitting down on the floor. She was about to read somebody the riot act. Focusing, while blinking back tears, she could not believe her eyes. It was no other than Himself.

She stared at him stunned. He was casually leaning against the busted doorframe, arms crossed staring back at her. And what the hell was he wearing – heels, full makeup and a lacy, ruffled get up with buttons and zippers all askew. She knew this was probably fashionable somewhere in the world but she could not wrap her head around how to describe this hippish, foppish, mishmash. Instead she went back to the wolf whistle, "I'm sorry, did you fall from the rafters and hit your head? We both know you would not know what to do with a big ass let alone a black ass. You of the waifish, exotic looking creatures. The very last thing you'd ever be seen with is a brown skinned, greater than size 2, sister with an attitude. PLEASE. Be gone. I am not in the mood."

He shifted slightly, "You do know I own this building, all the employees in here and everything in the adjacent compound?"

She faked a yawn, "And???? Does that mean I'll be getting my job back?" She had minimal hope in that last statement.

"Now why would I do that?" he taunted. "You don't seem to care too much about ME."

"You're right, I don't," she snapped, but then softened it, "I don't really know you and at this point, you're wasting my time."

He pushed off the doorframe to a standing position. It wasn't a sudden movement but the intensity of it made Cara flinch. Uncrossing his arms, he popped his collar, assumed his classic facial pose – pouty lips, sucked in cheeks and dreamy eyes – and gave an exaggerated sniff, "You're right, you don't know me." Then he was gone.

Cara let out a huge breath that she had not realized she'd been holding, then wondered when she had sucked in all that air. Well, at least he was gone and she could get up off the floor. Thank God she was wearing tights under her skirt and that it was to the knee and not a mini, but who knows what he saw from his view. She hoped it was something visually awful and that it scarred him for life, then laughed. At least she would never have to face him again. Still he had whistled. That just showed how he liked to demean and humiliate people. It was all about Him and what He wanted to do. Finally rising, her thoughts returned to her current situation. It was time to finish packing and get the hell out of Dodge.

Twenty minutes later with one bag on her shoulder and another being pulled along, Cara approached the door and looked into the hallway - empty. She still anticipated being accosted by the Director or his minions, but with the coast clear, she exited stage left. Briskly walking, almost at a small jog, she made her way to the theater's rear exit. So far so good. She thought she heard a sound behind her and so she bounded the last few feet and ran through the door. Unfortunately, the door locked on exiting and she found herself standing in pouring rain.

Running, as well as she could with all her of her paraphernalia, she reached her car. Minus one shoe, which she did not attempt to retrieve, and soaking wet, she found her vehicle on four flats. Throwing everything in the back seat, Cara slammed the door, started the car and the heat, and burst into frustrated tears.

Once she got started she could not control herself and bawled outright with an occasional wail at the top of her lungs for good measure. Who cared? No one could see her since she had fogged up the windows with her uninhibited hullabaloo. Everything ran through her mind: from her firing, to how long she would be able to make rent without a pay check, to who was going to help cover her mother's needs, to could she ask her sisters for assistance, to the unfairness of the whole situation, to which one of her co-workers had flattened all her tires, and lastly to her encounter with Himself and his lack of recognition of her value or her God given beauty. What the hell, maybe she deserved to be just where she was sitting.

Her crying spree tapered down from a roar to a rant to general sniffles. At first, she let the snot and tears run down her face but eventually it became too much, so she attempted to use her sleeve. It was so wet, it smeared everything around so she had to stop and search for something dry. Re-using several old tissues, as well as, a towel from the bottom of the car, Cara finally had to admit she felt better, like a burden had been lifted from her chest. Everything was going to be ok. She had only to get home, get dry and get a plan.

Retrieving her purse from the back, she found her expired auto club card. Great. Next she located her uncharged phone. Wonderful. Pondering what to do next, Cara thought she saw a motion out of her driver's side window. Wiping a small area with the tissue, she saw an approaching black limousine. Oh shit.

Slouching as low as possible while peeking through the steering wheel, she watched as the limo came to a stop in front of her car. Minutes passed and nothing happened. Maybe they were just looking at the flats and calling a tow service. Maybe she was about to catch a break. As far as she was concerned, they could tow her away with the car. Finally the limo drove away. Now all she had to do was wait. Cara let out a breath that again she did not realize she had been holding. She was going to have to watch that. Hypoxia was not a thing she could afford right now.

While closing her eyes and practicing her deep breathing, Cara drifted off to sleep lulled by the sound of the rain. Dreaming.... She had to be dreaming, because it was still raining only now she was in Hawaii with her sister and her family. The kids were splashing around on the grass and her sister was trying to say something to her but she could not make it out over a tapping noise. That's funny, she never realized there were woodpeckers in Hawaii. Wait, were there woodpeckers in Hawaii? The thought jarred her awake. She was then startled again when she realized there was a man standing next to her car tapping on the window.

Cara cracked the window, speaking through the narrow opening she said, "I'm ok, I'm just waiting for a tow," then immediately closed the window. The tapping resumed. She had just reclaimed a small amount of sanity and now someone else was attempting to make her go off the deep end, again. Rapidly rolling the window down, she tersely screeched, "Look, I said I'm okay. Please leave me alone." As she attempted to re-roll her window up, the man stuck a Billy club in the opening. Now she was really mad, not only was she getting wet, she was also getting cold again. The man bent to speak in the space. It was the same security guard from the fire, Brian.

"You are requested to step out of the car."

"I am not getting out of this car," and before Cara could say more, she was interrupted.

"If you do not exit the vehicle, we will be forced to remove you."

At the sound of 'we' and force, Cara began wiping the windows with her tissues and towel and there in front of her car stood a second security guard, as well as, the black limo.

Anybody being forcibly removed from anything could not be a pretty sight, but Cara was sure, in her case, she looked worse. First of all, she did not go willingly in any way shape or form. After they forced her window open and unlocked the door, she clung to everything and everybody she could lay her hands on.

Second, she was still wet and now absorbing another soaking in her transport, between the two guards that had tousled her out, from her car to the limo. Third, she had only been crying the last hour or so. So, besides having puffy eyes and a very red nose, her hair was plastered down in some spots and standing straight up in others. Last but not least, she had lost her other shoe, torn holes in both knees of her tights and her skirt was hiked up to her fanny. Nonetheless, she and her belongings were unceremoniously dumped onto the floor of the limo and the door was immediately shut and locked.

Cara never realized how dark the inside of a limo could be, and why should she, she had never been in one. Scrambling from the floor and attempting to straighten her clothes, she felt her way to the rear seat. She had just settled back, still tugging on her skirt, when she heard a soft chuckle from the front of the car. She squinted into the darkness.

"Your performance was greatly appreciated, but totally unnecessary. I only wanted to offer assistance." And with that the voice clicked on a side light.

To her astonishment it was HIM again, but not as Himself, as the Other.

Cara was dumbfounded, speechless, stunned. She stared into the shadows and he stared back. He was dressed simply in black slacks with a white button-down shirt, exposing the hair on his chest. His face was devoid of make-up and he watched her through dark framed lenses perched on his nose, just above his neatly trimmed mustache. There was no primping or posing and for a minute she actually thought of him as another person. But then she focused in on his glasses and remembered her own and wondered where they might be, probably with her shoes. Then she thought about how clean, calm and dry he looked and how disheveled, disastrous and downright dirty she felt, and she began to develop a slow burn.

It was as if he could read her mind, or maybe he felt the increasing temperature, because he smiled, choking back a laugh and said, "Please, let's not go there."

Again, Cara was thrown off balance. When he smiled, he truly appeared to be someone else. His smile was crooked and kinda goofy looking but there was also a shyness and vulnerability in it. The resemblance between him and Himself was nil to none. Just then, she lost all her steam and thought again about the thin line between sanity and insanity.

CHAPTER 2

It had been a few moments before Cara realized the car was moving. She wondered how long she had been staring at him; wondered if she had had her mouth open the entire time.

It was as if he knew her thoughts again. His smile intensified and he grinned from ear to ear, "I thought maybe you needed a ride home. Maybe something to eat as well," he said quietly. Somehow she never imagined him having such a deep soft voice. Then, she could not believe what he had just said.

"Do I look like somebody ready to go out and eat?" she asked sarcastically.

"No," he replied, "but you do look like someone who's been through a lot and might need someone to talk to."

Touché. Was that his way of telling her she looked like hell? Before she could issue a retort he held up his hand.

"Peace. We will get you shoes and dry clothes and then go for dinner."

Why did he set her so on edge? His statement came off as a command. "I do not need clothes. I need to go home," she huffed.

"That's ok too. We can do take out," he returned.

"What? No! Ok – wait. Apparently I'm missing a piece of this picture. You had your goons drag me out of my car so you could take me to dinner?" she questioned.

"No," he replied looking down, "I tried to have you rescued from an obviously nonfunctioning vehicle in the middle of a storm. I thought since we're sharing the same car, if it wasn't too much to ask, we could also share a meal."

Cara squinted at him. Something wasn't right with his story. "Besides being an errant knight, why would you want to have dinner with me?" she asked.

He gave her a side glance. "Let's just say, what better way to get to know someone. Everybody eats and I think it's time I expanded and explored a new palate."

He rapped on the window behind him sending the car into hyper-speed, but never took his eyes off her. Just before switching off the light, he gave her a questioning eyebrow, then plunged them both into silent darkness. Cara felt a sudden uneasy queasiness in the pit of her stomach.

The limo pulled to a stop in the front of a nondescript unmarked building. Brian got out, pushing a button to the side of the entrance. A light appeared at multiple windows. The Other slid across his seat to the door. "Come on," he said over his shoulder as he departed. Grasping the blanket that had magically appeared around her, Cara followed. Just as she was about to step barefooted from the car, Brian lifted her into his arms. Carrying her and a giant umbrella, she was deposited into an open hallway. Stepping gingerly, she noticed that the floor was warm with radiant heat and wiggled her toes into the sensation.

Following soft scone lighting, she made her way toward distant voices. Passing a mirror, she was aghast. She truly looked like something from 'Night of the Living Dead'. Her hair was helter-skelter all over her head and was beginning to frizz, all of her mascara was under her eyes which were bloodshot and swollen, and her clothes, now damp, were askew. Rampant, rapid raccoon was all she could think and then she remembered she had been sitting across from Him for the last twenty to thirty minutes and he had never said a word. Wait until she caught up with him. Rounding the corner of the last room on the left, she finally found her prey.

He must have seen the look in her eyes because he stepped

forward grabbing the front of her blanket and twisted it into a knot that he held firmly. She was both encased and constrained, and struggle as she might she could not break free. Cara was shocked. She had assumed that although he had a few inches on her, she carried the extra pounds and could easily take him in a rumble, but his strength had been camouflaged in his quiet unassuming manner. He seemed amused at her surprised expression and willfully tightened and loosened the knot, reminding her of what it must feel like to be squeezed by a python. He turned her gently towards the other person in the room.

To say that the man or the room was opulent would be an understatement. He was tall to their shortness, towering over them at 6'2. He was dark with a bald head and dressed magnificently in a red silk grand boubou. The walls were gold brocade with an ivory embossed ceiling dropping crystal chandeliers at integral points. The lighting was subdued but the light reflecting off the crystal and gold created a shimmering delight. "Ah," he began in a deep baritone, "You have been through some things, but I am here for you. I am Kafir." He made a lavish bow. "Let us begin, this way." Turning he glided toward an elaborately embroidered oversize ottoman. On it lay clothing in an array of colors and textures, cashmeres and silks, formal and casual. Stopping in front of a creamed colored linen suit, he turned back to them and said, "I believe this will do nicely." He lifted the suit uncovering delicate lace lingerie beneath, he lifted that too and continued to a door in the far side of the room. Still restricted in her blanket, Cara was maneuvered to its opening. Kafir had switched on the light and was laying the clothes on a glided bench in a beautiful Moroccan style bathroom. "We will leave you to yourself," he said tapping her imprisoner on the shoulder. As the Other relinquished his grip on the blanket, he pivoted silently closing the door behind him.

Half an hour later, Cara emerged, scrubbed fresh faced in her immaculate suit that fit like a glove, her lacy undies and a pair of shoes she'd found in the bathroom. She assumed they were for her because they too fit perfectly. If she didn't know better, she would almost believe they were made for her. But that would be impossible. She was very self-conscious with zero makeup and a pulled back frizzy ponytail. It was the best she could do considering her purse was resting on the floor of the limo. That and the fact that she was wearing lacy matching under things. Her underwear were predominately cotton, or on occasion nylon, and were never matching. There was something to be said for French silk lingerie. The feeling was amazing and it almost felt like a sin to cover it. It was so dainty, so soft and so beautiful, even in her size. Of course, she knew that they knew what she was wearing under her clothes, hence her self-consciousness.

Still, she opened the door and returned to the main room where she found Kafir and the Other in quiet conversation. The Other smiled as she approached. She felt a faint stirring of butterflies. "So Kafir," he said, "You were correct in everything." He then turned to her, "Shall we go?"

"Kafir," she started, "I don't know how to thank you," extending her hand. He grabbed it, brought it to his lips and kissed it softly.

"It has been my pleasure," he cooed. To the Other, clapping him on the back, he said, "See you in Paris." They exchanged handshakes and the door closed. The rain had subsided. A soft warm breeze stirred the night.

The interior of the limo had been cleaned. Cara's things were meticulously stacked to the front of the car. She and the Other settled into the back seat as the car slowly pulled into traffic. She stared out the window watching storefronts and lights blur by. She could feel the intensity of his stare but refused to turn and acknowledge it. The silence grew thickly between them. He murmured something so softly she could not understand. With an exasperated sigh, she turned from the window to face him. "I'm sorry, what did you say?"

"I said, where shall we go for dinner?"

So, they were back to dinner. Cara took a cleansing breath. It wasn't that she was ungrateful, but she never would have gotten soaked again, if she had not been removed from her car and forced into the limo. Before she could respond he grinned at her wickedly, "Surely, you would not begrudge your would-be knight?"

She was overwhelmed and exhausted by everything that had happened. Hazily she thought free ride, free clothes, free meal – what the hell. "Ok" she replied simply.

Expecting some frou-frou restaurant, instead the car glided to a stop in front of an up-scale deli. They were seated and he ordered wine, the exact type she drank. She arched an eyebrow in his direction and pursed her lips, "Why exactly are we here, again? I've caught your knight's tale but there's something not ringing true. We're at a deli, but supposedly you're vegan. You've ordered wine, but you don't drink. You've ordered my wine, but you don't know me. I think this is more about you and the games you like to play with people and less about you helping me!" Having gotten that mouthful out, she took a big gulp of wine. That was one way to finish this farce.

He casually looked up from his menu, "And you received all this information on me from whom?"

"Ok, you're right," she huffed "whispers, rumors, rag mags, whatever. But isn't that the shroud of mystery that you yourself created?"

He gave her a lop-sided smile but remained silent.

Another large sip of wine and she continued, "Who has anything to say about you? You must have a signed censor on everyone or a lot of people are sleeping with the fishes. Because nobody, and I mean nobody, ever gets more than two words out about you or anything associated with you before it's over."

"That's pure speculation," he said quietly and refilled her glass.

"Ok," she retorted, "let's have Reuben's and fries, and please have some wine."

"I ate earlier, so I don't need anything heavy, I'll just have a salad."

"And the wine?" she inquired sweetly.

"I'm nursing a hang-over."

"Liar," she snorted.

"Tell me how you really feel," he grinned.

"Well, I'll tell you what. I'm not going to sit here and gorge myself while you watch and play mind games. I'm out." She took one last swig and started to rise.

"Wait. Please wait," he implored.

"For what?" she questioned poised to depart.

"Just sit down."

"Why?"

"Just because. You have nothing better to do tonight and neither do I."

She sat back down. At least that part was true.

In the growing silence, Cara took a small sip of wine. She was warming up and relaxing all at the same time. She needed to slow down on the wine and keep her wits about her.

"I'm not Himself or the Other," he stated stiffly.

Cara's eyes snapped to his.

"Yeah, I know that's what I'm called," he continued, "I'm just me."

Taking a deep breathe, she exhaled while looking directly at him, "And who are you? Not the megastar or the artist but the man?"

Again the silence.

She thought this conversation was going nowhere fast. It was a labyrinth of unknowns, untruths and misunderstandings. So much for no more wine, she took another sip.

The waiter approached the table. "Reuben with fries, salad and more wine," he ordered.

She lifted both eyebrows in question.

"What?" he responded, "We're going to be here for awhile, this conversation is going nowhere fast."

Cara wasn't sure if it was the wine, or because he had just verbalized her thoughts or both, but she started laughing.

He started laughing too, "Oh, so you thought the same thing too." When they had both stopped laughing, he held out his hand and she shook it, "Nice to meet you," he grinned.

From there the conversation bloomed, haltingly at first, then more freely. They started with her firing and him admitting to being in the theatre and witnessing the whole thing. His comment was, 'Sometimes people need a good booting to get to their next place in life.' Before she could express her outrage, he recounted being booed as an opening act for rock bands. That experience helped him develop his musical style. Their discussion continued with him questioning her about her personal life or lack of it, which brought out questions about his espionage network. How he knew everything about everybody and nobody knew anything about him. He admitted in his line of business, he needed to know who he worked for and who worked for him. "Amen, brotha," she quipped, but he went right back to her current love life.

She felt he was prying into something that truly was none of his business, but before she could give him her heated reply he said, "Come on now, maybe a brotha could help a sista out." And they both started laughing again.

She reneged on her previous thoughts and blabbed her entire story. How her family was close, but she always considered herself the short fat squatty one. Three of her sisters had married

Dancing on the Edge of Moonlight

their high school/college sweethearts and now had kids while her youngest sister was gallivanting in Europe with her hot boyfriend. She, on the other hand, had had the great misfortune of returning to her college dorm room early to find the love of her life with her roommate/best friend. Forswearing love she had focused on her career. A career that had her stuck in stage design when her passion was costume design. The final blow was now she was jobless.

Upon completion of her woeful tale, Cara thought he looked like the cat that had swallowed the canary. So, just to take him down a notch, she gave him her readings on him. Most definitely it was the wine. She told him the only reason he was currently having dinner with her was because he was lonely and bored. That even though he had all the money in the world, he made bad choices, picking superficially beautiful women who cared a lot more about his money and status then they did about him. He quietly tensed and she thought he was about to explode when he said, "Damn girl, why you gotta be so hard on a brotha?" They both broke out laughing to tears.

And so the night continued. He had more brotha/sista one-liners than she had ever heard. He was quick witted with a wicked sense of humor. Try as she might, she could never knock him off balance or get a rise out of him and though she hated to admit it, she was enjoying herself.

Hours later, after they had dissected political rhetoric, re-examined philosophical themes, argued over geographic and historical importance of everything and then basically re-defined the meaning of life, the night finally came to an end. There was a small riff about taking home the leftovers she had packed up, but after some debate which included starving children in China, a compromise was reached and his security went back into the restaurant to retrieve them. Filled with food, wine and great conversation Cara tried not to fall asleep. Having already provided her address, she busied herself gathering her things in anticipation of her departure.

21

"I hate to admit it, but I had a really good time. Thank you," she said to the figure again hidden in the shadows.

"I know," came the reply.

"Modest as ever," she returned.

"Always." Then silence, only now it was a comfortable quiet. There was really no need for noise, satiation was enough.

The limo came to a slow stop in front of a storefront.

"Why would I not have guessed you lived in an antique store?" he chuckled.

"OMG!" she exclaimed, "your network must be slipping, apparently you don't know everything."

He insisted on walking her to her door. She did not complain, she had a lot to carry. She was surprised he was helping and not passing the errand on to his bodyguards. Half way up the flight of stairs he let out an exaggerated breath, "Damn girl, you must be tryin' to kill a brotha." Their laughter echoed throughout the hallway and they were still laughing when they made it to the top and to her door.

Cara fumbled with her keys, unlocked the door and turned to say good night. He was standing directly behind her. Since she had not opened the door, there was nowhere to go and although he did not touch her, she could feel the heat of his body and his warm breath just inches away.

"Can a brotha get a kiss good night?" he whispered. And before she could object, he kissed her softly on the lips.

He leaned into her sandwiching her body against his and the closed door. His kiss deepened and an arm slipped behind her back drawing her closer. Cara heard a low moan. Was that coming from her? And when had her arms encircled his neck? Trying to answer those questions, as well as, keep her body from responding was becoming a daunting task. She brought her hands down to his chest to push him away but somehow her fingers became entangled in his chest hair. It was much softer than she would have imagined and she could feel the hammering of his heart. Just then he broke the kiss but started a trail of butter-fly kisses toward her ear and then down her neck. She felt her knees get weak. Oh Lord, had his spy team been studying her erogenous zones too? This time she did moan and it was answered with a husky purr just south of her right ear.

Cara felt the door open behind her. The next thing she knew, they were in her living room and they were missing their shirts. That was shocking, but the feel of his hair and hands were both distracting and amazing. She was losing ground in this battle not to succumb or was the war already over? Confounded by thoughts and sensations, her next realization was they were both naked in bed. It was now or never. Gathering her wits about her Cara stayed all his activities.

"What are you doing?" she stammered.

"I'm showing you what a brotha can do with your big fat black ass," he growled softly, then entered her, making love to her gently.

Later in round two, things got a little rough. He flipped her over and entering her from behind, plunged deeply. Gripping first her shoulders and then her hair he rode her relentlessly. Just when Cara thought she could take no more, he yanked her hair and said, "What's my name?" She resisted saying it. This was classic bullshit. He slapped her on the butt, "I said, 'what's my name?'" Now she was pissed and attempted to buck him off, but he grabbed her by both shoulders again and plunged deeper still.

"Don't make me say it again,"

And as they both climaxed she yelled it out, "Julian.......Julian Starr."

CHAPTER 3

Julian Aristo Starr was born into an unhappy family. His father was an auto worker who wanted to be a musician, while his mother was a housewife that dreamed of being a movie star. Both felt trapped and blamed their inadequacies on each other. Into this brew came their one and only baby boy. They loved him as best they could. His father on swing shift, took time before leaving each day to play music for him or with him. His mother, who could not be bothered cooking or cleaning because she was studying her craft, at least kept him clean and dry and filled with plenty of milk. As he grew he remained on the small side. His father would say his long narrow fingers were good for reaching octaves on the piano. His mother called him her little pipsqueak. All was well, as far as he was concerned, until he turned five. It was then that he overheard his mother crying and telling a friend that his father had other children. At first, he was very excited to have brothers or sisters because he was an only child and that sucked. He waited for them to appear and after a while of nothingness, he asked his mother about them. She backhanded him across the mouth. The following day when his father asked how he got a busted lip, he told him what had happened. His father attacked his mother, first verbally then physically. As they fought throwing punches and household items, Julian hid under the kitchen table. Eventually his father stormed out slamming the front door. His mother came into the kitchen, she was missing a shoe and the ends of her dress were torn. She did not bend to retrieve him or try to comfort him, instead she said, "This is all your fault. See what you've done?" Then she shuffled to her room and closed the door. He remained under the table, falling asleep. When his father staggered home later that night he found him and put him in bed. After a few days things went back to normal and he became her pipsqueak again, but he never forgot that backhand.

Julian was about nine when he realized he was smaller than the other boys. With that realization he began to hate his pipsqueak moniker. He harnessed his anger and rage into a chip for his shoulder and honed his skills in everything he touched. In fighting he became a force no one wanted to mess with, in basketball although short, he was as fast as lightening and with his music he persevered. His parents' conflict continued to grow making his father stay away longer and longer while his mother developed a social life of going out with friends. The following year his parents separated. He remained at home with his mother who was 'out' every evening. He had had a few recalcitrant friends over but soon grew bored. Eventually he made his way to the basement and rediscovered his father's instruments. It was there he found his passion. He could create music. He also recognized that music could control people. It could make them feel good or bad, happy or sad, rowdy or peaceful. At night, he spent more and more of his time downstairs, alone with his music. By the time he turned twelve his mother had had a number of 'uncles' move in and out of the house. Julian was only allowed to stay with his father on weekends, which still left him alone at night, just in a different residence. He and his father did spend time together before his father had to go off, and that time was always spent over music. They'd have impromptu jam sessions, review and edit each other's sheet music and occasionally go over lyrics. Those became some of the happiest moments of his life.

The summer before starting high school his mother married Uncle Johnnie. Johnnie had been attempting to establish a relationship with Julian until they said 'I do'. Once he was officially in, he dropped the act and got down to the business of ordering Julian around. He was expected to cook, clean and get

a part time job to pay for his keep. By the second semester of
his freshman year, he had moved out and permanently in with
his dad. That lasted until his sophomore year, at which time
his dad finally caught a piece of his dream. He hit the road with
his band, leaving Julian to fin for himself in their apartment. It
was during this time he learned how pliable girls could be. Although he could not attract the beautiful ones, they required
cars and money for dates as well as titles: class president, quar-
terback, team captain, he found many willing participants who
were interested in extra-curricular activities in exchange for
attention, a meal or a song. Within three months, unable to
maintain the rent, he was evicted. He spent the remainder of
his sophomore year living in friends' basements and when push
came to shove on the streets. He dropped out half way through
his junior year. Hopping a bus to L.A., it was time to make his
dreams come true or die trying.

Hollywood and Vine had accumulated years of runaways, actors
and musicians. Julian became just another one, but he was not
about to be eaten up by those streets. He took all his talents and
put them to work as never before. Starting as a dishwasher, he
could afford to rent a room which he then charged his 'friends'
to sleep in, filling it nightly to capacity. He parlayed that money
into studio time, laying tracks. His next gig was as a waiter serving drinks in a thong, in an 'exclusive' club deep in Laurel Canyon. Initially he had been reluctant, but the friend that turned
him on to it assured him 'nobody had time for his skinny ass.'

Besides the thong, his required uniform included a mask and
the house rules included no fraternizing with the patrons. Julian found the experience liberating. The members also wore
masks, and little else. He assumed the anonymity of the situation broke down people's inhibitions, because the things he
saw became the fodder of future music, lyrics and stage behaviors. Even though fraternizing was frowned upon, who could
possibly keep up with it in the middle of Sodom and Gomorrah?
Julian turned a handsome profit in tips and fees for services ren-

dered to his female benefactors. He also had to kick a lot of ass, as the males in the house seemed to think him a possible conquest too. Thanks to the mask and the lighting, he was never identified as the perpetrator that had to put some M.F. in his place.

It was through this job that he met a contact that would get him into the legendary Mansion. A customer, extremely pleased with his services, suggested he meet her at a party there later that night. She provided the address and the golden token required for entrance. He never found her, in truth, he never even looked for her. Once inside, he worked the room like a three dollar whore and by morning he had made numerous acquaintances. He followed up with every single one, demo in hand, and by the end of the month he signed his first record contract.

The music industry is fickle at best, but Julian took all his life lessons and attacked it before it could get the best of him. During his street days in Hollywood he had used several aliases, J., Star Child, Ari. Now he reverted back to his God given name Julian Aristo Starr. In his initial gigs opening for rock bands, he was Julian Starr or Aristo Starr, but as his popularity and music continued to expand, he dropped all the excess baggage and became Aristo.

He found early on control was the name of the game. He knew plenty of musicians who had made it big but died penniless. He had no intention of being one of them. He wrestled the reigns from record executives, agents and financial consultants and in the end was able to call his own shots.

Because he avoided interviews, the press seemed to make up stories to fill in the gaps. It became easy to go with the flow. The more the reports grew, the quieter he became until he was one huge mystery man. Of course, he manipulated the media, planting pieces of information here and there, and true to any good journalist, they followed each and every lead. In the end, he was supposedly a self-made man from a biracial couple, with siblings he had lost contact with and a varied sexual ambiguity. He played heavily on the latter. After all, sex sells and he had a lot of selling to do.

His first album went platinum, the next two diamond. His concerts sold out worldwide. He won multiple awards but seldom attended to receive them. If he graced them with his appearance and a performance, it was usually so outrageous that he was not invited to attend the following year due to censor issues.

Women were at his beck and call. His associations with beautiful actresses, models, songstresses, au jeunes, rising stars and wannabe's were renowned. There were no lingering relationships, however, even with multiple marriages. The women were always expendable, they came and they went. He learned he had passive aggressive tendencies while under court ordered therapy. He never hit a woman, but would admit to a few hard shakes and a shove here and there. In one case, he had been driving while arguing with one of his madams. She had become overly aggressive, both verbally and physically. It wasn't his fault that she had not been wearing her seat belt when he hit the brakes. In court, she had maintained he had purposely tried to maim her. His side argued he hit the brakes to avoid a pedestrian. Since she wound up under the dashboard with a broken nose, she could not bear witness that there had or had not been someone crossing the street. The case was closed and would be expunged if he completed the therapy ordered by a suspicious judge. She was generously paid off.

Julian learned a lot from that situation: hire a driver, keep your hands and inanimate objects to yourself and generosity kills the cat. He had a greater understanding of himself too. Having grown up with a mother that was slightly neglectful and abusive, made him less tolerant of female antics. He preferred his women beautiful but quiet, enticing but obedient, flexible and open to manipulation. That all fell in line with the passive-aggressive thing, but in the end he did not see much wrong with it. He had a very simple rule, if you want to be with me, you do as I say. Given his net worth, there was never a lack of willing participants.

As time passed, Julian became the enigma he created. He returned to his hometown, created his own compound with multiple recording studios and established his own label. He collected women, cars, international homes and the respect and admiration of the world. Often, late at night or early in the pre-dawn of morning, he would roam his multi-thousand square foot homes. Contemplating lyrics, melodies, contracts or sometimes life, every now and then despite everything, he would feel once again like the little boy under the table, alone.

CHAPTER 4

Cara awoke with a start and a bad headache over her right eye. That was one hell of a nightmare. She slowly arose from her bed, groggily wondering why she was so stiff. While wobbling towards the bathroom she realized she was nude. Her headache spread to the other eye. Veering off her current path, she went into the living room. She found herself horrified. There were clothes, mostly hers, flung everywhere but most upsetting was the pair of a man's purple briefs lavishly spread upon the mantel. She squeezed her temples between both hands. It had not been a nightmare. She had lost her job, her car and her mind all in one night. The job and the car were replaceable, but a mind was a terrible thing to waste. Apparently, the wine had done most of the thinking, but still. She was totally disgusted with herself. She had never had a one night stand. She had barely had boyfriends, one unofficial attempt in high school and then that college lug. She was always a high academic achiever, so after that, she kicked into high drive completing her undergraduate degree in three years and her post-graduate degree in another two. She had dated off and on, but found that men in general had very short attention spans. Once they finished talking about themselves, they became preoccupied with the menu, the bar or the other women in the nearby vicinity. They also had very narrow bands of interest: sports, sex, food, sex, other women, sex, and more sex. She had yet to meet one that could maintain eye contact, a conversation or a thought long enough to develop a relationship.

Maybe that was it. She was deprived, maybe even depraved.

That would certainly explain her actions. Succumbing to a man she had just met, was trying hard not to like, who had an alter ego she could not stand. Cara returned to her room for a robe. Seeing the bed brought back memories of their scandalous behavior. There was a possibility that she would never complete the penance required to cover those activities. Bracing herself, she began cleaning up the mess. Somewhere between disposing of the purple peccadillo, discovering the remains of her precious French panties and devouring cup upon cup of coffee, Cara realized she had not run across any evidence of used protection. She panicked. Dumping every trash can and searching under every piece of furniture, she found nothing. The consumed coffee commenced gurgling in her stomach. Stay calm, deep breathe, and be rational. As far as she knew Julian, the Other, Himself – the entire trinity combined – had never fathered any kids and that included in the confines of multiple marriages. There was a great possibility that he was infertile, either by choice or circumstance. Small cleansing breath. He would never put himself at risk for STD's, let alone stray children. She may not know his precise plan of protection but she was sure he had one in place. Men like him did not rise to such heights without careful consideration of everything. She would wager that somewhere in her 'file' was her status, blood type and possibly her last PAP smear results. Bigger cleansing breath. If push came to shove, she could always go to the doctor for a checkup and a morning after treatment. Big exhale. Having cleaned her apartment and slightly settled a bubbling belly, Cara thought she deserved a break. She laid back down in the bed and promptly fell asleep.

Awakening to what she thought was early evening, Cara found she had actually slept through the night and was now encountering a new morning. Feeling great, she bounded out of bed to get started on setting things right: coffee, then to-do list, then out the door to get them done. She stopped short finding her car at the front curb with four functioning tires. She gingerly retrieved her keys from the bottom of her purse and thought, that's the least he could do. She was a new woman on a new mission and would not be deterred.

Cara accomplished her list and had time to squeeze in a 'catch-up' lunch with her girls. She received lots of support on her job loss, but stayed tight lipped about the other night's antics. Cara felt revived, like she could whip the world. Balancing packing boxes and groceries, she staggered down her hallway. Someone was spinning her jam, while the smell of something delicious was making her mouth water. She fumbled with her front door key trying hard not to drop anything. Finally, it opened.

In the kitchen stood Julian, stirring a pot and grinning like a fool. She dropped everything, vaulted into the room and angrily approached him.

"What are you doing in my apartment?"

"Cooking."

"You know that's not what I mean. How did you get in here?"

"You gave me a key last night."

"I most certainly did not. I only have one extra key and it's on my key ring."

"Is it?"

She looked at her keys, it was missing.

"You son of a bitch, you stole my key?"

"Did I?"

"You know you did and if you say 'Do I?' I'll jump this counter and beat the shit out of you!"

"Will you?"

Dammit this conversation was going nowhere, she was developing a massive headache and all her earlier bravado was slipping away.

"Please…" she started again, but before she could finish he came around the counter, handed her a glass of wine, pushed her gently down on the couch and took off her shoes while lifting her feet onto the coffee table. He then began gathering all the stuff she had dropped. This was better than counting to ten. Forgetting her resolve never to drink again, she sipped the wine. She was still angry that he had invaded her home without permission, but he seemed completely oblivious to her irritation. She had made it through the day with the thought that she would never have to face him again and here he was. Now what? She was practicing her mother's idiom – if you can't say something nice, keep your mouth shut – because in her head were a string of foul words aimed straight at her uninvited guest.

Julian, for his part, was enjoying himself immensely. He watched her steaming on the couch. He took his time arranging the boxes against the wall, rounded up the groceries then closing the door returned to the kitchen and stirred his pots. Just to push her over the edge he began putting away the groceries. It had the impact he expected. Cara jumped off the couch and charged into the kitchen. It was the perfect trap and she fell right into it. As soon as she got within arms' reach he grabbed her and pinned her to the fridge. Before she could let out the string of obscenities she had been working on, he planted his lips on hers. That brought out a fevered mumbled response but he persevered pushing his body onto hers and as he expected the tide soon turned and she melted into his arms.

A couple of hours later they were back at the table, she in her robe and he in his slightly ruffled attire. Cara was in a better mood and Julian was still grinning. She looked up between bites, "You didn't make this," she said emphatically.

"Sure I did."

"I thought you only ate rose petals, so how could you make quiche?"

"That's the other guy," he quipped.

"The other you or another person entirely?"

He kicked her under the table and retorted, "You know good and well the rose man would not be doing what we just did."

Cara blushed.

"I never thought I'd see it. A woman with the ability and the audacity to still be able to blush," he teased.

"What are you saying?" she challenged, "You didn't know black people could blush?"

"Au contraire," he countered, "obviously you're blushing." Her color intensified, she felt her cheeks burning. He continued, "In my life I have yet to come across a woman who lacked the experiences, the wantonness or the inhibition required for blushing. In other words, I've run with a pretty promiscuous crowd. You my dear, are a breath of fresh air that I intend to contaminate as quickly as possible." And he slid his foot up the inside of her leg toward her crotch.

Cara gasped, dislodged his foot and tightened her robe around her.

"A little late for that, isn't it?" he laughed.

She got up from the table, removed her plate and his too. She couldn't stand him or herself for that matter. All that encouraging self-talk earlier had done nothing with his reappearance. She could not even blame the wine. He aggravated and enticed her both at the same time. She had no clue what she was going to do. Cara fiddled with the dishes: rinsing, stacking, rearranging, and shuffling. Attempting to avoid going back to her chair. "You'll never fit into that garbage disposal," he called. She snapped the dishtowel she had been refolding for the fourth time and stomped into the room.

Easy, he thought, too easy. Again, he snatched her as she neared pulling her into his lap and kissing her into submission. She did not even struggle this time. I'm a sucker, Cara thought.

"You're in luck," he announced, standing suddenly and dropping her to the floor, "I have to go." He stepped over her, walked to the door and left. Just before closing the door completely, he reopened it and said, "Oh, I forgot to say goodnight. Goodnight." And he shut the door tight. Two seconds later, there was a loud crash and the shattering of splintering glass followed by a muffled shout. He laughed quietly as he strolled down the hall.

Cara was losing her mind. She wanted to pack up and get out of town as quick as possible, but she was dragging her feet. She did not want to see Julian again, but was disappointed anytime she came home and he was not there. It had been a week since their last encounter. Since neither provided the other with phone numbers, there was no way to predict his next breaking and entering episode. There was also the strong possible that he would never come again. He had that toying thing down to perfection, not so dissimilar to Himself. She had an involuntary shudder. She needed to get out - now. The plan had been to return home to her mother's. If she stopped procrastinating and finished packing, she could be gone and then she would never know if he returned or not. If he did, it would serve him right. That thought sent Cara into hyper-drive. She started in the kitchen, finishing quickly, then polished off the bathroom. She was in her jammies working on the bedroom, when there was a knock at the door. Figuring it was a neighbor, dressed in lounge pants and a t-shirt, she opened the door.

Julian stood on the other side with flowers and take-out. Cara attempted to slam the door, but his foot was already in it.

"First of all, that's no way to act," he started, "and secondly, we need to work on your sleeping attire."

She pushed harder against the door. She heard him laughing then the flowers were pushed through the narrowing opening. Cara loved flowers, but resisted reaching for them. Still, she leaned in a little just for a peek. The flowers hit her flush in the face, sputtering she lost her grip on the door. Julian came in closing and locking it behind him.

"That is no way to treat company," he smirked.

Although she was fuming, she did not rush forward. This time she took a step back.

"Ah, I see you have a touch of Pavlov going on."

She smiled sweetly but kept a piece of furniture between them. He walked casually to the kitchen but did not turn his back on her. Once he set everything down it became a stalemate. They both remained silent, neither moving, just staring. Cara finally blinked. It was as if he took that as a sign of surrender because he began unpacking the food.

She sighed, "This has got to stop."

"What?"

"This. This. Whatever this is. I don't want to do it anymore."

He stopped in mid-reach, "Have I done something to you? Hurt you? Offended you in some way?"

"No."

"Then why?

"Look I don't know what this is. It feels good but it also feels bad. You're here, you're not. You come, you go. You never call, you just show up."

"Would you feel better if I called?"

"Would you call?"

"No."

"Then what are we talking about?"

"Why does this have to have borders, terms, rules of engagement? Why can't we just do what we've been doing? Why do you have to feel bad? Is it because this is not the 'norm'?"

Cara stopped. Why did she feel bad? Obviously, she did not feel bad enough to escape. She could have been gone weeks ago, yet she lingered. The good must have outweighed the bad, and his coming and going really did not bother her. She was very self-entertaining and had tons of work to do. If he showed up, it was a pleasant surprise. If not, she just went on with her life. Maybe he was right. Maybe, it was because it was not the norm: I'll call you, you call me, we'll date, and we'll mate. She'd done that already and the outcome had not gone well. Why not try something different?

Julian was still standing there, mid–reach into the bag, watching her pondering her thoughts.

"Ok," she sighed.

He let out a big breath and came to her encircling her in his arms. "I'll tell you what," he whispered. She hated when he whispered, especially if it was close to her ears or neck, it gave her goosebumps.

"Let's have a date night," he smiled.

"Date night?" she questioned.

"Yeah, you know, dinner and a movie. No hanky-panky involved." He licked her neck then turned back to the kitchen.

"You know you are not right," she squeaked grabbing her neck.

"Ah, ah, ah, no rules," he chided. "Now find a movie."

Muttering, Cara approached her DVD collection and began calling out titles. Twenty movies into the process, he came over and viewed the choices for himself. Half an hour later they settled on Jurassic Park. There was a brief exchange of snide comments about film choices and what that said about a person, as well as, who was going to heat their food first in the microwave. That was followed by a discussion of the dangers of heating food with electromagnetic radiation, which sequenced into who was sitting where and why eminent domain should be applied. Once the movie started there was a brief interlude of quiet and tranquility, but once the meal was done the conversation veered toward the potential of genetic engineering and the reality of the current level of progress and so to prove points and win debates, laptops, encyclopedias and a few lifelines were employed. At the end of the evening, which was actually early morning, true to his word, Julian kissed her goodnight and left. Turning back to a room of scattered books, movies piled on various surfaces and a clutter of glasses and dishes on tabletops, Cara sighed. If this was the residual of 'the norm', she might have to rethink the situation.

Their association continued. Time together could be spent in wild sexual pursuits, date nights and/or, the newly established, quiet time. Cara felt remiss in calling it a relationship. Her opinion on the matter varied with her moods. On bad days, it was just a series of random booty calls and on good days, it was a social experiment on sexual liberation. Both came and went as they pleased and never did exchange phone numbers. While she tried to keep to a work schedule, there was no rhyme or reasons to his comings or goings. She neither expected nor relied on him. It was quite liberating. She had unpacked her work supplies, again, and began submitting costume designs to local venues, as well as, national projects. She did eventually get around to telling her sisters about her job loss and although they poo-pooed her decision to remain where she was a little longer, no one had much of a say in the matter since she was financially independent. Her six figure salary had been squirreled away the last five years. Her rent was minimal (there was an advantage to living over a store), her utilities were included (ditto) and while she did pay for her mother's companion care, it was provided by a family member that received nominal compensation in exchange for free room and board. For once she was free to do what her heart desired: costuming.

Cara spent hours in the fabric district milling through bolts for swatches. Sometimes she had specific projects with historical specifications and other times she was just perusing the goods. On rare occasions, Julian would come too. He'd just show up as she was on her way out and would invite himself along. At first, she was affronted because she had no place in his life, so why was he burrowing into hers? But he always had a way of weaseling in around her. He'd offer his car, pick up the tab or throw in a meal. His disguise in place, they browsed for hours. She hated to admit it, but he had a great eye and exquisite taste. She did not want to, but she started enjoying those times too.

Since there were no time indicators on either of them or their activities, it took a while before Cara realized that Julian had not been by. She actually had to think back, find receipts of what she had been doing, then go to a calendar to calculate the time. She was shocked, it had been over a month.

CHAPTER 5

Julian flew to Paris Fashion Week in his private jet. He had his entourage which included his standard bevy of beauties, as well as, personal assistants and body guards. Although there was a cacophony of excitement and commotion about him, he remained focused on the project at hand. Wearing enormous headphones he replayed melodies, wrote lyrics and arranged the background music in his latest endeavors. Everyone knew not to disturb him, so he remained a reticent isolated recluse in the midst of a populace of elation.

Landing at the Charles de Gaulle Airport, he was whisked to his Chateaux, a replica of Chateau de Malmaison, which he had built, personally supervising its interior design. Everyone drifted to their assigned quarters, he to his grand suites in the massive north wing. He occupied both floors and no one bothered him there unless summoned.

Travel did not particularly tire him, so he wandered throughout his rooms eventually arriving to his studio. He reworked some of his earlier compositions and because he remained restless he picked up the phone to call over some of his girls. They arrived dressed for success, lingerie, fantasy costumes and a few in nothing at all. He had pre-ordered a stocked bar, on his signal, they indulged. Getting comfortable he awaited the festivities. This was his assembly. A gathering of beautiful women, all handpicked for their height, how they looked in clothes, as well as, without them, how they handled themselves and most of all, for their deference to him. He had a vast menagerie of them, from different countries, cultures, with certain features and hair lengths, some with identical copies of themselves. It was amazing what you could collect when you had money: cars, houses, even people. As beautiful as they were, they all responded on the drop of a dime, day or night, without any kind of previous notification. They would arrive packed and dressed for whatever the invite indicated. They need only have a clean bill of health and pass a stringent medical exam before boarding the plane. A few had failed in previous years, they had been permanently deleted from the list.

Tonight, he was unimpressed with their antics. Part of his rules was that no one approached or touched him until he motioned for them. Dancing, rubbing, posing, acrobatics, even some coupling with each other were all occurring in front of him, but it was tedious at best. Maybe he had seen so much of it in the past it was no longer electrifying; maybe he really was tired. After a few hours he dismissed them all, some lingered in a continued attempt to entice him but he put those stragglers out too. The silent understanding was they could have all the fun they wanted with each other, but fraternizing with anyone on the staff or with anyone other than him while on a trip, was also terms for permanent termination. His rules were outrageous but if you wanted to play you abided by them. Apparently a lot of people wanted to play.

Julian went down to his private garage and pulled out in the steel gray Grand Sport Vitesse. What he needed was air. Night air to be precise, to help clear his mind. He was sufficiently outside the city proper to apply the speed that thrilled him, so he veered towards Orleans.

Top down, the wind whipped his hair and face. It was a nice night to be alive, especially nice if you were living his life, which he was. He wallowed in his vast fortune, his unprecedented accomplishments and his magnificent possessions. Time was inconsequential so he roamed on and on into the night. Just before dawn he stopped at a small café. Seating himself outside in the early morning chill, he had warm croissants fresh from the oven. His mind somewhat clearer, and with fatigue closing in, he headed for home. It had been a very long day and one hell of a long night. Slowly climbing the stairs and upon entering his room he began dropping his garments on the floor as he progressed toward the bed. Reaching it, he climbed in enjoying the cool soft sheets on his skin. Just before drifting off he wondered if 'she' had ever been to Paris. He dreamed of all the contentious conversations Europe would invoke. The thought roused him. Where had that come from? He would not be caught dead in her company. He had standards of appearance she could never reach. He slept fitfully after that, experiencing sporadic moments of pure joy replaying their times together and anticipating the times to come. He was still bewildered to find he enjoyed her curves. She was a cloud of warmth and softness that enveloped him to his core. He had relished her seduction but had become entangled with his conquest. He had to force himself to stay away. She was untried on so many sexual levels that the anticipation and challenge of taking her there was exhilarating. She was the opposite of his regular girls. She always had something to say and he had to joust her for the last word, but he found their conversations provocative, intriguing and sometimes downright blasphemous. As much as she could talk she could be quiet too and in those moments he found a peaceful reserve.

Julian awoke from a restless night with a sensation tantamount to a hang-over. He wore such a scowl that his entire entourage avoided him like the plague. It was a known fact that people had been eliminated for not recognizing the danger in approaching him when he was in one of his moods. His girls tiptoed around his perimeter inducing a deeper scowl as he regarded their thinness and a need for a meal. He gave up on human contact, locking himself in his studio. A collective sigh of relief was had by everyone left behind.

Music was Julian's solace, his constant companion and truthfully the love of his life. She was the one thing he could always count on. He took his confusion and melancholy to her. He wrote for hours frequently changing instruments, going from piano to guitar and when he was finished he had lyrics about a misplaced sexual connection with an unobtainable curvy brown girl. Rather than make the melody soft and slow he created an upbeat scherzando with an under tone and back beat in tenerezza. When he exited, his mood had improved. He took a nap, a long bath and prepared for the first of many fashion outings.

Hassani Kafir had been showing in Paris' fashion week for over five years. His collections drew the rich and the famous, from royalty to celebrities, old money, new money, big money. Space was at a premium so seating was by invitation only. This was Julian's final show, he had been in France for a month. The show was impeccable as always. He and Kafir met afterward at the private gala. Sitting in an exclusive area away from the bedlam of the party, they conversed.

Kafir, glowing with the success of his genius, began, "So tell me, how's the girl?"

Leave it to Kafir to jump in feet first. His show was so marvelous it was pointless to ask if you appreciated it, that was a given.

Julian smiled, "What girl do you mean? I have many girls."

"Don't play coy with me. You know who I mean, that beautiful brown thing you brought me to dress. I'm going to assume the outfit did the trick."

"Let's just say it came off as beautifully as it went on."

"And?" Kafir inquired.

"And what?" Julian countered, "You know me. I hit it and quit it."

Kafir watched Julian quietly. Something wasn't right. Something was different. "The reason we have gotten along so fabulously all these years is because we don't bullshit each other. I believe you when you say you hit it, you've been a dog for a while, but there's something not valid with the rest of the statement."

Julian had known Kafir since his first album. He had been a new hot designer, Julian's favorite by far. He helped establish his look, his identity, his flare. Over the years their working relationship had grown into a close friendship. Kafir was correct in claiming to be a no bull-shitter, he would call a spade a spade in a minute and let the cards fall where they may.

Julian silently took a slow sip from his glass. Kafir continued to watch him closely then smiled grandly and chuckled, "Ah my boy, don't tell me you've been sprung. Mm-hmm the power of a black woman's je ne sais quoi. Come, come, your reticence is very damning. Speak, and let not feathers fall from your mouth."

Julian grinned, "Really Kafir, feathers from my mouth? Where did you get that one from?"

"I made it up just now to get you to speak."

"Ok, ok. Some of what you say is true and some is false."

"Mm-hmm," Kafir inferred awaiting further explanation.

"I am quietly seeing her occasionally on the side," Julian finally admitted.

"On the side of what?"

"On the side of whatever else I'm doing," Julian snapped.

Kafir peered closely at Julian. In all the years they'd known each other, behind late deadlines, unfinished fittings and lost costumes, he had never seen Julian lose his composure. This was interesting indeed.

"Very well," Kafir quipped rising, "if you will excuse me, I have other guess to attend to."

"Kafir, wait. I'm sorry. Sometimes when you play with fire you get burned. I'm singed."

Kafir called a waiter for refills, resituated himself and waited.

Julian started again, "You know I do whatever I want, whenever I want. This time is no different."

"I beg to differ," Kafir inferred, "this is totally different."

"Kafir, please. I have no idea what's happening. She's impossible. She's stubborn as hell, doesn't listen, won't follow instructions and seldom stops talking. To top it all off, she has an open irreverence of me!"

Sounds perfect, Kafir thought to himself. Out loud he said, "How's the sex?"

"Phenomenal."

"Just booty calls, right?"

"Not always."

"Ah, so the real story begins."

"Kafir....."

"Unburden yourself, my son."

"Really?"

"Yes, really."

"Ok, we've had date nights: dinner and a movie, no sex."

Kafir choked on his drink, spattering liquid everywhere as he laughed.

"You promised not to laugh."

"I promised no such thing. Everything sounds ducky, why the long puss?"

"Because. You've seen her. What am I to do with the likes of her? She will never fit the bill in my life."

"Then why go back?"

"Because I can't stay away."

"You, my friend have a problem and I suggest you tread very carefully for your sake, as well as, hers."

CHAPTER 6

Cara had finished packing everything but her TV and bed. She initially intended to U-Haul it home then decided to have a professional company move her stuff instead. The rep had already surveyed her goods, given an estimate and booked a date. She had two more days to count down. All non-essentials had been sold off on Craig's List. There were a few odds and ends here and there, but what wasn't packed, wasn't coming. Since everything was done, she had nothing to do but catch up on her on-demand programming.

She had given up on Julian ever resurfacing and was not surprised that it didn't hurt that much. What surprised her, was that it hurt at all. She had stopped trying to talk to herself about it and had created a box in her mind in which she stuffed those thoughts and memories. Every time one creeped out, she visually crammed it back in. She had been using this technique for the last week, so she barely thought of him at all. Instead she chose to focus on all her new plans. She had sold her car, which needed replacing anyway, and was going by train. First to her sisters' and then back home to mom's house. She was super excited about the trip and had her sketch pads and novels ready for the ride. Feeling she deserved something extra special Cara had booked a sleeping car with its own bathroom for her adventure. She was ready to shake off this city and all the memories associated with it.

There was a knock at the door. Wearing her red silk pajamas that you know who had given her, she walked to the door. She had never worn them until his disappearance. The last thing she wanted was for him to think she needed him to dress her. Please. She was perfectly capable of dressing herself, it might not have been to his tastes, but oh well. She stopped in mid-stride, put all that in the box, lid close, deep cleansing breath, focus. Finally reaching the door, she opened it. There stood a man in a trench coat leaning on the door frame his head bowed into the crook of his arm. Cara's heart stopped. Son of a bitch, it couldn't be. Julian looked up. He had grown facial hair in his absence. He had one of the most gorgeous goatees' she had ever seen and up until that moment she did not know she had a thing for men with facial hair. Her next thought was Dumas – if he did not look like a musketeer then she didn't know who did.

Julian watched her watching him. She had taken so long answering his knock that he believed she was gone. How many times had she been partially packed when he'd been absent a few days too many? He had come straight from the airport with the hope she was still there but with the expectation that she would be gone. He noticed she was wearing his pajamas, she must have realized it at the same time because an expletive escaped her lips as she crossed her arms over her chest. A slow smile grew on his face.

"So you like it." he stated.

"Like what?" she queried.

"Don't play with me. You've been staring at me for half an hour," he commented as he pushed himself off the wall. "And, you forgot to slam the door in my face."

Stunned, Cara reached for the door.

"Too late," he smirked and crossed the threshold.

Julian stopped. The room was completely empty except for boxes stacked against the wall. He really had made it there just in the nick of time. He continued strolling towards the bedroom and the sound of the TV.

"I see you've kept my favorite piece," he teased.

47

Cara slammed the door.

Julian removed his coat, looked for a place to put it then dropped it on the floor. Sitting at the foot of the bed he began undoing his shoes.

"Aren't you going to ask me where I've been?"

"None of my business," she answered coming into the room and stopping at a standstill on his coat.

He looked at his coat, then up at her with a raised eyebrow. "You're mad, huh?"

"Not at all. I'm just not sure why you're here."

"You know why I'm here. I'm just not sure why you're standing on my coat."

"Oh, am I standing on your coat? I thought I was standing on the floor."

Having removed his shoes and socks he got up to retrieve his coat. Cara did not move. He gave a few timid tugs then looked up at her.

"I think you should put on your coat and leave," she declared.

"Ok," he responded.

She stepped off. He picked it up, hung it on the door and re-sumed his seat. Pulling his shirt from his pants, he began unbut-toning it.

"You said you'd leave," Cara stammered.

"You didn't believe that, did you?"

"Look, I don't know what you think is going to happen here, but you can't be gone that long and then think you can just waltz back in here and get back into action," she huffed.

"How long?" he questioned as he continued undressing.

"How long what?

"How long is too long to return to action? I've been gone days, weeks at a time and that's been ok. Is there a designated number? What is it? You've never said anything about it before," he chided.

Cara was mad enough to spit bullets. If she wasn't apprehensive about approaching him, she would have slapped him. He saw the look on her face and laughed as he removed his pants.

"Do you need help getting undressed?" he inquired as he began to turn down the bed.

"Look," she yelled, "it's not happening."

"Oh yeah," he grinned, "it's happening and if you make me come over there to get you, you're gonna pay."

To hell with this Cara thought, I'm out. She turned, ran to the front room and bolted out the door. As soon as she was half way down the hall she slowed. He'd need to get dressed before pursuing her. She was feeling very impressed with herself when a hand clamped over her mouth and an arm encircled her waist. Julian, clad only in his underwear, was hauling her back. He lifted/dragged her down the hallway and into the apartment, slamming the door with his foot as he continued to the bedroom. He did not release her until he fell on top of her as he shoved her face down on the bed. When he did let go he grabbed the front of her p.j. top pulling it from under her, ripping off all the buttons and flinging it to the far side of the room. Dammit, he was destroying her only silk pajamas. As if she was not mad enough, this enraged her more and she struggled to turn over, get up or something.

"Uh, uh," he scolded and pushed her back down.

Did he have his knee on her back? This was terrible positioning, she could not get any leverage to make a difference. Just then she heard the ripping of her bottoms. Shit, Shit, Shit.

Having completed his task he flipped her and pinned her to the bed. "I told you this would go badly for you" he admonished.

"You need to get the hell off me. You can't do this. This is force," she accused.

"I don't hear you screaming. In everything you just said, I did not hear you say no," and he fastened his mouth to hers.

She struggled, but that wasn't working because all the movement was causing friction and the friction was creating an intense heat that was getting hotter by the minute. Being still was worst because that initial kiss had turned into a soft supple sensation while the beard was making an impression of its own. Finally Cara gave up, gave in, gave over – who was she fooling – she wanted this as much as him. Her body must have relaxed in a way that he read as assent. He loosened his grip and rolled to her side.

Cara opened her eyes. Julian was staring at her. "I missed you," he said softly.

"Why didn't you just say that to begin with?" she objected.

"Because we would have missed all this fun," he taunted.

"You destroyed my silk pajama," she complained.

"I know," he said, "I always keep my word about pay back."

"I paid with my pajamas?"

"No, that was just the beginning," he whispered lowering his lips to her neck.

Oh boy, Cara thought, but to her surprise and pleasure he began rubbing his beard along her neckline. That would have sufficed, but she soon learned where the punishment was going as he proceeded to rub her entire body with his bristles. She was hanging on for dear life when he finally approached her nether region, blowing softly in advance of his descent.

"Whoa," she said bolting up right and covering herself with both hands. "That's nice, but not necessary." She would have gotten up but he was laying on her legs.

"What?" he teased watching her intently, "What's wrong?"

"There' nothing wrong, it's just I don't want to do that."

"Do what?" he grinned.

"You know what I'm saying. That, that, I'm not doing that."

"Why?"

"Why not? You said I could say no. I'm saying no."

"You can't say no now."

"What?"

"You had to say no at the beginning. You can't just reach a point and then say no. What about the other person?"

"What about you?" she simmered.

"Yes me, I'm not ready to stop."

"Well do something else, cause I don't want to do that."

"Ok, I'll stop if you tell me why."

"I can't tell you why and you never do what you say."

"That's not true, I'm making you pay."

"Yeah – whatever."

He blew into the tops of her hands. The heated air went right through her fingers. She would have pulled his hair but that would have meant using her hands and they were both otherwise occupied. He seemed to guess her quandary and continued blowing.

"Ok. Fine," she surrendered.

"We're going to do this?

"No. I'm going to tell you why I don't want to."

"Ok, why?"

"Because I don't want to do everything with you."

Julian was stunned, "If not with me, then whom?"

"Someone who plans to be around and have some significance in my life."

"What if you never find that person?"

"Whether I do or don't, it has nothing to do with you."

"I beg to differ, especially in the position I currently occupy."

Cara attempted to wiggle her legs from beneath him."

"No, not happening," he scolded, "so getting back to this other guy. Why him and not me?"

"Because we've done enough," she stated.

"Oh," he interrupted, "I get it. You're saving something for somebody else. How sweet."

"Laugh if you like, but why should I be used up on the likes of you?"

"Used up? Likes of me? I'm hurt. I'm here sharing my experiences in the tutelage of the art of love."

"Art of porn is more like it. Should I ever meet someone, I don't want to have to explain my skills level because messing with you feels like edging into a professional category."

"You poor misguided child," and he blew here for emphasis, "we have yet to do anything outside the norm."

"OK, well let's just say I am not prepared to venture into your norm, because little old me from back wood city is not trying to keep up with the world jet setter, you. I'm sure my eyeballs would combust and fall out if I saw half the stuff you do."

Julian remained silent, but thought she was probably right. Her eyeballs would definitely explode on viewing his history. "Still, why save it? You could croak tomorrow but I can take you to heaven today," he purred.

If she had been able, she would have kicked him in the head.

"Come on please," he whined.

"I'm sorry, did you just say please? Could I get that engraved or on a t-shirt – The great Julian Aristo Starr said please – just for historical reference, you understand."

"I was trying to be nice," he sulked.

"You were trying to get your way. There's nothing nice about you. Nice is not blowing into someone's crotch."

"I think you're wrong there and if you'd move your hands, I'd show you how nice I can be."

He gave up on his verbal tactics and began sucking Cara's fingers. Hey, they were down there.

"Julian, please," she hissed

"Please what, my darling?"

"I am not your darling."

"You're not? Then what are you?"

"I don't know. You tell me."

Julian quieted.

Cara understood the game, better than he realized. She knew his boundaries and accepted that she existed in the outer perimeters of his life. Still, he could not acknowledge her perceptions so he took a new tack, a cruel one.

"Ok, so you're saving what's left of yourself for your husband? You tell him to call me and I'll tell him where your sweet spots are."

"You know what? You need to get the hell off me," Cara bellowed.

"Or what?" he tested and he wrapped his arms around her upper thighs awaiting the storm.

It came.

She moved her hands grabbing two fists full of hair. It was the moment Julian had been waiting for. He wrenched her thighs apart and sunk his head into her privates. Now it was a war as to who would give up first, him from the pain in his head and her from the lick of the clit. In the end it was Cara, but now she understood why there were so many photos of Himself with his tongue out. Apparently all his personalities shared the same talents.

When Cara awoke the following morning Julian was still there. That had never happened before. She thought she was the first to awaken and delighted in them just being spooned together, but then he ruined it by saying, "It's about time you woke up."

"Really? You could have slunk away as usual at any point," she retorted.

"I said I missed you," he stated.

"And?"

"You didn't say it back. Didn't you miss me a little?"

"Look Julian, I can't say I miss you because I can't miss something that's not mine. You're elusive, secretive and manipulative. Here today, gone tomorrow."

"I guess I should go," he grumbled.

"I guess you should," she reinforced.

He attempted to look affronted but did not move. Cara leaned over the bed retrieving, then handing him his underwear, shoes and socks. He wasn't putting any of it on.

"Can't a brotha at least get breakfast?"

She didn't bother to answer. Instead, she bolted from the bed naked and marched into the kitchen. Julian followed a few minutes later, still undressed, now sporting her towel. In his hand he held a stunning Kimono which he wrapped her into.

"Oh, it's beautiful, thank you" she said pulling her arms through the sleeves.

"Don't thank me, it's from Kafir."

"Of course. Why would I think you brought this for me?"

"I'm offended," he objected, "I did bring you something," and he presented a tissue wrapped packet.

She hesitated reaching for it. Julian always wanted immediate gratification – you had to put it on, try it out, and wear it down. Finally, accepting the package, Cara tore the paper. Beautiful French lingerie fell to the floor. "Gee, thanks," she croaked.

"Don't mention it," he beamed, "now back to breakfast – let's go out."

Two hours later they were back in bed. Laying side by side Julian resumed the earlier topic. He leaned in close to her ear and whispered, "Tell me you missed me."

"Julian, I'm not going to say it," she insisted, "I know you want to hear me say it, but it's not going to happen."

"You missed me," he persisted, "and if you weren't such a stubborn bitch you'd say it."

"Well it takes one to know one and don't call me a bitch."

"Or what?" he taunted.

"Or this," and she pushed him down and sat on his face.

Four days later Julian came strutting down her hallway to find the delivery man taking the couch he ordered out instead of in. The landlord presiding over the activities advised him Cara had moved out two days prior. He had underestimated her. He had assumed she would unpack yet again upon his return, but she had surprised him. She had taken her happy ass on. That was ok, because deep down he wasn't sure how it was going to work anyway. On the other hand, no one walked out on Julian Aristo Starr. He was the person who did the leaving, even with his ex-wives. He had texted one, called another and had the last one physically set out on the curb. He was not a man to be crossed. He was seething. Upon returning to his car, he set a plan in action. Picking up the phone he called his private investigating services. He requested a skip trace and surveillance on her and all her family members. He was going to find her one way or another and when he did, he would make her pay.

CHAPTER 7

Traveling by train was a world unto itself. The motion, sound and visuals quickly enfolded Cara, encasing her in a blissful rhythm of eat, sleep, work, walk, sleep, eat and stare out the windows. It was not mindless but it was carefree. She established a schedule of being first in the dining car for breakfast because he did not want to share the table, conversation or the view with anyone. She usually took coffee back to her room but seldom finished it. The smell was a little off. Next, she'd take out her sketches and work until after lunch which she picked up at the snack car. She would wait until the absolute latest to do dinner. The staff caught on quickly to her timetable and became very accommodating. Cara felt brilliant, liberated, and exhilarated. Her plans for freedom had gone off without a hitch even though Julian had made a surprise reappearance. She had kept her cool, kept everything under wrap and made her great escape. She would have loved to see his face when and if he ever showed up again to find her apartment empty and her gone. The great manipulator manipulated. Oh well, you can't have everything. Julian, the thought of him gave her pause. He probably thought she would unpack and hang out again upon his return and she probably would have if things had not changed.

Trying to use the last of her medical benefits before their expiration and switch to Cobra, Cara had gone for a physical. She received a call back on her lab results and had to double back for a MD consult. She was slightly nervous. She was hoping she did not have a funky pap smear or worse yet an STD. There would be plenty of recrimination and name calling if either of those proved true but instead she got a good old down home diagnosis. She was pregnant. The doctor gave her a slight read down because not only was she pregnant, but she had completed her first trimester apparently without prenatal care. After a sound reprimand the consult continued with scripts, volumes of information and referrals. Cara missed everything after the word 'pregnant' and although she could see the redness of the doctor's face and hear the inference of his voice, for the life of her she could not understand a word he said. There was a sound of an incoming wave in her head and she was waiting to see if it would overtake her. By the end of the session he had assured her everything was ok, encouraged her to eat right, exercise and keep a positive attitude and outlook. Easier said, then done. She had staggered out the office and made it home just in time to drop on the couch. Thank God she had cut back on the drinking. A couple of hours later the impact of the pregnancy hit her and sent her into full panic mode. It wasn't that she was having a baby as a single woman. She could handle that. She was of age, had a great bank account balance and had a career that only needed to get back on track. The problem was she was having Julian's baby and by default also Aristo's offspring. Who knew what that would mean to either of them? The best thing for her was to get out of town as quickly as possible. Hence, there was no unpacking once Julian returned. It had taken all the will she could muster and several trips to the loo to get through those last few days. Of all the things she and Julian had discussed, a family and kids had not been one of them. That would have been an odd conversation indeed in the midst of their wild sexcapades. In any case, the infertility that Julian purported and she believed, obviously was not true. Maybe she should drop him a note – Oh, by the way......... By the way what? If she knew what was good for her, and she did, she would keep her mouth shut and put as much distance as humanly possible between them.

Cara had safely departed, as planned, and now had multiple

things to think about. First, she had to figure out how to break the baby news to her family. Her sisters would flip and their mother would not be pleased. That was not an insurmountable issue, it's just that she did not want to concentrate on that just yet. Instead, she chose to revel in the mastery of her plan, enjoying her sleeping car and, for once without guilt, eat ice cream. Secondly, she was going to have a baby. A baby. She had always wanted children but had kinda pushed the idea to the back burner. Career, lack of boyfriend or perspectives and a waning biological clock had bumped it so far down on her list of things to do, that she had stopped counting on it at all. She was super excited. Her and her baby – the two of them against the world. Sounded like fun. The things they would do, and share and explore. In a little less than six more months somebody would be sharing her life. There was a stack of baby naming books piled with her other stuff. Who knew there were so many names? You need only pick a country, a language, a religion, a historical time period or a gender and names fell from the heavens, which was why she had a small library of baby monikers. Her third thing to think about was a bit more difficult and mesmerizing. She had made a stunning discovery while stripping her bed just prior to the moving company's arrival. She'd turned the top mattress over on its side and in the middle of the box spring sat multiple bundles of one hundred dollar bills. She was still staring at them when there was a knock at the door. Like a thief caught in the act, she'd jammed them into her overnight bag and set it on the kitchen counter. Overseeing the movers that came in, she forgot about it until she was finally ensconced in her room on the train. The only person she knew who could drop that kind of cash and had access to her bedroom was Julian. But why?? Searching for her night time paraphernalia she again discovered the bundles. What the hell was this? Was it reimbursement for services rendered??? The thought made her both mad and sad. Was it some kind of way for him to negate whatever it was they were doing? Did it make it better if he was paying for it?? Then he would not have to feel anything at all? Cara perseverated on these thoughts and questions. While she was at it, she finally counted the money. It was worse than she could have predicted. Each stack had one hundred bills in it and she had a total of twenty stacks. She found her phone for the calculations. Holy shit, it was two hundred thousand dollars. She had never seen, let alone held so much cash in her life. It was frightening and she began to tremble, which brought on a bout of nausea that advanced to vomiting that cleared out everything she had eaten that day. Thanks Julian.

Try as she might she could not conceive of an idea as to why he had done it. She was totally flabbergasted. After another round of projectile vomiting she returned to the bed where the counting and calculations had occurred and laid down across the whole mess. Screw it. Why was she trying to figure out Julian? It would never happen, it was a waste of time. Instead, she should be trying to figure out what to do with it. There was an inkling in the back of her mind that you could not just show up at the bank with that much cash, bundled cash at that, and not have to answer a whole lot of questions. She wondered if she could be detained, if her answers were not fast enough or correct enough to satisfy the interrogation. Would the police be called? Geez, it was the stuff of nightmares. Tossing and turning fitfully Cara nudged all the bulky items behind her, finally finding a micron of comfort she began to doze off, telling herself to think happy thoughts, happy thoughts and then she had one. Thanks to Julian's generous donation she would be able to stay home with her baby perhaps until preschool, if she managed things right. She smiled and fell peacefully asleep.

CHAPTER 8

Julian sat at his desk reviewing the Cara files supplied by his investigators. Julian had initially been excited by the challenge of the chase but once he cooled down, he found he had used up most of his energy imaging his retaliation. He'd had all kind of fantasies from kidnapping to bondage, but as the weeks wore on the illusions faded. He had provided every personal contact listed in her employee folder but so far zilch. Although her family had received some vague inquisitions, that band of Bohemian banshees had circled the wagons and zipped their lips so tight there was not a peep to be had among them. He suspected Cara was headed to her mother's but by what route and on what time schedule remained to be determined.

It still irked him that she had left, although he had to admire her walking away. He was highly aware that many around him were there for what they could get; there were very few who took a personal interest in his wellbeing. He imagined in their eyes he was a money bag that everyone followed around waiting for a seam to rupture or a bill to blow off of. Cara had been his breath of fresh air. Other than the opening request for her job back, she had neither duplicated that request nor asked for anything from him. It was her total disregard of his wealth that intrigued him. She willingly shared whatever she had and was not affronted when he showed up with take-out or they stayed in for movies. She seemed to enjoy his company for what it was without expectations of anything else. For that reason he tried to shower her with things. First small trinkets – flowers, DVD/CD's, lingerie, lounge wear but being the stubborn thing that she was, only the flowers made an impression. She adamantly refused to wear anything he bought her if he was around, only on occasion and strictly by accident did he witness that she actually wore any of it. When he did catch her, she would blush a divine rose color and attempt to excuse herself with any lie that necessitated her leaving the room. He recognized the rouse and would not let her out of his sight. She would get steamed and he would get hot and in the end it all came off. Still, it was nice to think she liked it, used it and thought she could keep it from him.

He was beginning to miss their tete a tete's. They had had conversations, arguments, and debates on subjects as wide and varied as the wind. She never backed down or bowed her opinion for his, in fact, she appeared to play the devil's advocate often taking the stance that was the polar opposite to his. They could rage for hours and frequently did, late into the night and then into the early morning. He was a night person but she was not so he could depend on her throwing in the towel, not a surrender, a postponement for future deliberation. Julian found he missed her apartment too, all five hundred square feet of it. There had been a whole lot of life jammed in that tiny place. Her floor to ceiling bookshelves had been crammed with an eclectic assortment of books and albums. On finding one of his once, he questioned her about his music. She freely admitted she liked the music and more importantly the lyrics but then went on to add that she'd heard the artist was an ass. He had just stared at her and apparently for too long because she got up, turned around, pointed at her butt and repeated ass. He knew then she would always say whatever she wanted to say and it really didn't matter who he was. He had laughed it off then but it had also stung a little. He knew he was an ass, he just didn't want her to think that. When had it started to matter? He had taken to visiting Cara's apartment even if she wasn't there. She was so regimented in her schedule that he knew when she went out, she would not return until dinnertime. He could also monitor her activities by the surveillance equipment he had had secretly installed. It was audio only, but he could hear her doing all kinds of things, talking on the phone, singing, cleaning, dancing and fussing. She had a penchant for talking to herself and some of her most outrageous conversations were about him. He really enjoyed those and although he had never gotten her to admit anything about her feelings towards him, her-self discussions led him to believe something was afoot. Every now and then he'd drop some speck of her internal voicings in their conversation. She would stop and stare at him, giving him a very suspicious squint. Once she had retorted 'And you came up with that all by yourself, did you?' Her verbalizations decreased for a while and it sounded like she was tipping through her place. With time she resumed her regular pattern of behavior. He was more careful after that.

Julian knew better then to be secretly traipsing through her life but he couldn't help himself. There was something about being there and hearing her bumping around that made him imagine it as a 'home'. Not his home, he had tons of those scattered all around the globe, but they for the most part were quiet and empty. He started thinking of her place as their place, although he'd never ever mentioned anything like that to Cara for fear of being tossed or blown out of the residence. Still, the thought made him smile. He had grown so comfortable going in and out of Cara's apartment that the couple that owned the antique store and lived next door responded to him like he belonged there. That was an enjoyable sensation too. He had thought he'd be caught, but it never happened. Sometimes he'd have tea and listen to albums, other times he'd read or simply look out the window, studying people as they passed on the busy street below. He had snooped through her things not believing she had not been involved with someone. Search as he might he could find nothing, but he did discover a lot about her. She liked lists. Lists of things to do, places to go, books to read, movies to see and so on. He had noted and read several of the books on her list and when he inserted them in one of their discussions she was impressed he'd beat her to the readings. He wasn't sure at the time if she was suspicious, but the following week there were four additional reading lists: the top 100 reads before you die, the top 100 sci-fi, the top 100 black diaspora and the top 10 self-help books. He'd laughed because she didn't have one self-help book on her shelves so it made him think she had included it just for him. She had then started inquiring about his reading pursuits.

He had looked through her mail, bank statements and other things labeled "important papers". She was meticulous with her bills, they were organized, filed and paid on time. The bottom of her closet was a mess, but the bathroom had a spit shine on it. The kitchen was lived in, there were tons of mugs and cups that he suspected had been lifted or acquired at second hand stores. They were from multiple cities/countries, gave sage advice and sometimes wished certain unpleasantness on specific noted individuals. The plastics area was an avalanche waiting to happen and there was a stash of chick peas, olives and tuna that could possibly keep the neighborhood going in case of disaster. In a stroke of luck he had happened upon a box of photos. Where most people had gone digital, paper still remained supreme at her place. He studied her sisters, their kids and spouses, her mother and a varied host of others. They appeared to be one huge smiling unruly crew, but the happiness, fun and love they shared was evident, even to him. His favorite was an old pix of Cara and her sisters in their school uniforms. Catholic school, if the nun beside them meant anything. All the sisters stood demurely smiling at the camera except Cara who had pulled a face and crossed her eyes. He pocketed that one.

There were many things that Julian had been, tranquil was not one of them, yet in this tiny cramped apartment full of things stuffed everywhere, he found a certain kind of peace. His homes were expansive exquisite architectural wonders but had a museum feel to them. Here in Cara's apartment there were no off limit areas. Together they had tested every surface including the walls in their escapades. Maybe he had a quality of life issue. He had enjoyed everything about her but had not attempted to push it past their initial arrangement. He would argue it was her mouthy stubbornness that had foresworn him away, but in truth he just didn't feel the need to take it any further. Now he did.

Julian looked again at the pile of investigative reports. Hell, he could have found out this much of nothing. She was traveling-no duh. Where? By what means? She was using her card to eat through a catering service at least once a day. What service was that? And when had she taken to catering? Was she on a job? Last of all, why hadn't she said good-bye?? It was foolishness, he knew, but it still ached just around the edges of his heart that she could walk away like he could. Damn her. Flipping through the papers he found stupidity stacked on insufficiency, dumped on ineffectiveness. He paid hard earned dollars for this B.S. and he was not pleased. He called for his secretary – no answer. He clicked for security – no response. He paged his personal care attendants – nada. Apparently everybody was giving him the breath and width of freedom so as not to get fired. He understood. In truth, he had been in a foul mood since Cara's departure. He ensconced himself in his suites and studio with the designation of no interruptions except for incoming reports. For now he would grant everyone immunity and work on going over the current stack without further reminiscing.

These reports were bogus. He would either be receiving reduced rates or finding services elsewhere. Pissed, tired and wired he finally found a piece of information. There at the bottom of the last pile he found a receipt. He stopped, wiped his glasses and then looked again. His heart rate increased as he continued to stare at it, mesmerized. It was a receipt for prenatal vitamins.

CHAPTER 9

Cara deliberately stayed mum about her current situation while visiting her sisters. That was not what those visits were about and mentioning it would have changed the dynamics, so they had a good old fashioned time.

In Seattle with her oldest sister, Tina, they did the wharf with her five kids. When her husband, Charles, was available, they left everybody behind. The two of them did every bookstore, coffee cafe and antique shop within driving, walking or crawling distance – it was the bomb.

Then on to Oregon, to Patrice's with her 'perfect' family of one boy, one girl, for the great outdoors: hiking, light camping, canoeing and fishing. Her husband, Ralph, was the outdoors man supreme, pitching tents, cleaning fish and doing all the cooking. She asked Patrice if he had a brother. He did, but he was gay. Sounded like a great trade off if he would be providing similar services as his brother. Her sister had laughed the notion away but Cara stowed it in the back of her mind for later consideration. Families were not what they used to be, there was far more openness, flexibility and dimensions. No need to be in a rush to cross someone off just for a slight variation. This off beat attitude was probably what contributed to her current predicament, but she was a woman in need of a plan.

Each visit had been stirring. Talking about old times, making plans for the holidays and, of course, sharing dreams and aspiration of future adventures. Returning to her sleeping car after each stent was like returning to a time out – peace, quiet and tranquility before the next frenzied session. Still, she had had such a good time that she really regretted her two younger sisters not being there. Jenna was still scouring Europe with her hot boyfriend, Fernando and Erica lived in Hawaii with her family. No train services there. Those visits would have to wait until Xmas and by then, the cat would be out the bag, the bun out the oven, the baby in plain view. She would need to sleep on that one. Since she was sleep deprived from all the activities, the overnight junket to California would provide the opportunity to do some serious thinking and sleeping.

On her arrival to Seaside, Cara found her mother and aunt waiting for her at the gate. She was pleasantly surprised but slightly irritated; she was supposed to take a cab home and surprise them. After group hugs and kisses all around and a track to the baggage claim area, her mother finally revealed that it was Patrice that had blabbed about her arrival.

"I should have known Patrice couldn't keep a secret, the big mouth," she snorted.

"Now Cara, be kind. Your sister is going through some things," her mother reasoned.

"Really?? What?? I was just there and she didn't say anything," she questioned.

"Well, sometimes people have their own time schedule on things they need to share."

Enough said on that point, Cara zipped her lips and walked on silently.

Aunt Effie, at seventy-six, had driven the van. Her mother, who was four years older, had stopped driving after her last accident. Age didn't seem to have slowed either of them down. They were walking without devices, lugging bags and filling her in on family and neighborhood happenings, as well as, the night's menu, sleeping arrangements and eligible young men in the near vicinity. Cara was assigned to the back seat with the rest of her bags that had not fit into the rear compartment. She had not realized until that moment just how many bags she had. There were things that needed to go with her for fear of loss and/or damage. Apparently it was more than she imagined. The advantage of being wedged between bags and having the rest on her lap was that it blocked her view of Aunt Effie's driving. She closed her eyes and prayed through all the rapid accelerations and jerky braking. She thought of Mr. Todd's Wild Ride but couldn't remember if that had ended well. So, she tightened her grip, kept her eyes squinched shut and went back to praying.

Arriving safely home, Cara found herself ensconced back in her old bedroom – de ja vu. All her pictures and knick-knacks had been removed or lost in transitions but the old furniture brought back memories. There were still three twin beds in the room. Oh joy. Her two oldest sisters had shared a room, leaving the remaining three to duke it out in a single room. There had been much hair pulling, name calling, flying objects and clothing thievery. She would have liked to say that all that had made her closer to her siblings, but in three's there is always an odd man out and Cara was it. Those two had banded together like pirates leaving her to defend herself, her property and her peace of mind by any means necessary. No wonder she had anger/temper issues. There was many a ruckus that had to cease suddenly before the arrival of their mother. By the time she opened the door although hair was standing on ends, whelps on arms and legs and buttons scattered across the floor, everyone confirmed everything was ok. She would give them the stink eye and say 'don't make me come back up here' and that would be the end of that episode, because everyone knew if mama came back it would not matter what was said or how anyone looked, everyone was going to get it.

Cara laughed at the thought. She had come full circle to return to the room of chaos. She thought about asking for Patrice and Tina's room, at least they had full size beds. She would have to think about how to approach that subject, in the meantime, she began unpacking. There was a sense of comfort being home, but also a feeling of disquiet. Trying to find a place to put her stuff

without disarranging the current set-up was proving to be difficult. It was like trying to move into a museum, just how much
could you displace in an exhibit? She was beginning to feel
stuffed in an off space. Maybe she should have rented something
on a month to month basis. That idea immediately eliminated
the pressure she was feeling to conform to the space without
messing with her sisters' historical presence. She ceased all activity and decided to get a paper.

Deciding to walk, she changed into Cali attire: shorts, sleeveless
T, and flip flops. She had to poo-poo her mother and aunt's ideas
that they should go with her, she should drive or she should put
it off until tomorrow. Guaranteeing she would not be late for
dinner, she backed out of the house and power walked to the
corner to avoid further suggestions. Her mother lived about a
mile off an old fashion main street and while you couldn't see
the beach from their location, you could smell the sand, surf
and salt. Cara enjoyed the excursion. After her train adventure,
the use of her legs in such a novel idea as walking, was wonderful. She studied the new people who had moved in. Waved and
was way-laid by persons who had lived there since her birth.
Picked up a few shopping lists, lots of gossip, a couple of hook-
ups and put out several bags of trash. By the time she made it
to Main Street she was exhausted, famished and regretful she
had not taken the car. The shops on Main were pretty much the
same as she remembered. They called this Old Town Main versus Main because the newer, upbeat, yuppie shops were another
two to three miles away where the road forked. They would not
be seeing her today. She made her way to the local diner, took
a window seat, retrieved a paper and got comfortable. She was
on her second scoop of ice cream. Hell, she deserved it after that
hellacious walk and she was eating for two, when she thought
she caught sight of a black car out the corner of her eye. It hadn't
passed directly in front of the diner but cruised by on a side
street. She stopped mid-bite due to the elevation in her heart
rate. Breathe, she had to think about her techniques which she

had not needed in a while. She was being ridiculous. There were probably hundreds of millions of black cars in America. So what, that it was a big black car. It did not necessarily have to be a limo, and even if it was, she was in California. Probably the limo capital of the world, considering all the stars that lived there. And what month was this? Maybe it was prom season? Cara felt better, but the initial panic had turned her stomach. It was just as well, she really should not have been eating all that ice cream.

On the walk home Cara had more regrets. First, she would be late for dinner and did not look forward to 'that' conversation. Secondly, by the time she picked up and dropped off the few things to a few neighbors, she was exhausted, again, and her feet hurt. Which brought her to the third thing – she should have worn tennis shoes.

When she finally made it back, the door swung open before she could reach for the knob. Boy, she thought, they really are upset about the dinner.

"I'm sorry, I know I said I wouldn't be late but..."

"Never you mind about that," her aunt interrupted. "We have company."

"Oh well, I'll let you visit and go upstairs, I'm really bushed. Sorry again."

"No, no" her aunt insisted, "You have to come in and say hi."

"OK" Cara shrugged, she was going to make this short and sweet. Perfect, somebody else to consume that sit down dinner.

Her aunt led the way down the hall. Making a right into the living room, she stepped to the side to make space for her to enter. Cara stopped short just inside the doorway. She heard the sudden roar of an approaching wave in her ears. There sitting next to her mother was Julian, sipping something from a cup with a saucer. He smiled at her over the lip of the cup. It was the last thing she remembered. The wave over took her and she fell into

Leandra Simone

darkness.

CHAPTER 10

If Julian had wanted to make an impression, he had succeeded beyond his wildest dreams. The expression on Cara's face had been priceless and the fact that she had swooned into her aunt's arms could not be duplicated. He was delighted, although externally he remained as cool and collected as ever. He arose, placing his cup and saucer on the coffee table and advanced to help. He attempted to soothe her relatives while nudging them aside to gather Cara in his arms. He suggested water and a cool towel and they both jumped into action going to retrieve the items. No sooner had they departed then Cara started to revive. Her eyelids fluttered rapidly but when she was finally able to focus and saw him smiling sweetly down upon her, they snapped open. She scrambled to stand, rising quickly, which brought on a bout of nausea that sent her running to the bathroom, arriving just in time to puke. His grin deepened, this just kept getting better and better. By the time he made it to the bathroom door he met up with his assistants and their supplies. He thanked them profusely, took the items and assured them he would take care of Cara. They all made sweet eyes at each other and the older women departed towards the kitchen discussing how they did not make men like him anymore. He opened the door, not bothering to knock. She was way too busy gripping the toilet to respond even if he had. He promptly threw the towel in the sink, then sat on the side of the tub sipping the glass of ice water. Cara had overheard his conciliatory statement to her mom and aunt and their positive reactions to his bullshit. What was the matter with them? They were some of the most cautious women she knew and had a reputation for being quick to dial the police to dispatch questionable characters. Yet here sat one of the worst, smiling broadly, giving her a "cheers" signal and drinking her water. The thought of fluids brought out more upheaval. She was shocked by how much was coming up. First, she thought it was the ice cream and it would be over, but that was followed by some kettle corn, grilled chicken and a few nachos. Damn, when had she eaten all that??? She finally felt it was coming to an end, when the breakfast biscuit from the train showed up. She eventually stopped calling Ralph, his brother Raul and their uncle Earl. She was so exhausted, she could not muster the strength to be mad. Holding onto the sink, she rose slowly, running cold water over her face and into her mouth.

"Julian," she whimpered, "Why are you here? Better yet, how did you get into this house? My mother and aunt never let strangers in."

"I'm not a stranger," he said grinning, "I'm your fiancé."

With that, Cara went back to the toilet for a few additional dry heaves.

"Don't be like that," he continued, "they loved the flowers. Roses for your mom, lilies for your aunt, right? Wild flowers for you. They were a little apprehensive at first but the limo ride, along with the sad story of how you abandoned me, running away and forcing me to come after you, did the trick. By the time we got back, I was invited in for refreshments and dinner."

Cara gripped the sides of the toilet with all her might. She wished she had the muscles to rip it out and hit him with it. Better yet, she wished bad thoughts came true, so he would auto combust leaving only a pile of ash. Since none of that was happening, she tried again.

"Julian, why would you tell my mother that? She's never going to let that go," she grimaced.

"Why should she? What did you want me to say? That we were in the middle of a non-committed sexually liberating experience with no holds barred, when you left without saying good-bye, forcing me to find you and drag your happy ass back with me," he sneered.

If she could just wipe that pretentious self-satisfied expression off his face, she just might survive. Otherwise, if things continued on this same bend, she could die right there hugging the toilet while the Cheshire cat grinned on.

She rose slowly again, forgoing the water for her face and mouth, then headed for the door. Maybe she just needed air, but she only got a few gulps before being surrounded by her mother and aunt. They were twittering around her: she should lay down, she needed to take better care of herself, she ought to get herself together for the man that loved her. The last comment stopped her dead in her tracks. She turned for a retort, finding Julian leaning in the doorway behind them, eyebrows raised. She realized the uncontrolled string of obscenities that were on her tongue and pressed her hand to her lips, which made everybody step back a notch.

"You probably need to go to your room with Julian so you two can discuss things," her mother offered. Now it was Cara's turn to raise her eyebrows.

"Thank you," Julian said solemnly, "I'll help her up," and on passing her mom and aunt, kissed them on the forehead. Oh shit, Cara thought, everybody's lost their minds.

Cara did not argue, she let him encircle one arm around her waist and tenderly guide her upstairs. If she hadn't puked so much before, now would have been an evoking opportunity. No sooner had she indicated the door to the right and they were out of sight, then he swung open the door, pushed her in and closed the door soundly.

"What?" Cara quipped, "Is the performance over?"

"No, no, no," he retorted, "the show is just about to begin.

She did not like the sound of that. In fact, his whole demeanor had changed. While the self-satisfaction remained, an intense darkness had crept into his expression. Cara backed away.

"Surely, you know I didn't come all this way to bring you and your family flowers and have tea," he sneered.

"I'm sure you didn't, so why don't you just tell me why you are here?" she insisted.

"I'm here because you left with something of mine, and you know how I feel about people taking my stuff," he warned.

Clearly the lunacy continued.

"What Julian? What do I have of yours?" She stopped mid-question. The money. He was here for the money. "I have your money."

She walked past him, approaching a desk by the door to retrieve a safe deposit key.

"Here's the key. You can get it and go. It's all there. I didn't use any of it," she reported as she extended the key towards him.

"I'm not talking about that," he jeered as he slapped the key from her hand. He grabbed her wrist swinging her around and pinning her between his arms to the door. The intensity of his glare was almost too much. She had the feeling he was trying to convey something with his eyes but she remained clueless under his scrutiny. Finally, taking one hand from the door, he stroked his goatee then gingerly placed his hand on her waist slowly moving it to her lower abdomen. There was something vaguely disturbing about his hand placement and its lack of movement. She looked down and started. He could not possibly know, she thought. But when she looked up and met his gaze, he lifted his brow in question. For a minute, she was stunned, then she was downright outraged. Pushing his hand aside, she walked around him to the window.

"Sorry, but there's nothing there that belongs to you. If it's in me then its mine. Possession is nine-tenths of the law," she murmured.

"We can argue law if you like," Julian retorted leaning casually on the door, "I retain a stable of attorneys, but let's cut to the chase. I want you to come back with me, you and the baby."

"Julian, this is my baby. What makes you think it's even yours. You've been out of town for months at a time. I could have been busy with anybody," she scoffed.

"Oh, it's mine and its coming home with me," he commanded.

Cara refused to back down, she hotly stammered on, "First of all, you don't know it's yours. Secondly, it's in me and I'm not going anywhere with you. I just got here. So, I guess this conversation is over," and with that she turned her back to him.

"This is far from over," he warned.

Cara could hear him approaching but refused to turn around. The odd thing was the closer he got, the softer his voice became.

"We can settle this nice or we can do it ugly, but either way, I will be getting what's mine."

By the time he finished his statement she could feel him standing directly behind her, still she refused to turn. Refused to be intimidated. He leaned in, not touching her and whispered snidely in her ear, "If you didn't want to deal with me being the father of your child, you should have taken precautions." The statement created its intended effect.

Carla whirled to face him. Having no place to go, they stood toe to toe.

"You have the audacity to blame me?" she snapped, "I didn't see you using anything."

"Why should I?" he chided, "I wasn't the one who was going to get pregnant."

Cara was so angry she was at a loss for words. While she was sputtering for some to respond to his ludicrous statement, he smoothly withdrew a manila envelope from within his jacket and laid it on the windowsill beside her. Leaning in again, he continued his whispered threats.

"Inside this," and for emphasis he nudged the envelope up against her, "Is the legal motion requesting primary custody of my sole heir. It makes a few disparaging remarks against you, as in, you have no job, no current source of income and no stable residence. It could be argued that you could obtain all that, but if you're working full time to provide it, who's taking care of the baby? I, on the other hand, have multiple residents around the world, an unimaginable source and amount of wealth that could provide 24/7 care for my child. It also allows that the baby could be with me, wherever I am and therefore, I only seek to provide a life, education and experiences that a child of mine should be accustomed to."

Cara felt her heart flutter, then drop. He leaned back looking directly into her eyes. What she saw there made her shudder. His eyes had the intent, she imagined, of a serial killer's.

"Here's us doing it nice," he reasoned, "My car will pick you up tomorrow morning at ten a.m. and we will fly home. In exchange for you playing nice, I don't file for primary custody, not now, not ever. We will work something out, but together, and yes, you will get it in writing. Or we can get down and dirty. It's your choice."

Julian leaned in one last time, kissed her on the top of her head then turned and left, not bothering to close the door behind him. She was too stunned to cry. She stood there mutely staring out into the hallway.

CHAPTER 11

Cara was inconsolable the rest of the afternoon and evening. Eventually, she snapped out of her stupor but had lost all courage and hope. She received a deluge of advice. Her mother and aunt propped her up at the kitchen table, where, for once, dinner was forgone for whiskey. She had to maintain on water because apparently, Julian had also dropped hints of her condition. They went through a brisk review, not of what she should do, but of a list of obvious observations: Julian had come after her, he could have bided her a good riddance and gone on about his business; he had wealth and was willing to provide for her, plus he could be a charmer. He had overwhelmed them and apparently her too, which would explain her current situation. Gee thanks.

Next came the calls from all of her sisters, even the one in Spain who was living la Vida Loca. How had that gotten out so fast? Her mother and aunt must have been relaying a play by play while it was actually happening. Patrice and Tina were like – 'What's the problem? You've got it made.' Erica wanted to know who the father was and what was his net worth? Jenna offered sanctuary with her and Fernando on the road, wherever they were headed next.

None of any of that helped. She had not divulged Julian' name or identity. There was no way to explain that she had become involved with somebody's alter ego, or was this his true ego, or was this just two of many? Maybe she just hadn't met the others, yet. Trying to explain that would have made her sound insane, so instead she made up an alternative background story – in other words, she lied.

Julian, became Alexander, and she wove a tale of his frequent use of aliases and even presented doubt that Alex was his real name. Such behavior was questionable and cast a very shaky shadow which was why she could not just believe in him. Next she disclosed that he had had multiple previous marriages and it was unknown if any of them had been legal and/or dissolved, so that took care of the question of marriage. Last of all, while he sported the trappings of wealth, none of it was his. He was actually using his employer's stuff, car and reputation to further his own image and agenda. He was nothing more than a background musician who had the great fortune to look similar to his employer and therefore frequently played the decoy for the infamous artist. That bipolar twisted story backed everyone up for a pause. In the end though, she did the only thing she could. She packed her bags and got ready for the car to pick her up in the morning. No way was she gong to risk custody of her baby and she had no doubt that Julian would file for it if he didn't get his way. Cara knew she could not afford a legal battle against someone with unlimited funds, obsessive control issues and a jaded vengeful spirit. Trying to get around Julian would be like trying to drink ice water in hell. He was good at saying he made people pay, but up until then, she had only glimpsed the edges of that statement. Now she was one of those people, targeted, vise gripped and trussed. Only time and Julian would indicate what her sentence would be.

Cara was up at four a.m. She had gotten tired of tossing and turning the night away, so she thought, to hell with it, and got up. She had found her mother and aunt in the kitchen having coffee. She was unsure if they had gone to bed or just stayed up all night. She also suspected that the coffee might just be a cover for the continued consumption of whiskey. Everyone was solemn and silent, which was just as well because Cara was all advised, thought and talked out. She was resigned to her fate and just wanted to get it over with. She avoided the coffee because her stomach was still doing somersaults, but had 7-up and crackers. She had to consume something. If not for the sake of the baby, then at least to keep from passing out again. Although, she doubted food had anything to do with that episode.

In between sips of whatever people were drinking, they made plans for Christmas. Everyone was coming home, including Erica, Nahoa and their kids from Hawaii and even Jen, who had promised to shake off her world travel adventures to be there too. It sounded like fun. Complicated, but fun. Could Cara remember all the stories she'd invented? She would have to write them down. Would Julian allow her to leave, could she take the baby, would he have to come too? God forbid. The more she thought about it, the more her stomach rumbled so she chose to put those thoughts aside. That was a future endeavor, she had enough currently going on that would kill a weaker person, but she was bound and determined to survive. The next time she got the upper hand, she would not forget to make Julian pay.

The car arrived promptly at ten, a black limo, of course, perfect for the mournful atmosphere. She kissed her mom and aunt as they helped her load her bags. She assured them everything would be ok and that they were right, Julian would take good care of her and the baby. That seemed to lift their spirits. Although she was choking on those words, if they felt better than she felt better. Cara even mustered a smile with her wave as the car pulled away. Once out of sight, she fell listless into the backseat. The quiet, the motion and the fact that she had hardly slept crept up on her and she drowsed into a deep sleep.

There was a voice from far away, followed by a slight shake. Cara roused slowly and could not figure out where she was or who was shaking her. When it all came back she bolted upright. Brian smiled down at her, "we're here." Wiping the slob from the side of her face, as well as, the dampness from her neck, she departed the car. Surprised, she stood on an airfield. She had assumed she was flying a commercial airline but here was a red carpet leading to a flight of stairs into a private jet.

CHAPTER 12

If nothing else, Julian was exposing her to a whole lot of firsts: first firing, first time meeting Himself and then the Other, first limo ride, first one night stand, first French lingerie, first no boundary liberating affair, first extended period of un-employment, first cunnilingus, first cash donation greater than one hundred dollars, first pregnancy, first custody fight and now first private jet ride. It was questionable if she could survive too many more firsts, especially with Julian introducing them.

Cara had promised herself she would not be lugubrious, so she stiffened her back and her upper lip, put on a brave face and began the climb up the stairs. Just inside the door, Brian directed her to the left second row. Apparently she had assigned seating because another row after that the plane opened up into a large lounge with four oversized chairs that obviously stretched into beds, with tables and TV's interspersed between them. Brian took up the seat directly across from her. At least she had a window, but the soft leather butter cream chairs she had glimpsed were calling her name. Maybe someone would take pity on her and invite her into the exclusive section. She looked out the window, nothing but airfield, no planes, no hangars, no cars. She felt like she'd been placed in a corner. Those feelings did not improve because two hours later she was still in the plane on the tarmac looking at nothing. It was useless to attempt to ask Brian anything, it was like talking to a mute. He made vague gestures without words so she had no clue as to what was happening. Obviously, they were waiting on something or someone and since Julian had ordered her there, she was going to assume it was him. But why have her sitting there knowing take off was nowhere near the appointed time?? Flash of an answer- because he could. Cara started to simmer. She asked Brian about the bathroom thinking she could at least take a tour of the exclusive area under the guise of a potty break. She was directed to a small closet just across from the door. Of course, how could she be so stupid? There would be one for the prince and one for the paupers. She got in and out, no fun there. It was then she noticed her assigned set of seats had their backs to the main lounge, this must be the help's section – see no evil, hear no evil, report no evil. She asked Brian for food. He opened the cabinet above his seat and handed her a large paper bag in which she found a box of saltines, several 7-ups, a large bottle of water and a barf bag. Her simmer escalated into a full boil.

"What the hell?" she started, only to be cut off by the sound of people ascending the stairs. It was the captain, co-pilot, and two beautiful air attendants, followed by a caterer. Everyone acknowledged and dismissed her in passing. She had to kneel in her seat to keep up with what was going on. The attendants immediately began arranging the lounge, adding pillows, blankets and flowers. The caterer, besides stocking several cabinets with food, beverages and sweets, also began preparing large platters of sumptuous fare. Cara looked at her brown bag and had a very distinct feeling that she was not going to be invited to any of that. Her rage had softened with all the action, but now it returned with a vengeance. What had she been thinking? She'd convinced herself that she and Julian would talk on the flight, exam expectations, logistics and the responsibilities of each other. She had to be crazy to think that. This was all about payback and if it was like this here and now, she did not even want to think about what was to come. Good thing she was still on the ground to have this change of mind. Cara began gathering her stuff and picking up her bags. Brian immediately rose from his seat and blocked the aisle.

"Look Brian, I appreciate everything, but I've got to go. I know you and I have tussled in the past, but unless you're prepared to wrestle with a pregnant woman, I suggest you get out of my way."

Brian's eyes widened and while he did not get out of the way, he did back up. She kept moving forward and he kept moving back. She made it out of her row and to the end of the next one when Brian bumped into a giant of a man behind him.

"Move it," was all he muttered. Brian advanced on her, arms spread wide, forcing her backward until she was back where she started. Before an argument could ensue, three gorgeous nymphs came around the large man and advanced into the lounge. They passed without any eye contact or recognition, apparently she had grown invisible too. Both Brian and the other man immediately stepped aside, and there coming through the door, making a princely entrance was Himself – Aristo.

Cara's mouth flew open, then she promptly clamped it shut, dropped into her seat and looked out the window.

Aristo stopped before the men, "Tell the pilot we're ready for take-off," he said, then continued down the aisle. He was wearing some funky outfit, with full make-up, built up shoes and shades. He gradually walked by, passing her as if she did not exist. Cara let out her breath. No sooner had she finished then he backed up, cocked his head, pulled his shades down on his nose and stared at her. She was so startled by his return, she forgot to look away and their eyes met. He kept staring, then suddenly made a V with his fingers in front of his lips and wiggled his tongue. His nymphs broke out into a salacious laugh. She could feel a redness and heat rising on her cheeks and spread across her neck and chest. She had no idea what that meant, but knowing whom it came from and the reaction it garnered, she was sure it was something nasty. Aristo continued his intense scrutiny, raising his eyebrows.

"Tsk, tsk, tsk," he sneered. Pushing his glasses back in place, he pimp walked down the aisle and into the lounge.

When she shifted her eyes away she caught the men in the back looking at her, they avoided eye contact. Cara was horrified. For a brief moment she had dared hope that the situation could be worked out, but now she realized how hopeless it truly was. She was embarrassed beyond words. What was going to become of her and her baby? Obviously, she was dealing with someone who was not playing with a full deck, but the really scary part was that he held all the cards. Her stomach began to rumble and she developed a severe headache. Maybe she'd stroke out and it would all be over. Brian must have read the dilemma on her face, he extended a blanket and pillow in her direction. There was nothing for her to be proud about, so she laid down and covered her head while hot tears of humiliation leaked from her eyes. Somewhere between her leaky eyes and her attempting to overhear what was going on in the lounge, she fell, once again, into a deep sleep.

Aristo/Julian knew he was treating Cara badly. It had not been his intention to retrieve her with his entourage in tow. He actually had been in L.A. on business when her location and arrival had been reported. The coincidence was too much to be overlooked. He hopped his plane in L.A. to arrive just after her train pulled in, put eyes on the ground and slid in with her family as soon as she left the house. By the time she returned, the damage was done, he was in like Flint and the rest was history. After their encounter, in which he served her phony custody papers, he left his plane there and took another limo back to Los Angeles. He was over the top with his success and knew she would bend to his will. Why not enjoy the fruits of his labor? It was not his entourage's fault they were caught in the middle, so he proceeded on with business as usual. He wrapped up his legal dealings, signing contracts and fulfilling promotional schedules, picked up his girls, did the night life then rode back to Seaside to board his plane. He knew he would not return by Cara's designated pick-up time. He suspected the wait would piss her off. He had worked on getting her to submit to him, and her resistance, as well as, her audacity to leave him needed to be checked. This was payback. Which was also why he arrived as Aristo. She had an unhealthy disregard for Aristo and a preference for Julian. Whether she wanted to accept it or not, he was one and the same. He had given her an extreme reality check. He could see the shock of it on her face and for one split second felt sorry for what he was doing. It passed, and he antagonized her further with his obscene gesture. She probably had to Google it, but it made her blush a royal rose color and he loved it. Julian promised himself he would make it up to her soon, very soon. He really was glad to have her back.

Cara roused slowly. She felt like she had slept the sleep of the dead. Awakening on the seat she remembered where she was, but why was it so dark? As she rose, she discovered she was alone. Apparently in everyone's haste to depart, they had forgotten all about her. Her bags were missing too. Instead of following the light and going out the open door, she turned back into the lounge. Obviously the cleaning crew had not arrived. She sat, then leaned back into a lounge chair, it felt just like she imagined. There was a blanket over the arm – cashmere. She felt the intense desire to lift one, then hotly shot the idea down, then thought – what the hell. She picked it up, folded in tightly and jammed it into her purse. There was something to be said about having an oversize purse, besides losing things in it, you could also appropriate necessary commodities. The thought made her smile- she had moved from being invisible to become a cat burglar. She found her shoes, put them on and departed.

At the bottom of the stairs stood a black limo. Brian immediately got out and opened the door. If she survived this experience and escaped this situation, she promised herself to never ride in black limos again. This one was blessedly empty. When she finally got comfortable she checked the time, it was three in the morning.

Arriving at the compound Cara had a sense of deja vue. She had made all these great plans and actually carried them through, only to wind up back in the same place. The only difference was the limo pulled into the front gate while she usually entered through the rear gate to the back lot. Dawn was still some minutes away as Brian cruised slowly in the darkness avoiding the main residence and offices. Forking to the left, he followed its curve around to the right. In the end they wound up at a house directly behind the main building but separated by at least an acre and obscured by brush and foliage. The house had a southern New Orleans style, large windows running from ceiling to floor with iron balconies. Cara imagined the lighting would be divine. The car pulled to a stop directly in front, Brian opened her door, put her bags on the steps, handed her some keys and drove away. In the darkness Cara fumbled to open the door, then searched the wall for light switches. When she finally hit the correct one, she found a huge open space completely devoid of furniture except for a couch sitting before the fireplace that looked suspiciously similar to her old one. She continued her tour finding countless bedrooms and baths, an enormous kitchen, and multiple multi-functional rooms – all empty. Finally she arrived at the master bedroom. There she found an enormous magnificently intricate wrought iron bed covered in pillows. She had always wanted a wrought iron bed although she had never imagined one so big or so beautiful. Had she ever mentioned that to Julian? She had left all the lights on while exploring the house, but now on viewing the bed, she had a sudden sensation of needing a nap. She pulled back the covers, displacing several pillows and jumped in ready rolled. She did not think twice about burning up all that electricity. After all, she wasn't paying the bill. As she tossed and turned pillows continued to roll, fly and fall in all directions.

CHAPTER 13

There was a snake under the foot of the bed, Cara was not afraid because she knew she was dreaming. She watched it as it slithered in and out of its hiding place, changing colors to match the background environment. At one point a bird flew low chasing a small lizard. The snake sprung out snatching the lizard from the bird's grasp. She could feel her heart rate increase. Dream or not, that was a little scary. She decided to distance herself from the snake. She got out of the bed on the opposite side, but she had to pass it to get to the door. She was tipping quietly along, the snake absorbed in something in the other direction when she stumbled over the pillows on the floor. The snake turned and sprung at her, sinking its fangs into her face. Cara screamed to the top of her lungs. Opening her eyes, she found herself sitting bolt upright holding her cheek.

"Bad dream, huh?" came a voice from a pile of pillows on the bed.

Turning, she discovered Julian, sporting a five o'clock shadow, draped casually at her side. She dropped back on the bed. One hand still holding her dream injured face, the other over her heart, whose rate was so fast she could not yet speak.

"That bad? Hope I wasn't in it," and he smiled one of his rare, full faced, open smiles, not the snide sneer, sly sexy or self-satisfied concoction. It was simple, but radiant. Cara, happy to still have a face, a decreasing heart rate and not having to face Aristo, without thinking, smiled back.

Julian immediately took that as a good sign and sat up.

"We have a lot to do today," he said pulling her up to a sitting position, "I think you need to furnish your house. Maybe we could start with the baby's room. As if on cue, the baby kicked. Cara had felt fluttering, but this was a full jab, she grabbed her abdomen.

"Are you alright?" he questioned.

"The baby kicked," she whispered.

Julian reached to touch the spot but stopped short. She looked up and their eyes met, he seemed to be waiting for permission. Now that was different – Julian waiting – Julian seeking permission. She placed her hand over his and guided it to the busy spot. Two to three seconds later it happened again, they both erupted into laughter.

"Ok, we better hurry," he exclaimed, "because somebody is going to be here soon."

"Not that soon," she mused.

"How soon?" he doubted.

"Oh, about six months, give or take a few weeks," she stated.

"I'm not sure I can wait that long," he teased.

"Well, you're gonna have to, because I can't cook it any faster."

They were both standing by the bed when he looked at her in yesterday's slept in clothes. He shook his head.

"We have a long to-do list, but I see doing something about your sleep wear is still on it."

Cara and Julian fell into a semi-comfortable zone. It was not what it had been, but the new parameters were workable for all. Julian appeared genuinely excited about the baby. He still came and went as he pleased but it seemed he came more and left less. Cara let go of her residual anger and resentment at being forced to acquiesce to him and concentrated on getting ready for the baby.

Initially, it was all about the shopping. Although Cara loved fabric and books she was not so excited about furniture. She loved Ikea because the rooms were predesigned and you could just walk through, pick it out and take it home. Julian was having none of it, but he was Architectural Digest by design. The gap was too wide. It took many weeks, arguments, compromises and sneaky maneuvers to come to a resolution and get something done and that was just the baby's room.

Days flew into weeks, then it was time to add Lamaze to the mix. By then, she was showing, big time. She had gone from barely there to big belly baby on board. Somewhere around that same time Cara realized that Julian didn't touch, actively seek to seduce or even really look at her any more. They had conversations, arguments, meals, movies and now classes, but that was the extent of their interactions. When she counted the weeks to months since their last physical encounter she was terrified. She had never considered this new phase in their relationship would be platonic. She was no saint but she wasn't a nun either. The ramifications of her current living situation were staggering. Somehow she could not imagine Julian letting her off the compound for a pleasure seeking adventure. She tried not to think of his alter ego Aristo and the fun he was having. Her mind flashed to the nymphs on the plane. Obviously, she was the only one getting the short end of the stick. Was he just not into her anymore because basically he had won, the game was over and he was on to new conquests? Or was it he had initially found her curvaceous but now she was down-right humongous? Or was he just not into pregnant people? What was wrong and how could she fix it? Or if there was nothing to fix and he was just done with her, then what?

Cara had just finished getting dressed for the Lamaze class. Julian would arrive to retrieve her in a few minutes. She sat at the kitchen counter attempting to wipe the worries off her face. Julian was very perceptive of her facial expressions, body mannerisms and thoughts. Sometimes she suspected he could read her mind. She was attempting to create a neutral face when he walked in. Julian had keys to her house, and to Cara's surprise, also a secret passage that led from his residence to hers. Again, this was an area of TMI, so they both took a don't ask, don't tell stance on that piece of info.

Julian came in smiling, stopping just short of her, which she knew he would. What would happen if she just threw her arms around him? Fear, pride and the possibility of humiliation kept her in her chair.

"You ready?" he asked.

"Yeah, let me run to the bathroom again."

"Ok, I'll be in the car."

Grabbing her bag and mat, she walked out locking the door. Julian negated the necessity of that activity, but a habit was a habit, she always locked the door. He was sitting out front in a Mustang convertible. She was no longer surprised that he was driving, he had been doing that since they started Lamaze classes five weeks ago. What surprised her was that, so far, he had never driven the same car twice. She had heard he had a thing for motorcycles, apparently his interests also included cars. Initially there was a red Corvette (too low), then the white Ferrari (too fast), followed by a black Benz 350 (too bourgeoisie), tempered by the Navy BMW Z3 (her favorite – so far). She had to admit he was a great driver, because he usually got them there in half the time. She was never frightened by the speed, he was in control, as always.

Their private Lamaze lessons were informative but dry. Obviously, the instructor had been subjugated to a stern gag clause, which she no doubt accepted for a considerable amount of cash. Only now, it appeared she was choking on her restrictions. These classes reflected none of the fun her sisters had always talked about. The best part so far was getting to sit between Julian's legs during the breathing exercises. Today the instructor was advocating for Kegel exercises to strengthening the bladder muscles, emphasizing continued practice either by stopping the flow of urine in mid-stream or tightening the muscles during sex. Still propped in the breathing position, Cara listened idly while Julian softly stroked her abdomen. They had been through this so often, in their detached way. She considered it his way of rubbing the baby, while she was just an interloping barrier. When the instructor turned to point out something on the board, Julian leaned forward.

"I hope you're practicing your Kegel's," he murmured in her ear.

"I am," she replied, attempting to bat him away from her ear.

"By method number one or number two?"

"By method one, since two is obviously not an option," she sneered.

"There are always options," he purred and his hands dipped low into her mons pubis.

Cara yelped. The instructor whipped around, but they had resumed the correct position and both looked up innocently.

"Gesundheit," Julian said, patting Cara on the shoulder.

"Thank you," she replied rubbing her nose while rapidly blinking her eyes.

The instructor turned back to the board with a remark that sounded like "bullshit" to which they stifled giggles. Class passed quickly after that.

Riding back, predominately in silence, Julian acted like nothing had happened. Cara pondered the meaning or lack of meaning his actions entailed. Something was wrong, but she wasn't sure if it was her or him. He made a quick turn and drifted to a stop in front of her door. It was strictly a stunt move. Sometimes he came in, sometimes he didn't. Today he decided to come in, which irritated her to no end. She abruptly opened the front door, marched straight into the kitchen and began angrily searching through the cabinets. She heard the front door click shut. Why did the way Julian close doors affect her so? Was it the quiet intensity in which he did it or was it the old expectation of what use to follow? She was super sensitive to it now especially since nothing ever followed.

He sauntered into the kitchen, lazily leaning on a counter stool.

"So, are we a little tense today?" he started.

"No, we are not, but I'm......." she stopped. What was she? Agitated? Angry? Humiliated? Horny?

As she considered her response, she watched him watch her. She was sure he was doing that mind-reading thing again so she tried quickly to go blank.

"Nice try," he smiled.

He reached into his jacket and pulled out a phone, placing it on the counter and sliding it toward her.

"This is for you."

"I already have a phone."

"This is your personal connection to me."

"Why don't we just exchange phone numbers? I like my phone, not interested."

"You can keep your phone, you'll just have two."

"I don't need two. One is enough, almost too much."

"Cara, stop being difficult."

Now she was intrigued. She came over to the counter to inspect it.

"Why is it so important that I have this phone?

"In case of emergency."

"My phone can make emergency calls."

He sighed silently.

A thought bloomed in her mind.

"Oh, this is one of your 'special' phones. It probably has GPS, tracking, motion sensitive recording: audio, video, and photo. And there's probably an auto destruct capacity, just in case I'm not a good girl. Tell me I'm wrong."

Julian grinned, "All that is most certainly not true."

"Only part of it though, right? I don't suppose you'll tell me which features are true?"

"No. Now take it."

"I've heard you don't like to be called and won't answer your phone. Who will be answering??"

"It's my direct connection to you."

"But will you answer if I call?"

"I can't say."

"Then I won't take it."

He frowned.

"Ok fine, I'll take it, but I won't use it. How will you know what I'm calling about if you won't answer? The baby could be coming, the house could be on fire, or the world could be coming to an end. I've never called you about anything."

"You never had my number."

"The point is, I never asked for it either. I am not a frivolous caller."

"OK," he huffed, "I'll answer if you call."

"You promise?"

"I said I would."

"But do you promise?"

"I promise."

"Cross your heart and hope to die?"

"Cara...." he started.

"You know you have a history of saying anything to get out of a situation."

"Ok, ok, ok. I give my word I will answer your calls."

"Fine," she quipped picking up the phone and turning back to the cabinets.

He huffed again as the chair scrapped back and she heard his footsteps head toward the door. This time when it closed it was not so intimidating. Cara was proud of herself. She had grilled him good and for once gotten her way, but what good was that? She was still alone. First she was mad he had come in, now she was sad he'd left so soon. She was losing it. She stood quietly in the kitchen. Now what? She stared at the phone a few minutes, made a decision, picked it up and hit dial.

Julian had just cleared the driveway and put the car in full throttle when his phone went off. He began cursing a blue streak because he recognized the tone to be Cara's and she had just said she would not call. He stopped, slammed into reverse and drove back the way he had just come from. He vaulted over the closed car door, kicked open the front door and bounded into the kitchen. Cara was so surprised by his volatile return, she still had the phone to her ear, open mouthed. He came without a word, took the phone from her, turned it off, placed it on the counter and turned to leave. He was closing the door behind him when Cara re-found her voice.

"I was just calling to say I missed you," she yelled out.

She had no way of knowing if he had heard and as the seconds turned into minutes, she guessed he had not. Given his first reaction, she was not about to make a second call. Besides she didn't think she had it in her. It had taken a lot to admit she missed him, make the call, then try to say it out loud. That had been a disaster, but at least she had tried. She opened a drawer, put the phone in and shut it. She would not be carrying or using that thing again.

Cara was still in the kitchen trying to think of a snack that sounded good after losing her appetite. She thought she heard the front door squeak. Julian had probably not shut it all the way on his jaunt out. She was glad it was still on its hinges. Rounding the corner to check it, she found Julian standing in the open doorway, head down as if deep in thought. She stopped. He looked up in a sultry way she had not seen in a long time.

"You were saying?"

"I.....uh...I......" she stammered. Cara recognized she was stuttering. She who never lacked for words and responses.

He seemed slightly amused. She closed her eyes, took a deep breath and started again.

"Julian," she murmured, "I miss you."

"How can you miss me? I've been right here. We've been doing all kinds of stuff together."

She should have known that he wouldn't make it easy.

He watched her closely. Her face revealed all the doubts, confusion, longing and misgivings that he himself also felt.

She took another deep breath and tried again.

"I miss the way we used to be. You're here but in a detached sort of way."

"What is it you want from me?" he queried.

Oh boy, he could not have been any more direct. This time she sighed letting all the air out.

"I don't know," she admitted softly. "I just know I miss you and how we used to be."

This time it was his turn to lean in to catch the words she was whispering. She blushed when she finished and the room fell silent.

Julian didn't move. In his mind he was going through the list of things she had refused to share with him, things she was saving for the man she felt was 'the one'. Things she felt were too intimate to impart on a fling. Bathing together, breakfast in bed, fantasy play, massages, hair washing/brushing, and fellatio were among some of the things on the no-no list, although he had gotten his way on the cunnilingus. He had wanted to partake in all that, and the thought of someone else receiving those benefits created a low burn around the edges of his heart. In short, he guessed he had wanted to be her 'one'. He felt a warmth engulf him.

"So you want me to be 'the one'?" he inquired.

"I didn't say that."

"Then you just want my body?"

"Julian, please," she sighed.

"Please, what? You called me, remember?"

Julian remained staunchly in the doorway.

Cara felt a tightening around her heart. What did she want? She still wanted all the things she had dreamed of – a husband, children, a house, a career. Now everything was botched. She shrugged, there were just no words. She turned back to the kitchen.

Clearing his throat, Julian stayed her exit. "I've been waiting for you to admit you love me."

Cara baulked, "That's not going to happen."

"Why can't you just believe in us, whatever we are? It's worked fine up until now."

"Fine??!??" she scoffed.

"Granted there have been a few kinks, but for the most part we were having fun." Julian reasoned, "It's not your typical life, but it seemed to be working and you just admitted you missed it."

Cara thought about it. It was far from typical – they had separate residences, he came, went and did who knew what with whomever, but he was kind, generous and funny as hell. He had a life, career and lifestyle that she would never fully be a part of. She would always be on the fringe and he would always be the center, a controlling perfectionist, a master manipulator. Still he had come for her, using his wealth and power to force her return, when he could have just as easily used it to make her disappear. That must mean something. She had actually enjoyed their previous arrangement. She got to be herself and he got to be all the people he was, and when they were together it was just them. Maybe it could work, people were living all types of life-styles, why was she so stuck on the conventional?

"Ok," she relented.

"Ok what?" he insisted.

"Ok, I'll try it your way," she admitted.

"So, I'm 'the one'?"

"Julian, in my wildest dreams you will never be 'the one'," Cara clapped her hand over her mouth.

"That's ok. You keep that 'one' fantasy because I'm your real-ity," he said tersely.

Cara felt a chill run down her spine. He was her reality. There would never be 'the one' as she had imagined, and if he did hap-pen to show up, Julian would make sure he was never seen again. She had a sudden sinking feeling that Julian would be the only 'one' she would ever have.

Julian watched the truth dawning across her face. He had her right where he wanted her, here in his compound. He had all the time in the world to wear her down.

She closed her eyes and held the bridge of her nose, when she opened them, he was standing directly in front of her. He re-mained stealthy as ever.

"You were saying?" he asked smiling broadly.

She opened her mouth to retort but before she could, he kissed her. It wasn't a wild sexy kiss but a soft exploration of where they currently were and also where they might be going. Cara sighed and drifted into it and his arms. This was a whole new feeling. It felt like something she could get used to, believe in, and hold on to.

Julian suddenly pulled away, pressing her back by the shoulders, "There's something serious we need to discuss."

"No, Julian, not now," she whimpered refusing to open her eyes.

"No, Cara, now," he said shaking her gently. "This has to do with you, me and the baby."

She opened one eye, then the other. He looked serious.

"Ok, what?" she snapped.

"I've been thinking about those Kegel exercises and I think we should start practicing immediately – option two."

He attempted to lower her to the couch. That didn't work. It was a whole new experience dealing with a pregnant body configuration, but Julian, persistent and creative as always finally found the right positioning. In no time they had no clothes on, and it was becoming a hot and heavy situation. Just when she felt she could not hold on any longer, Julian suddenly groaned and shouted out, "Kegel me, baby" and she did.

CHAPTER 14

Aiden showed up and showed out just like his father. He arrived two weeks early and made a spectacular entrance. In the middle of an argument over Bach versus Mozart, with Julian attempting to win unfair advantage with unnecessary caressing, Cara's water broke. The gush was so large it soaked both of them.

Julian, the consummate controller, remained calm. He seated Cara in a kitchen chair, started the timer on the contractions and cleaned the floor. Next, he went upstairs, changed clothes, returned with her pre-packed bag and clothing which he helped her into. She was always amazed at how efficient he was. He surrounded himself with people that did everything for him when he was perfectly capable of doing it himself. Maybe that was the extravagance of wealth, why do it yourself when others could be paid to perform the task. That revelry was cut short by a strong contraction.

"Julian, they're starting," she called out.

He was on the phone and the limo pulled up two seconds later. The interior was well padded.

The contractions were progressing along when suddenly they stopped. Everyone was reassured and Pitocin was started. Cara should have known the baby would be fickle, just like his father. Two hours later the contractions were back on track and they were moved to the delivery room. Somewhere between their arrival at the hospital and their transfer to Labor and Delivery, Cara and Julian fretted about positioning, disagreed on the breathing, nixed the use of drugs and developed a strong dislike for one another. On the final push, with Julian pressing her forward as she bared down, Aiden popped out.

Julian cut the cord, held the bloody baby and wore a look she had never seen. After wiping the baby, they placed him on her breast. Cara thought he was the most beautiful baby in the world and Julian hugged both of them to his chest. They kissed, the doctor harrumphed, they grinned and Aiden cried.

Once back home Julian lavished Cara with everything she could possibly imagine: flowers, chefs, clothing, and jewelry. He had insisted on a nanny but Cara declined, this was her baby and she was going to take care of him. Besides, if she needed help, she always had Shelly.

Julian had had a shit fit when Cara had initially brought Shelly home. He had insisted that 'you could not just pick people off the street' and bring them into your life without extensive background checking. But that's just what Cara had done. She and Shelly had met several months after her forced return from California. Cara had been sulking in a coffee shop when Shelly's ex pulled his car to the curb and unceremoniously threw Shelly and all her stuff in the street. Although Cara had been thinking her situation sucked, when she saw Shelly she knew hers was worse. Cara watched as the car pulled away, Shelly sitting on the curb crying while people either walked through or drove on her belongings. Thinking she could at least offer words of encouragement and maybe a cup of coffee, Cara had approached her. She had convinced Shelly to come in and what started with a lot of tissue, tears and scones turned into dinner, coffee and an employment opportunity. It turned out Shelly was a linguist, taking a sabbatical from her doctorate program, to drive across the country with her significant other. Two states out she realized he was not so significant after all. In fact, he was downright rude. When she began to call him out on his behavior, he became increasingly angry, agitated and verbally abusive, cumulating into the witnessed ejection from his car. Shelly was totally bummed. She had no clothes, little money and no plans.

Cara came up with the idea that Shelly could assist her with the upcoming baby and eventually become his tutor/teacher. Cara had stumbled through her Spanish classes. She wanted her children to be multi-lingual and Shelly seemed like the perfect start. Shelly jumped at the suggestion and they struck a deal.

Julian had hit the roof when he found Shelly in Cara's house. He had ranted and raved, threatening to check her out and return with security. He found nothing untoward about her and eventually added her to his payroll, although that initial affront left a bad taste in everyone's mouth. Cara got over it first, especially since she had gotten her way.

Life changed. Cara had imagined that she would have Aiden pretty much to herself. That a crying, messy baby would cut into Julian's creative flow. To her surprise, it was just the opposite. It seemed he enjoyed being a dad. Julian's appearances began to mimic Aiden's schedule. Anytime Aiden was awake or feeding, Julian was there.

One night Cara awoke to find them both gone. By then, she had found and toured the tunnel linking her house to Julian's. It had been purely accidental. She was sneaking a midnight snack when the wall slid aside and Julian emerged. Caught, he was gracious enough to show her how it worked and gave her a tour. It was the first time Cara had been in his house. The exit actually connected to a private studio off Julian's bedroom. His house was massive and highly decorated with his initials, insignias and colors. Her remark about him not being able to forget his name had led to an abrupt end to that excursion. Some people just could not take a joke.

Anyway, with her baby missing Cara took to the tunnel. She found father and son in the studio. Aiden wide awake watching Julian play the piano while crooning softly to him. Both looked up sharply upon her entrance.

"You were sleeping so soundly that I didn't want to wake you, so Aiden and I decided to spend some guy time together."

She smiled, so did he and Aiden gurgled.

"Ok," she said and turned to go.

"Well, since you're here, you're welcomed to stay."

"Ok," she grinned and made herself comfortable on the couch. Eventually, Cara drifted back to sleep. When she woke up, they were gone again. This time, however, there was a note:

We're downstairs in the kitchen having breakfast. You are welcome to join us if you can refrain from comments on the décor.

Cara laughed. She did join them, without comments. She was surprised to find that Julian had stocked his kitchen to match hers, with baby equipment and food. Imagine.

Cara had gone on a boot camp exercise program due to her excessive weight gain. Julian had insisted on one of those nudie pregnancy portraits. He looked fine as hell while she thought she resembled a beached whale. Whether it was the exercising, the breast feeding or a combo, Cara dropped the baby fat fast and became rather toned.

Julian was all over that. His daily baby visits gave him a bird's eye view of her progress and he marked that along with the required abstinence period in his mind. He had not forgotten her 'saved for the one list' and was making plans to claim all that was rightfully his.

One day Cara returned home from an extended walk around the compound to find a large elaborately decorated box in the kitchen. Opening it, she found her long lost picture of herself and her sisters in uniform with Sister Mary Claire. That sick son of a bitch had had her photo all along. Under the pix was an adult size school uniform: skirt, blouse, sweater, knee socks, oxfords and white cotton full briefs and bra. The only thing missing was a beanie. At the bottom of the box was an envelope with a note indicating a date and time. Apparently, she'd been summoned. Her original agitation turned into intrigue, then enticement and finally lust. When was the last time they had done it???

When was the last time she'd played dress up outside of Hallow-een??? Other than with her sisters as little girls – never. The date was for the following day – she would be ready.

Cara was waiting in uniform, at the appointed time on the front steps, sucking a tootsie pop, when Julian pulled up on his motorcycle. Leather outfitted with shades, he stopped, pulled them down and gave her a long lascivious gaze.

"Hey baby, you want a ride?"

Cara stared at him. "Excuse me?" she sneered. "Are you talking to me? What kind of girl do you think I am?" She spun around, flicked her ponytail and went inside.

Julian began to curse. Why couldn't she follow the damn plan? He turned off his bike, kicked the stand and marched into the house behind her.

Cara whirled horrified, "You have to get out of my house before my father comes home. He'll be here any minute."

"Cool," Julian replied as he flounced on the couch, unzipping his jacket and beginning to unbutton his shirt. "I can't wait to meet him."

"Look, I'm going to call the cops. You're trespassing."

Julian faked a yawn, "I think I hear a car."

"Ok, ok. Please, would you please leave? I'll be grounded for life if my dad finds you in here."

"I'll leave if you come with me and do anything I say."

"What? I'm not that crazy!"

"Tsk, tsk, you're wasting time."

"Ok, ok, I'll come with you, just leave."

Julian got off the couch, shirt tails flapping, "See you out back."

Cara went to the kitchen and poured a glass of water. That was kind of invigorating. She'd worn a uniform all her life, but it had never felt like this. She heard the bike start and rev around to the back of the house. Time for scene two. She put down her glass and exited through the back door.

Julian did not acknowledge her, sitting stoically with his shades covering his eyes, bike idling. Cara had never been on a motorcycle. She approached it nervously, struggled to climb on, and then attempted to settle herself upon it. She had just found where to put her feet and was adjusting her skirt when he suddenly took off. She immediately wrapped her arms around him and held on for dear life. He drove at a high rate of speed or maybe it was just the sensation of having nothing encasing you but the wind. Cara was terrified. She could care less that her skirt was whipping up to her waist and her hair was being lashed about her head. She would have screamed but she was using all her energy squeezing tightly unto Julian.

He did not go far, pulling over to what looked like an abandoned building. Julian stopped, kicked the stand, and cut the power. Cara tumbled off and regained her footing on shaky legs. Julian continued to stare at her silently from the bike. Cara could not read his expression due to his shades but she had an intense sensation that the fantasy was about to go awry.

As if on cue with that thought, Julian dismounted, grabbed her wrist and pulled her inside. It appeared to be an old office building. He dragged her from door to door until he found one with a couch. He ushered her in leaving the door open. Cara went to the couch and sat down creating a cloud of dust moots and a bout of uncontrolled coughing.

"Not to your liking, huh? Well that's ok cause it's not for you. Get up."

There was something amiss here. She could detect a hint of distain in almost everything he said and she wondered how many Catholic school girls had run afoul of this man. She got up as instructed. Julian promptly took her place, stretching out while opening his jacket, shirt and pants.

"It's time for you to get to work," he jeered.

Cara stood motionless.

"You promised," he added as he shimmied his pants down and pulled his member free. It was flaccid but the more Julian studied Cara's discomfort the harder he became.

"I don't have all day, bitch."

Cara flinched. This was far from her idea of a fun fantasy, but it wasn't hers, it was his. She had been feeling it, until then. Maybe she just needed to get back into character. She inched forward. His sneer and erection intensified. Obviously, he was expecting fellatio. She had been working on overcoming her indifference to performing that. It wasn't the action itself. It was the fact that Julian was not exclusively hers. Who knows who or what he did when he wasn't with her and the thought of putting her mouth on that mix was disturbing.

Again, as if reading her mind he grinned maliciously, "That's right, you don't know where it's been but that's not going to stop you from doing it. Now get over here."

Cara closed her eyes. She could do this. She was grateful this was not a high school experience but a play fantasy with the father of her son. She walked to the side of the couch and started to kneel.

"No, get up here."

Maybe there was hope yet that this would play out into a happy ending. With that thought in mind she mounted the couch. It was crazy positioning, she had to kneel between his legs and he insisted her booty stay in the air while her mouth came down and around him.

"You're going to have to work it better than that," he cajoled. "Think of it as your lollipop."

Cara clenched her eyes tight, adding motion and suction to her task at hand. Within a few minutes she could sense a change in Julian's body tension, as he relaxed in the moment and began to moan. She was just beginning to feel empowered. So, she could control him too. Suddenly, he grabbed her hair and drove her down deeper, making her gag. She began to struggle. He did it twice more, then came in her mouth, releasing her. As she sat back and attempted to spit the cum out, he sat up too, clamping his hand over her mouth and grabbing the back of her neck. She fought to pull his hand away. He squeezed her nostrils shut. Cara swallowed when she ran out of air and he immediately released her as she sputtered and gasped for air.

Julian got off the couch, straightened his clothes and said, "Let's go."

She quietly followed him out, controlling the desire to hit him in the back of his head. He dropped her home without a word and drove away.

Cara was overwhelmed with confused emotions. She felt angry, humiliated and betrayed. The small amount of power she was enlightened to, was snuffed out by the ending of that scene. She was finished with fantasy and to prove her point, she burned the entire outfit in the fireplace later that night.

Julian showed up the following day as if nothing had happened. He took Aiden and played with him most of the day. Cara tried to avoid them, moving several times, but Julian kept moving too. Eventually she gave up. Towards the end of the day he asked about dinner, which was his way of indicating that he would be eating with them. Shelly, Cara's live-in personal assistant vs nanny vs friend, begged off. She was not very particular about Julian, and he pretty much felt the same way about her. Aiden went to sleep early which left them together alone. Silence was nothing new between them but there was a heaviness to the quiet. Julian finally broke it.

Cara was at the stove sautéing veggies when he came up behind her, gently wrapped his arms around her, nuzzled her neck and attempted an explanation.

"I'm sorry," he whispered kissing her softly along her neck and shoulder. She shivered.

"Tell me I didn't hurt you. I would never want to hurt you."

Cara didn't turn around, but continued stirring slowly.

"You must have something serious against Catholic school girls or maybe it's the uniform?"

She felt him grin and as stupid as it sounds, she grinned too. She had a hard time staying mad at him. After all, she had enjoyed it until the end.

"Let's just say girls of that caliber wouldn't give me the time of day. They were highly verbal with their rejections and condescension that someone of my abjectness would even try approaching them."

Cara was stunned by his admission. This was the most personal information he had ever revealed in a conversation. She turned in his arms.

"I'm sorry. Not all Catholic school girls are like that," she soothed, "Some of them are worse. You've yet to meet my sisters."

They laughed, then started kissing. Serious kissing, but nothing more than that happened. The vegetables burned, so they had to stop and call out for dinner.

Two days later, Cara found another beautiful box in her bedroom. It held an almost identical outfit, only the color of the plaid was different. The card at the bottom said: 2 pm today – I owe you. That sounded uplifting and so against her better judgement but still in the mood to play, she was standing clad in her assigned outfit in the front yard. She heard his bike way before she saw him, and to her surprise Julian rode right on by. She was pissed. She threw the binder and notebook she was holding on the grass and stomped into the house. No sooner had she slammed the door then the bell began to ring. Julian stood on the porch, his back to the door. She slammed it again and threw the lock. The bell started immediately but she ignored it walking straight through the house to the kitchen where she found Shelly and Aiden. Shelly took one look at her outfit, picked up the baby and left. Cara almost laughed. Just then Julian came through the back door. He solemnly grabbed her wrist and pulled her downstairs to the basement. Her house was five thousand square feet. There was more than enough room on the first two floors. She had never been in the basement.

There were walls and doors everywhere. It was a dark maze of confusion.

Julian searched until he found what he was looking for. The room looked like a movie scene. It was made to mimic an old fashioned basement. There were rafters, a tacky couch, a TV with an antenna, as well as, shelves with books, tools and knick-knacks. Cara scoped all that out under a single 40 watt bulb hanging in the middle of the room. She stopped short of entering. Julian released her. Stepping into the room, he switched on a volcano lava lamp and killed the bulb. He came back slowly with a stalking approach and a sly grin.

"Don't be afraid. It's ok, my parents are gone for the night." He waited.

Cara understood. If this was going any further, she would have to acquiesce. She shook her head no, sending her ponytail flying.

"I'm not sure," and she began backing away. She realized then that the hallways were all dark and she had no idea which way to go. She stopped. Julian grinned.

"I have refreshments. A little something to help you relax," Julian purred.

"Really, like what? Valium?"

He snorted, "You know me better than that. I have your favorite, wine, and one of the best – Boone's Farm."

"Boone's Farm? Are you kidding?"

"No, seriously. Strawberry."

Cara didn't believe him. She was forced to come into the room to see the bottle. Well not forced, but what the hell, who could turn down a throwback cocktail of Strawberry Boone's Farm?

The old school vibes, the uniform, Julian looking fine as hell and her feeling frisky as ever, got the best of her. What would it have been like to be in someone's basement when their parents weren't home? She sat on the couch creating another dust cloud. Perfect.

Julian came around the couch carrying two paper cups. Hers appeared to be filled to the brim while his was low? Empty? Slowly easing down on the other end of the couch he handed her the beverage. She sipped warily as he watched her over his cup. Awkward, just like high school. Finally, he got up and put some music on. The song was every teenage boy/young man's anthem: Marvin Gaye's Let's Get It On. If Cara had heard this song once, she had heard it a zillion times and always in a similar situation. A guy trying to get some. It had not bode well for the previous guys, only now she had a feeling her luck was about to change. She took a huge swig of wine – yuck.

Julian did not return to the couch but rather wandered around the room. The distance gave Cara little comfort because she had the distinct impression he was stalking her. She choked on her next sip of wine. Coughing through watery eyes she lost track of him. By the time she had recuperated, she found him nestled next to her on the couch, pinning most of her skirt under him. She was so restrained she could not reach the coffee table to place her cup. Julian took it, crumbled it and threw it on the floor. Somehow that made her more nervous. She began fidgeting, straightening her hair and attempting to pull her skirt free.

"What's the matter?" he cooed. "Am I going too slow or did you drink your wine too fast?"

Cara stalled the answer, "Maybe you should drink yours."

He reached for his cup and turned it up. It was empty, just as she had suspected.

"I'm done," he whispered, "It's time to get busy."

Julian placed his arms gently around her waist and pulled her to him. He began with feather kisses about her eyes, cheeks and forehead. This wasn't bad, Cara thought, and began to relax into her role. Julian immediately sensed a change in her attitude and increased his ministrations. His kisses trailed to her ear lobes and down her neck. Cara squirmed. He knew her weakness for that spot on her neck. She sighed. This was going great. Maybe this time the fantasy would turn out right. No sooner had the thought crossed her mind than he moved to her lips.

Julian was in no hurry. He began again with the feather kisses to her lips and down the front of her throat building slowly in pressure and depth. Cara got lost in the moment and by the time she resurfaced her hands were tangled in his chest hair, her blouse was open and her skirt was hiked up almost to her waist. She gasped. At least, she still had on her granny panties.

Julian chuckled, pushing her down on the couch. Now she realized his mishap of sitting on her skirt was a calculated move. The lower she got the higher her skirt became. By the time she was prone it was bunched around her waist. She groaned and she thought she heard him snicker. His hands were everywhere. They started with her breast, palming, smoothing, and caressing until they were free from their cups. Next they traveled down her abdomen and around to her back, kneading and pinching their way down until finally they were massaging and squeezing her buttocks.

Cara was all for foreplay, but she was fast approaching the climax and conclusion of her fantasy. She pressed herself to him, fumbling with the front of his pants. He moaned, but pushed her hands away.

"Do it," she urged.

"Do what?"

"Do me!" she exclaimed and grabbed again for his crotch.

He pushed her down grabbing the front of her panties. At last, she thought, but instead of pulling them down he jammed his hand inside, fingering her clitoris. She immediately grabbed his wrist. That was not the type of release she had been asking for and he knew it. This was another one of his sick games. Julian laughed and plunged his fingers deeper. Cara came almost immediately. Julian rolled off of her.

"Why did you do that?"

"Do what?"

"You know what. This is beginning to feel like a vengeful fantasy."

"You seemed pretty hot with it. You just didn't get what you wanted, the way you wanted."

She sat up, straightening her panties and skirt. Pulling her blouse shut, she stomped to the door. She again faced the dark hallway, but her anger overcame the darkness and she headed down the hall. Cara made it about ten feet before she ran into a stack of boxes that sent her sprawling to the floor. Scrambling, she noted the small amount of light from the room was gone and now she was in complete blackness. She took a deep breath. Served her right. She should have stuck with the initial 'no'. Attempting to rise, her foot caught on something and she went down again. From behind she felt Julian encircle her waist and pull her to her feet. She attempted to break free but he held her firmly.

"Are you still working on your anger management exercises?" he teased softly in her ear.

"Ugh," she growled fighting against him which only made him tighten his grip.

"Stop it, baby," he cooed. "Playtime is over."

They eventually made their way back upstairs. Julian excused himself as soon as they cleared the door. Shelly shook her head, picked up Aiden and left.

Cara soaked in an extremely hot tub of water. It was pointless trying to ponder the where and the what-for of Julian's fantasies. She burned that outfit in the fireplace too.

CHAPTER 15

A week later, Cara found another gorgeous box, with another uniform in a different plaid. She called Julian to personally tell him she was no longer interested in fantasy sex play. He did not answer the phone. She left a message. Later that evening she got a text with a date, a time and a message: The third time is the charm.

If she wasn't so horny she would not have even considered it, but it had been an extremely long time since they'd had sex. Julian kept working her into a frenzy and then avoiding contact other than in their role playing. Cara felt part of Julian's fantasy was the tease. She was not sure of much else. Still, she would never find out if she didn't play. She remained intrigued. So, on the appointed time and date, she found herself once again outside in a new uniform. This time though, she had given up trying to be cute and coy. She was tired of playing her part nice. This time she was going to play it ugly. Her hair was loose, in a tumble of curls. Her uniform waist band was rolled, the blouse tied in a knot at the waist and her knee socks slouched. Instead of standing expectantly, she was stretched out on a chaise lounge in shades, drinking lemonade. She heard the sound of the approaching menace.

Julian slowly rode his bike around the circle driveway a few times, then back to her designated spot. Clearly, he was enjoying the view. Neither addressed the other. He glared at her intently. This was a different girl from the other two forays. The shy, hesitant creature, willing to try, had been replaced with an angry, frustrated bitch. This was the girl he had been waiting for. He gave a low wolf whistle.

"Glad you liked what you see," she quipped between sips from her straw. "Because that's about all that you'll get, a visual."

He cut the bike and dismounted.

"Oh, come on baby, don't be like that."

"You must have fallen off that bike and hit your head really hard, if you think I'm your baby."

"What is it that you want from me?" he questioned.

"What could you have that I would possibly want?" she jeered.

Julian smiled slyly as he approached the chair and knelt by its side.

"The other day you asked me for something."

"You're delirious, I most certainly did not."

"Maybe you don't remember and need a reminder," he whispered taking her hand and licking her palm, then continuing up the inside of her forearm.

Cara shivered. He never played fair. She jerked her hand away, pulled her shades up and squinted at him.

"You're chances are over. Bye-bye."

He arched an eyebrow then leaned forward to purr in her ear, "I promise to be good."

"You are one of the most untrustworthy individuals I have ever had the misfortune to meet."

"Please..." he was a good actor, it almost sounded like a whine.

"I don't think so."

"You know when I'm good, I'm REALLY good," her whispered in her ear.

Cara felt goosebumps on her arms. That was no lie, he was really good. "Ok," she sighed, "but if this doesn't work out, I'm never going to talk to you again."

"Is that a promise?" he grinned dusting the knees of his pants. He attempted to assist her, but she batted his hands away, making him grin harder. He mounted the bike starting it immediately. As soon as Cara's ass hit the seat he took off. She grabbed hold of him tightly, cursing under her breath as her clothes fluttered around her.

Julia drove several miles, pulling to the side of the road near a field flanked by forestry. He kicked out the stand but continued idling as he ordered Cara off the bike. She dismounted then turned to Julian in question. He continued up the road then turned back towards her. Pulling alongside her, he removed his shades, tucked them into a breast pocket and considered her.

"I have something to tell you."

Cara felt her heart hit a slow hammer.

"This is it for us. I got what I wanted and I'm finished."

"What?" she yelled. "You just promised to be good."

"I lied," he smirked. "You're too easy," and he pulled away.

Cara was totally irate. She looked down, found a rock and threw it at him. On a good day, she couldn't hit the broad side of a barn, but today, as luck would have it, it struck Julian in the back of his head. She cheered, then yelped and took off running into the field after she'd seen the murderous look on his face. For some odd reason, she felt she would be safe if she just made it to the trees, but as she glanced back, she found Julian had not gotten off his bike. Instead, he was riding through the field, hot on her heels.

Cara was not a runner. There was a good possibility she'd have a cardiac arrest before he had a chance to run her down. To her surprise, she made it to the trees. Stopping to suck in as much air as she could, she put her hands on her knees and looked for an escape route. Hearing the motor die she took off again through the bushes and bramble. Hopping over logs and dodging branches she had the emerging hope that she would escape his angst. That was until she stumbled in a hole and fell flat. Rising to continue, she was tackled from behind. This time the weight of her pursuer knocked all the air and fight out of her.

Julian was upon her like a madman, which was exactly what he was a mad man. They rolled around until Cara found herself pinned on her back with Julian straddling her. He looked crazed and when he raised his hands, she cried out for fear he'd strike her. Instead he grabbed her blouse, ripping it open and sending buttons flying in all directions. She began to struggle beneath him when he reached into his boot and pulled out a knife. Cara froze. She'd heard of snuff fantasies. Did people really get killed in those? She was hoping this was not one of them. He grabbed the knot and the front of her bra, cut it up the middle then stabbed the knife into the ground next to Cara's head. She looked at the knife then back at Julian. He was busy yanking her skirt up and her panties down. She forgot about the knife when she felt her panties rip. Cara began her struggles anew but Julian's weight was driving her into the sticks, stones and pine needles beneath her. She suddenly felt him shift and position himself between her legs.

"Cara," he snapped.

She stopped and looked at him. He stared intently at her, waiting. At first she was confused, then it dawned on her, as crazy as it sounded, he was waiting on permission. So there were boundaries with this fantasy.

Yeah, she wanted it. How many weeks had he been stringing her along? "Do me," she wheezed.

Julian plunged into her roughly. She arched and came almost immediately, but he continued, pummeling into her relentlessly.

Cara began to feel the bramble and debris pushing into her with reach stroke. She had the sensation of her skin breaking in multiple places. It occurred to her that they were so stupid and new to each other that they had never established a safe word. Now she began to struggle again in earnest and to her horror he drove still deeper. She was in pain everywhere.

She yelled his name, "Julian."

He stopped immediately, blinking at her blankly.

"You're hurting me," she whimpered.

He took a deep breath then closed his eyes. Cara thought it was over. He began to withdraw but gave one final thrust, coming violently in her. Cara screamed. He laid quietly on top of her while she hot tears ran down her face.

Eventually, Julian rolled off and unto his feet. He picked up her ripped panties, cleaned himself, dropping them back on the ground, adjusted his clothing then turned to leave. Cara struggled up to her elbows.

"Hey, what about me?"

He turned back with a very maleficent expression, "I already told you, I'm done with you."

"You are such an ass," she retorted.

"And you are an easy ass whore. We're finished."

Cara felt her heart tightened. For a moment his fantasy and their reality seem to meld together. What was he saying? She wasn't sure. She closed her eyes and when she opened them, he was gone.

Cara wasted time believing Julian would come back. They had been playing. It was a fantasy. When she heard his bike rev up and the sound disappear into the distance, she knew he would return. She was wrong. Struggling to rise, she found her right ankle three times its appropriate size. That made all her activities harder. Being unable to bear weight on it, she was forced to crawl around in an attempt to redress. Abandoning her bra she tied her blouse closed. Her panties were toast and she could only find one shoe. When the sun began dipping behind the trees, Cara realized how long she'd been alone. This brought back the fear that maybe Julian had meant what he had said. In which case, she would have to save herself.

Mustering what strength she had left, Cara attempted hopping on one foot. That motion sent a jarring pain to her injured foot and ankle causing her to drop back to the ground. She crawled around searching for a stick that could be used as a cane and found her other shoe. Eventually, she found a branch but discovered she was unable to hold it in a way that provided the support she needed. Finally, sitting on a log wondering why she didn't bring her phone and how she got sucked into this fatalistic fantasy, she realized she was holding the shoe she couldn't wear. She tied that to the top of the stick with strips from the panties, sole up, put it under her arm and used it like a crutch.

Julian had let things get out of control and that was something he hadn't done in a long time. His reaction was to regroup ASAP, leaving Cara to walk home. He drove home haphazardly, going straight to his personal quarters, disrobing along the way and not stopping until he was standing in the shower under a spray of hot water. Head down, under the ministrations of the heat and steam, he replayed his actions in his mind. Somewhere along the way, he had allowed the focus of his fantasy to cross over to his past realities. All his internal inadequacies, self-doubts and insecurities had roiled up within. He had been so busy thinking of himself, he had failed to recognize her discomfort. He felt abominable about what he had done and ashamed that he had done the one thing he had promised not to do – hurt her. He tried to sooth himself with the thought that part of this was also her fault for playing along, but he did not really believe it. He exited the shower slowly. He would eventually have to face Cara again. He would need a plan and an explanation. It was then he noticed his phone ringing. It was Cara's tone. Plan or no, he needed to speak with her. Answering on the fifth ring, he was shocked to hear Shelly's voice.

"Is Cara with you? She never came back and it's getting dark."

Julian didn't bother to answer. His heart seized as he pulled on jeans and a t-shirt at a rapid rate. Bounding down the stairs to his garage, he took the nearest car, the Camaro, and had it tearing down the road in seconds.

Cara had just made it out the tree line to the field when she heard a car approaching. She wanted to think positive thoughts, but the truth was she would not make it to the road in time to signal for help. At the speed the car was going, it would drive by without seeing her. She caught sight of the car and gasped as it left the road, barreling into the field toward her. The speed at which it approached frightened her. She thought about moving back into the trees but was frozen to the spot. Having worked so hard to make it out of the forest, she found it ironic that she would be taken out by what appeared to be a drunk driver. She closed her eyes, awaiting impact. She heard the squeal of tires, the swish of grass and the slamming of a door. Cara opened her eyes to see Julian running towards her. In all her hours of struggling, she had not shed a tear but as he reached her and clutched her to his chest, she began to cry hysterically. She heard herself babbling. It almost sounded like someone speaking in tongues. What the hell was she trying to say? She was clueless. It didn't seem to matter to Julian, who was holding her like he was a drowning man and she was his life preserver. Unbeknownst to Cara, she was holding him just as tightly. Julian eventually pulled free, swooped her up in his arms and deposited her in the front seat. He silently returned to the driver's seat, taking off at a breakneck speed.

Arriving back at her house, he carried her into the den. Shelly took one look at them, picked up Aiden and left. As soon as Julian had arranged her on the couch, the doorbell rang. The compound EMS hurried in with a portable x-ray machine, equipment bag and blankets. Cara was covered, x-rayed and examined within a matter of minutes. There was a brief quiet conversation with Julian as he walked them to the door. Since no one did anything with her ankle she assumed it wasn't broken. Thank God.

Cara watched Julian as he stoically returned. He gently lifted her off the couch and carried her upstairs. Cara, who had always imagined she was too heavy to be carried, sat back and enjoyed the ride. Julian must have been running on a heavy dose of adrenaline. He by-passed the bed and gingerly seated her on the side of the tub. He turned the water on and began to undress her. He gave up on the knot holding her blouse together and opted to cut it and the skirt off. Julian inhaled deeply. Cara was a canvass of abrasions, cuts, scratches and blisters, all embedded with debris. He slowed visually when he spotted the nick on her chest that he had personally delivered when cutting off her bra. She watched him survey the damage. Finally their eyes met. For just a second Cara thought she saw moisture in his eyes, but it was gone in a blink. He agilely helped her into the tub. The hot water on all the open areas made Cara bite her lip in pain as tears rolled down. Julian left and came back with a glass of wine in one hand and the bottle in the other. He placed the glass to her lips gazing at her as she slowly sip it. He did not move it until the glass was empty, then refilling it, he placed it on the side of the tube. Then, taking up a brush began to remove the sticks and debris from her hair.

Cara began to relax. She gazed up at him but they both remained silent. Finally, Julian opened his mouth as if he was about to speak, then shut it, shook his head and shrugged. Cara knew exactly what he meant. There were just no words.

The grim task of removing the embedded debris, cleaning the wounds, as well as, the application of antiseptics and dressings, took hours. Julian did it all himself. In a way it was his penance. It was also a cathartic experience for both of them. When Cara wasn't crying, he was. They were exhausted by the end of it, tumbling into bed and into each other's arms. He held her again, as he had when he found her, like he would never let her go.

Two weeks later, Cara found a plain white box on the kitchen counter. She did not even approach it. Julian happened in and pushed it over to her. She pushed it back.

"Open it," he demanded, pushing it back her way.

Cara took a deep breath, exhaled and reached for the box. It had a card on top. That was different. Opening the envelope, she read the message:

Maybe we should just work on being ourselves.

She looked up at Julian and opened the box. It was empty. They both smiled.

CHAPTER 16

Of all of Julian's friends, Kafir was the only one who could just drop by and actually get into the compound on any given day. He appeared at Julian's front door just as he was finishing an all-night studio session. Welcoming him in, Julian ran up to shower and change. Upon returning, he found Kafir comfortably ensconced on his couch, sipping a beverage from a baby cup.

"I'm thinking we have much to talk about," stated Kafir, raising the cup as if to toast.

"Kafir, I have no idea where to begin."

"From the beginning my boy. Always from the beginning."

"There are not enough words nor do you have the time. Come with me."

Cara was playing with Aiden when she heard the knock on the door. Irritated as to why Julian was knocking, she picked up Aiden and started for the entrance. He was babbling and laughing in advance to who it might be. At least Aiden was excited to be having company.

"Julian, why didn't you just use your key?" she fussed whipping open the door. To her surprise there he stood with Kafir, who bellowed out a huge laugh. Aiden cried out "Da-dee" and Kafir laughed again, only louder, if that was possible. Julian walked in took Aiden and continued into the house. Kafir wrapped Cara in a bear hug and swung her around in a monumental circle.

"Ha, Ha. I knew it, I knew it. I knew you'd be the one," he said finally setting her down with a kiss.

"Oh Kafir, it's so good to see you," Cara smiled leading them through the house in search of Julian.

"You knew nothing of the kind," Julian called out from the kitchen area. They turned in that direction.

"Feathers, my dear boy, feathers. Now, when is the christening and what am I to wear?" Kafir continued.

Julian and Cara looked blankly at each other. There was a lot going on. Other than Shelly and Brian, no one knew about them or the baby. Kafir picked up on it almost immediately.

"I'm good with secrets," he expounded, "but it will cost you."

"I know you are not trying to blackmail me," countered Julian.

"My boy, you are just where I have wanted you for years."

"Between a rock and hard place?"

"Between a woman and a baby," Kafir chided. He could not contain his giant smile nor did he try.

Cara was just returning with refreshments. "What?"

Julian was agitated. He'd been surprised and Julian did not like surprises.

"I graciously accept to be the godfather," he said magnanimously. "Now, give me my godchild and be gone."

Aiden went to Kafir as if he truly was his long lost godfather. They hugged and gurgled together as if they had the world to catch up on. Cara shrugged and returned to the kitchen with Julian sulking behind her.

Aiden turned six months just before Christmas. It was time to decide if they would be attending her family's gathering or not. There were many logistical issues, the main one being Cara had not told the truth when Julian had met her mother and aunt. And like any good lie, it had snowballed out of control. She loved her family and really wanted to go, but there would be so much explaining to do that she might need a screenwriter? An attorney? A publicist?

Julian, who was not family oriented other than his individual unit, could care less. This would be Aiden's first Christmas and he thought he should be home. Julian liked his space and serenity under his control and neither of those would occur at her family function. The environment was always too small. The participants too loud and usually slightly inebriated. There would be a large number of children, all under the age of eighteen, highly excited by the season, the expectations, the sugar overload and each other's company. Cara had a dilemma. She wanted to show off her beautiful new baby boy, but she did not want to be under the scrutiny of her sisters. There were four of them and they would not be as easy to convince as their mother. Also, she was having trouble remembering just what she had said. So, all of the exaggeration, rumors and insinuations added by her mother, aunt and sisters were sure to trip her up. She really wished she could just pop in, say "hi" and retreat, but flying to California with Shelly and the baby, with or preferably without Julian, would be a task.

Since Cara could not pin Julian down, and since he seemed to be leaning towards not only "no", but "hell no", she proceeded making plans to go. She would stay the minimum amount of time and sleep anywhere other than her mother's house, where everyone else would be dispersed to rooms, couches, cots, porches and any other spare floor space that could accommodate a sleeping bag. The actual celebration was on Christmas Eve, so the plan was to fly home first thing in the morning getting Aiden back in time to spend Xmas with his father.

Cara made arrangements to stay in yurts built into the cliffs on the beach not far from her mother's house. No sooner had she booked two then Julian decided he would accompany them, but not attend the party. Cara refused to cancel her reservations. Julian was outraged that his son should be in such quarters but she advised that next time he needed to make up his mind in a more timely fashion. Case closed. Her entourage of three would be in their yurts and he could go where he liked. Julian eventually acquiesced but that was many days, demands and threats later. Next, he decided he wanted to take his private plane. No argument there. Cara cancelled all the air arrangements and the packing began.

As the time to depart got closer, Cara's initial trepidation turned to dread, then into downright panic. She finally put together a semi-plausible storyline of their lives. Julian continued to be Alex D., the impersonator/decoy for Aristo. They resided on Aristo's compound and Alex's travels were dictated by whatever Aristo's needs were. Cara had attributed some schitzy components to Julian's character, but she could not remember what those were. She would just have to wing it. Try as she might, she could get neither Julian nor Shelly to learn their lines or practice their roles. Julian advised he would not be attending and Shelly quipped she would just pick up the baby and leave. Cara developed a burning sensation in her upper gastric area.

Julian continued to complain about their accommodations. The flight included an argument that not everyone belonged to the bourgeoisie, and the common people just wanted to expand their experiences and have fun. Of course, Julian wanted to expound on the expanded experiences but Cara was not in the mood. Everyone fell into a sullen silence and drifted off to sleep, except Julian who donned his head phones and floated off to music land.

The standard black limo awaited their descent from the plane. Brian, always on hand, was backed up by another large man. They took care of the luggage while the rest of the party got comfortable in the back seats. Julian insisted on carrying Aiden, who slept through most of his first great adventure. His continued somnolence was another good reason for everyone not to talk. The drive to their resort was breath taking. It followed Pacific Coast Highway along the curves, cliffs and rocky beaches until finally reaching a dirt road that appeared to fall off the edge. As Cara began gathering her purse to check in, Julian handed her the baby and said he would take care of it. Tired and not feeling up to further disagreements, she settled back on the seat next to Shelly who gave her an eyebrow, but remained silent. For all they knew, he was cancelling everything. After an extended period of time Julian returned, had a discussion with his boys, who in turn began unloading and carrying bags to their prearranged spots.

The yurts were scattered on the hillside leading down to the beach. They were situated in a way that secluded each from the other with trees, shrubs and flowers. Each yurt had its own private pathway, deck with chairs, fire pit and outdoor tub, as well as, inside fireplace, skylight, kitchen and king size bed. Julian, still reticent from the flight, took Aiden and led the way to their yurt. Upon entering, Cara took a brief tour of their lodgings then headed for the deck. She took in the ocean, the sound of the waves and the gulls, the smell of the salt, sand and surf. Inhaling deeply she let out a cleansing breath and began to fill the tub. By the time Julian finally decided to appear, Cara was neck deep in the hottest water she could tolerate with a cool glass of white wine. The stress of the trip and the anticipated Xmas dinner had finally begun to wan.

Julian by passed her and went directly to the rail without a word. He stood silently with his back to her, which was fine with Cara. Eventually, he turned and stared at her. "Are you nude out here in that tub?"

"That's the only way I know how to bathe," she answered.

"But you're outside in the open."

"In case you haven't noticed, these yurts are pretty isolated from each other. Besides, everything is under water."

"Is this your idea of expanding your horizons?" he questioned snidely.

"As a matter of fact, it is. I bet you've never been in a yurt or nuddie booty in a tub outside, hanging off a cliff."

"No," he relented, "but I've done plenty of other things."

"Oh, I'm sure you have. The question is not what you or I have done in the past, it's what are we going to do now and in the future, together? It's not just you and me anymore, we have Aiden. What horizons are we going to open up for him?"

Julian was silent. In actuality, he had considered Aiden's future and summed it up in one word – successful. After that he had been too busy being excited, proud, astounded and exhilarated by the fact that he had created life. He loved to look, hold, bathe, tickle, dress, and just stare at his little boy. This idea of exposures and horizons was new to him. It was not part of his childhood experience. He sank slowly into one of the Adirondack chairs, pulling the hair under his lower lip while looking at the sunset. The possibilities were endless. He could show his son the world. The thought brought such a sudden brilliant happiness that he smiled. Cara had been watching him closely. She had no idea what was flowing through his mind. Something was ticker-taping its way around every fiber of him given his intensity and when he smiled, she let out a breath. Apparently whatever it was, everything was going to be okay.

Julian steepled his fingers and stared at her. "I like your sense of adventure."

"Why thank you," she grinned. "You know you can join in at any time. In fact, maybe we could plan some things together.

"Together?" he inquired and then his smirk turned lascivious. "I'd like that."

Cara was not concerned, although she did sink a little deeper. Her water was way too hot for him to even attempt a plunge and she had no intent of getting out any time soon.

"Trips," she clarified, "work together planning trips." She enunciated slowly so he could catch her drift. "Expeditions, adventures, excursions..." She was in the middle of her list when Julian suddenly got up, grabbed the hair piled high on her head and kissed her deeply. She forgot the rest of the words on the list.

Later that evening, when Cara finally abandoned the tub, she found Julian in bed, directly under the skylight bathed in moonlight and little else. She initially thought he was asleep but as she approached, found him gazing stoically at the moon. She dropped her towel and wordlessly crawled in beside him, pulling the sheet up to cover them both. She was still waiting for him to comment on his yurt experience, but refused to ask him or disturb his silence. She was drifting off to sleep when he reached over and pulled her to him.

CHAPTER 17

The Xmas party was slated to begin at five. Hoping to get in and out ASAP, Cara, Shelly and Aiden showed up at four. Of course, everybody was already there. They were attempting to get out of the foyer with all her sisters oohing and aahing over the baby, when the bell rang. Since she was closest to the door, Cara answered it. There on the porch stood Julian. She attempted to push him back as he advanced and her sisters noticing the commotion, turned their attention to the action.

"I thought you said you weren't coming," she hissed.

Julian pushed past her, smiled charmingly and said, "I changed my mind."

All of her sisters stood agoggled.

"This is Alex D," she stammered. Silence.

"Aiden's father." More silence.

"He's not who you think he is. He's Aristo's decoy/impersonator." Continued silence. And then they all broke out laughing.

"Of course, he's not Aristo," said Tina, her oldest sister.

"Yeah right, Aristo would never be with someone like you. You worked for him, for what five years, and he never even spoke to you," piped in Patrice, her next oldest sister.

"Me, maybe," chimed in Jenna, her youngest sister, "but you?" They all started laughing again.

Julian felt Cara sag beside him. He snaked his arm around her waist and pulled her against him.

"Now, now ladies," he cooed, "your sister got the best of the best. She got me and everything associated with me, which is kinda like getting Aristo and everything associated with him." And to make his point Julian flipped out his phone, called Brain and requested he return with the flowers, liquor and desserts he had forgotten in the trunk of the car. Cara knew there were no such items there, but within ten minutes, Brian arrived hauling cases of beer and wine, multiple bouquets, and a wide variety of desserts. The mention of additional alcohol brought her brothers-in-law out front and center. They gave Julian a hand-shake in passing to assist in retrieving the goodies from the car. Julian presented the largest and most elaborate bouquets to her mother and aunt, who had joined the chaos, and then with a flourish gave one to each of her now hushed sisters. The evening was off to a bang and everybody was still standing in the foyer.

Having cleared the introduction hurdle, dinner was a breeze. Questions were volleyed from everyone, but Julian as Alex D, handled it as the true performer he was. He was pretty quick on his feet and Cara gave up attempting to keep pace with or re-member all the tales he was spinning.

After dinner, everyone gathered around the tree for the kids to open their presents. Aiden was enthralled with the other chil-dren, the wrapping paper, ribbon and bows, as well as, all the extra attention he garnered. Shelly volunteered to help clean the kitchen, thereby assuring her peace and tranquility since everyone else was around the tree. Julian tolerated most of it really well considering the number of people, the volume of noise and the closeness of quarters. Cara, on the other hand, had developed a vicious headache. Leaving the baby with Julian, she made her way to the nearest bathroom. Once inside, a brief survey of the medicine cabinet proved no relief would be found there, so she placed a cool damp towel on her forehead. No sooner had the vise begun to loosen when there was a knock at the door. Cara pulled herself off the side of the tub. Opening the door she found Erica, her second youngest sister.

"Are you okay?" Erica asked.

"Yeah, just a headache. I think I'm overly tired."

"Are you sure that's what it is?"

"What do you mean?"

"I mean maybe you're pregnant."

"What? That's a jump."

"You're tired, you have a headache. I bet you've been irritable too. And you're drinking. That's something you need to know," and Erica pulled a pregnancy test out her purse. Cara pulled a face.

"What? Girl, I'm always in a need to know state. At least I'm prepared."

She tossed the test at Cara and left. After her sister's departure she thought, sure, why the hell not and took the test.

Merry Christmas, it was positive.

Part of their family tradition included adult time after all the children and elders had gone to bed. Cara attempted to leave before this faction began, but Julian, truly out of character, had made best buds with her brothers-in-law and put the kibosh on that idea. He sent Shelly and Aiden back to the yurts instead. Starting with cocktails, advancing to games and finally to presents, everyone coupled up with their mates for the final count down. Having not prepared for this part of the evening, Cara was relaxing next to Julian when her sisters presented him with a box. "Welcome to the family," they all smiled.

"Well, it seems you've made an impression," Cara teased.

Julian graciously accepted the box and began to slowly unwrap it. There was tissue paper, and tissue paper and more tissue paper. Cara was beginning to believe it was a gag gift when he reached in the bottom and pulled out a Ziploc bag that contained her positive pregnancy test.

"What the..." he began. All her sisters began to giggle and laugh at once.

"Let's see how mister big stuff likes that," sneered her oldest sister.

Cara was enraged. She forgot to breathe. Instead she slapped the baggie out of Julian's hand and bolted off the couch. She would have vaulted over the coffee table had not Julian grabbed her around the waist.

"You are a bunch of sick bitches," she shrieked.

They continued laughing as Julian began dragging her to the kitchen. Frustrated, she kicked her feet out sending one of her shoes flying into Erica's forehead. She yelped and grabbed her face.

"Yeah, laugh about that," was Cara's final retort before Julian closed the door. Standing in front of it, Julian released her. Cara paced one direction, then the other muttering obscenities under her breath. Julian the consummate observer merely watched. Finally, in about her seventh rotation, he reached out, took her firmly by the waist and sat her on the end of the kitchen table. Cara refused to meet his gaze. She was flush with embarrassment, anger and her cardio workout.

"Well?" he said softly.

"Well what?" she snapped.

Julian put his index finger under her chin and lifted her head up until their eyes met. Cara had an overwhelming sense of foreboding. Julian remained silent, waiting.

Finally, she took a deep breath. "It's not fair. It was mine to tell."

"Ok, so tell me," he coaxed.

"Julian, we are going to have another baby," and with that she broke out into a full sob.

Julian grinned, but Cara couldn't see that through the tears. He hugged her tightly, burying his face in her neck and hair.

"You know I love you and Aiden," he whispered. Cara gulped for air.

"You know we can afford as many babies as we can make." Cara sniffled.

"You know my name is not Alex D. You do remember who I am?" Cara laughed.

On hearing her laugh, Julian kissed her deeply and began nibbling on her neck. Somewhere along the way, he lowered her back onto the table and that's just where they were when her siblings busted in.

"I know you're not doing what I think you are on my momma's table," exclaimed Patrice.

They sat up immediately to find everybody jammed in the doorway.

Julian gave them his most lascivious smile, "That all depends on what you think we were doing." He shamelessly pulled Cara off the table, holding her close so that she literally slid down his body. She heard her brothers-in-law quick intake of air.

"In any case, we've got to go. It seems we have some celebrating to do," announced Julian as he ushered Cara out by the small of her back. She would have laughed at all their gawking faces, but seeing her sisters again put her back in a foul mood. Julian held out her sweater and opened the door. The limo was out front waiting, Brian by the open door. Just before exiting Julian turned back to his silent audience.

"Oh, by the way we have some extra yurts on the hillside, maybe you'd like to come by, maybe spread out some," and he dropped five sets of keys on the side table. Cara was seething by the time they reached the car.

"Why would you do that? I can't stand them," she grimaced.

"Because I can." Julian grinned, "Because now they're my family too, and because it's going to drive your sisters crazy to see just how big my stuff can be."

Cara and Julian settled back into their yurt. Cara could not shake the sense of gloom and doom. Julian, perceptive as always, pulled her into bed and held her tightly.

"Don't over think it Cara. We have another room to decorate. Aiden will be a big brother. Shelly will get a raise. You'll get to breast feed again and I'll get to talk to your tummy. Things are not that bad. I think we've been doing ok. Whatever we have going on is working."

Cara exhaled loudly. All of that was true. Maybe it was just a matter of letting go. After all, she was knee deep in it now. She was just about to voice her apprehensions when the quiet of their haven was disrupted by the shrieking voices of those banshees she called sisters. Apparently, all of them had tucked away their pride enough to take advantage of Julian's offer. Cara huffed and attempted to pull away.

"Uh-Uh," Julian chided and hugged her tightly, "we're all family now."

Cara could not sleep. She tossed and turned, awakening to find Julian gone. Since she was wide awake, she went in search of him only to find an impromptu smoked filled, liquor fueled poker game in yurt #12. She was quickly driven out by the questioning claim that Julian had confessed she had given it up on their first date. Her immediate whirl to face him was the wrong response. It sent the room into a roar. Julian merely shrugged as she stormed out. Returning to bed, her agitated state resumed. There was so much on her mind. What would happen to her and her babies? Julian would always be Julian, doing whatever he pleased, but what would happen if he should tire of them? Right now everything was new and novel but when the shine wore off, what would occur? Her mind reeled from one issue to another. What if Julian tired of her and decided to seek sole custody? Could she bear being separated from her babies? Never. At least she had one answer. Why were her sisters being such bitches?? When was this baby conceived?? How far along was she?

Cara woke the following morning with a massive headache, a rumbling stomach and a heart full of misgivings. Julian had still not returned. Dragging herself from the bed, she spent an hour under the pounding spray of the shower, alternating the water temperature from scalding to cold. When she finally got out her headache was gone, her GI distress had turned to hunger and her misgivings had diminished to wayward thoughts. Quickly dressing, she went in search of her child, her man, and a meal. Although the yurts were designed for privacy, the meals were served beach side on a deck large enough to hold all that ventured that far. It was there that Cara found the rest of the yurt inhabitants, including Julian, in full regale, tables laden with every breakfast food imaginable. Cara was about to forgive and forget all the previous night's atrocities when she stopped short. There in front of every adult was a large white box with variations of exquisite bows. Julian appeared behind her, ushering her forward from her rooted spot to a chair that also had a box before it.

She wheeled on him, whispering vehemently, "What have you done?"

"I'm sharing grown-up entertainment with grown-up people, who requested to play, I might add," he countered as he continued pressing her into her chair.

Cara watched with a growing dread. Every sister had a Catholic school uniform of a different plaid with the white cotton under garments. Cat calls bellowed forth as the granny panties flapped in the wind. The guys had a variety of "manly" costumes: fireman, cowboy, policeman, etc. Cara immediately thought: The Village People. No one noticed Julian did not have a box nor was Cara attempting to open hers. The conversation quickly turned to organizing a party. Since all the children had been conveniently left to visit their grandmother and aunt, it was time to dress up and show out in their new gear. Cara felt a throb in her left temple, her hunger had turned to nausea and she again felt hell hounds on her heels. She excused herself leaving her box behind, kissed Aiden on the way out, returned to her bed and covered her head. Julian found her that way several hours later.

"Come on. Get up. I brought you food."

She heard it, then her covers flew off. "Julian," she squeaked.

"Eat, then we're taking Aiden for a walk. You do remember Aiden, don't you?"

Wallowing in self-pity, Cara had not forgotten Aiden. He was with Shelly and well cared for. He was on her happy list. She was currently bogged down going through her unhappy list. She sat up, then laid back down. "I don't feel well," she whined.

"Well, you're not going to get any better in here. Let's go," Julian demanded.

He began undressing and dressing her. Cara usually would have been outraged, but she laid there like a lump, forcing him to do everything. By the end he got a little rough and rolled her off the edge of the bed, sending her into an unexpected free fall to the floor. That snapped her out of it. She jumped up infuriated only to find Julian by the door holding her shoes. She snatched them as he opened the door, leading the way out.

Their walk was invigorating and as usual Julian dispelled all her dark thought clouds. Upon their return, Cara was hyped up for the party. They had finished their fantasies. It would be interesting to see if her sisters fared any better. Aiden stayed with them the remainder of the afternoon and into the early evening. Cara was dressed in her French maid outfit, adjusting her stockings when Shelly came to the door. Shelly shook her head, took Aiden and left. Julian had spent an inordinate amount of time in the bathroom. She had no idea what could be taking him so long. He had entered with silk pajamas and a smoking jacket. Cara thought he was going as Hugh Hefner. She was wrong. When he withdrew from his preparations, he was none other than Aristo. Cara was stunned. He was clean shaven except for a small mustache, professionally made up and sporting some leisure high rise heels.

"Oh, no," she muttered, "I'm out."

"You most certainly are not," he chided.

"You know I do not particularly care for Aristo," she stated.

"And you know that's also who I am."

She sat down in a huff on a chair. Julian continued preening in the mirror. He opened the top three buttons of his top, setting his chest hair free. Cara studied him in the reflection. She really could not stand Aristo. Was it the makeup, the hair, the clothes, the attitude? It all rubbed her the wrong way. She recalled watching a concert he insisted she attend after her recovery from California. It was there she realized Julian/Aristo, which ever he was, would never be hers. Standing in the side wings, she could feel the intensity and energy of the crowd. While Julian was magnificent as a musician and consummate as performer, she believed he was channeling the synergy of the audience. It explained a lot of things about of him. The many days and nights it would take to disperse so much energy, accounted for his sleepless nights and manic days. His vibe was purely sexual, so his countless women were also spot lighted. To be fair, how many panties thrown on stage, secreted into pockets or passed on by your entourage could anyone take? Cara accepted then that he would never be hers, not in the way she wanted. The only saving grace was he would never be anyone else's either, no matter how beautiful. His first love, his undying devotion was to his music and himself, and everyone could just take a ticket after that.

The longer she watched him, the more she realized this had nothing to do with sharing fantasy. This elaborately concocted event had everything to do with him and what her sisters' had said about him being a poor copy of Aristo (which was a hoot, since that's actually who he was). Apparently he had been insulted and somebody was going to pay. In a way, Cara almost felt sorry for her sisters, but thought better of it and was glad to be a part of the opposing team.

"Let the games begin," he exclaimed.

Cara and Aristo made their way slowly down to the party venue. They were way past fashionably late, but rushing was not a part of Aristo's vocabulary. Besides, this was all about a calculated entrance. From the clamor below, it sounded as if everyone had overindulged in the offerings. Cara knew both parties all too well. Her sisters, as well as their spouses, would attempt to empty the coffers. Julian, on the other hand, had bottomless resources. He would keep them supplied even if he had to send his security out to the store. There was no way this would end well and that was an understatement.

Upon their entrance, it seemed, everything stopped. Cara's heart certainly did. Then everything resumed at a higher speed and noise level. Her sisters immediately surrounded Aristo, their view of him as a poor imposter had obviously changed. They were all over him and Cara had a sudden attack of possessiveness. She attempted a verbal rebuff that was hugely ignored, then elbowing them aside, which was also ineffective. Finally, she used her feather duster as a weapon, driving them back. Aristo was casually draped over his chair. He appeared highly entertained by the drama.

"All you heifers need to back the hell up," Cara demand, "I do believe all your men are behind you."

"You don't have to be so snotty," snapped Erica, "we were just trying to say hello."

"Well, you've said it. So take your boobs and booties out of his face."

"Damn girl, you need to relax," scoffed Patrice.

"Don't tell me....."

"Ladies," Aristo purred, "There's no need to fight. Personally, I have had my fill of Catholic school girls. (Here he winked at Cara, who blushed profusely). My tastes have expanded to French cuisine." He held his hand out to Cara, who pranced her ass very provocatively to his side.

"Her?" All her sisters chimed at once.

"She does exactly as ordered."

"What?" The group again, questioning.

"Kiss me," he demanded, and did not bother to turn his face toward her.

Cara thought, two can play this game. She bent to kiss him extravagantly, including a lot of tongue that tapered to his lips then trailed along the side of his face, ending with a body roll, her boobs brushing his face. She heard her brothers-in-law groan and she would have laughed, but she had to maintain her role in the face of all her sisters' stunned expressions. Instead, she smiled sweetly and said, "Next time maybe you girls should strive for something more exotic." Her sisters turned as a single unit and huffed off. Aristo took her hand and kissed her wrist.

"I like your possessive green side." he murmured. "Even for the likes of me."

Cara attempted to pull her arm away, but he held tight, working his kisses up her arm. She felt her heart rate quicken and in spite of herself, she shivered.

"Mmmm," he whispered, "look how easily you've forgotten Julian."

"You are Julian," she snapped yanking her arm free, "and you're still an ass!"

He laughed.

The party continued in full swing. Her brothers-in-law really resembled the Village People and they must have realized it because they kept breaking out into the YMCA. Her sisters on the other hand, had all adjusted their uniforms (like good Catholic school girls), except Tina, who wore hers exactly as it was supposed to be worn, including pinning a tissue on her head in place of the missing beanie. The libations continued and Cara could calculate the number of drinks consumed by the deterioration of the characters and the raunchiness of the dancing. Julian sipped some concoction while quietly observing the scene. He had ordered her something special, a glass of milk served in a stem glass with an umbrella. She gave him her deadliest smile. He laughed.

Apparently, witnessing debauchery was not on Aristo's to do list. Just over an hour after their entrance, he rose to go. Cara having nothing better to do followed. It was half way up the trail that she faltered. She had not considered that she might be sleeping with Aristo. In all their time together, she had only been with Julian.

"Uh-Uh, it's too late to think of that now," Aristo chided, grabbing her wrist and tugging her along.

Damn him and his mind reading abilities. Still, she got slower and slower the closer they came to their yurt. In the end, Aristo was behind her pushing her forward. Cara stopped at the door, not bothering to open it. Not to worry, Aristo reached around, turned the knob and threw it open. She was stunned. The room was covered with rose petals and candles.

"It seems I've developed a predilection for pregnant women," he whispered, his breath hot on the back of her neck. Cara shivered.

"Ah, still virginal, and in your condition."

She turned to give him a hot retort, but he pulled her into his arms and kissed her. Her initial struggle evaporated, he felt just like Julian.

By the time he released her, they were inside, her uniform was missing and all he had on were his pajama bottoms. He dropped those, climbed atop the petal covered bed, and motioned to her. She hesitated.

"Don't over think it," he urged.

It sounded just like Julian, so she went to him. He pulled her down and they rolled around until all her underwear was gone too. Aristo proceeded to kiss every square inch of her. Their night together was long, hot and steamy.

In the morning, Cara awoke to find Julian staring at her. Make-up free, perfectly mussed hair, already sporting a five o-clock shadow.

"Tramp," he exclaimed.

"What?"

"See how easily you can be dissuaded to forget about me?"

"Are you insane? You're the one always saying I should accept that you and Aristo are the same person."

"I said accept him, not sleep with him."

Cara groaned, this conversation was truly bizarre.

"So, who's better?"

"You, of course," she quipped.

"Why?"

"Really?"

"Yes, why?"

"Because Aristo's love-making was staged. I felt like I was just one of many who had received that same set-up and perform-ance. With you it feels like it's about me, and what happens between us is personally ours. Which means, neither of us has experienced anything like that with anyone else."

She had certainly let that cat out of the bag, but what the hell. She had one baby with this man and was expecting another. It seemed pointless to pull the punches now. Julian stared at her and she stared back. Two people could talk just as crazy as one.

Finally, a grin appeared on one side of Julian's face and grew until it encompassed his whole face with a huge smile. Cara loved it when he smiled like that.

"Touché," he said and began rubbing his scruffy shadow all over her and he did not stop until he had covered every square inch of her.

Cara and Julian were still lounging, picking stray petals from obscure places when Cara suddenly sat up.

"What's the matter?" He inquired lazily.

"Something's wrong," she stated.

"What?"

"No really, listen," she insisted. And there was nothing but quiet.

Cara bounded out of bed searching for something to put on. Julian casually watched her frantic actions.

"So let me get this straight, just because it's quiet you think there's something wrong?"

"Julian, please. You've met my family. Have you ever heard them quiet? Listen, there's no talking, snoring, fussing, farting, whispering – nothing. Unless we've both died and this is heaven, there's something going on."

Dressed in shorts, a tank top and flip flops, Cara headed for the door.

"Wait for me, this ought to be good."

"You're going to take too long," she whined. Julian never just threw clothes on.

"Wait," he demanded. "Whatever it is, it isn't going anywhere." He sauntered off to the bathroom.

Cara paced the room a thousand times before Julian emerged in a silk walking suit and sandals. She attempted to rush out the door but he insisted they walk arm in arm, slowing her down tremendously.

"Remember, whatever happens it's going to be ok," he soothed, but that just made her heart beat harder and faster. What premonition had made him say that? He continued to hold her back. Once they cleared their private path the silence became eerie. Cara had a sudden overwhelming fear that everyone had been murdered. Julian assured her his security team would never let that happen. Still, they checked on Shelly and the baby first. Shelly was groggy and Aiden was still sleeping. Cara was afraid to knock on any other doors instead opting to go directly to the deck below. It was empty. Her heart seized. Continuing to the beach they finally found her youngest sister, sitting on a rock crying. Cara rushed to her.

"Jenna, what's the matter? What's happened?" she asked shrilly.

Through massive amounts of sniffles and occasional breakdowns, Jenna relayed the finale of the party they had missed. Right after their departure, wild bawdy dancing broke out. Inebriated revelry deteriorated into confusion, complications and confrontations. Couples got mixed up, foul words were exchanged and finally fists started flying. Jenna had kept her head but Fernando, overwhelmed by her sisters' extravagant attention, doubted if he wanted to have anything further to do with her family or with her, for that matter.

Cara looked immediately at Julian, who only raised his eyebrows but otherwise, looked extremely pleased. She frowned. Turning back to Jenna she said, "Maybe you should come home with us."

"No," Julian interrupted, "She needs to stay here and wait for Fernando's return." Cara pulled Julian aside.

"This is all your fault," she hissed.

"It most certainly is not," he replied flippantly. "All these gray ass people are old enough to make their own choices and decisions. Me and mine were where we were supposed to be. If others over indulge, over compensate and/or over react, that's not on me, that's on them."

Cara huffed. He was right, they were all adults, but something about him had a tendency to lead people astray. Julian suddenly decided it was time to go home. He flipped out his phone and set the ball in motion. By the time they corralled her sister up the trail to her yurt and helped her pack, security appeared with Shelly and Aiden, their packed packs in tow. Julian and Cara's things were already magically in the car. Jenna was dropped at their mother's house on the way to the airport and an hour later they were in the air. Cara played with Aiden, Shelly napped and Julian fielded phone calls.

That was a Xmas to remember. It was several months before Cara heard from any of her sisters, and when she did, they were not so bold or brazen as usual. No one mentioned the yurts and no one ever accepted an invitation to stay there again.

CHAPTER 18

Quinton was born one month after Aiden's first birthday. He arrived with the flare of all the other men in her life, early and in the ambulance before they reached the hospital. If Julian had been overjoyed with one son, he was ecstatic to have two. 'His boys' became his best friends, confidants and band mates, and they were only a newborn and a one year old. Cara smiled at the thought of things to come.

Six months after Quinton's birth, Julian insisted on a commitment ceremony. He had continued to ask her to marry him, and she had consistently declined. Cara was a bit flustered. She was living on his compound with their two children. He had open access to come and go as he pleased and to her knowledge he had not relinquished his girly entourage. What was there to commit to? Still Julian persisted and Cara, who could not see what difference it would make and to avoid further discussion on the matter, agreed.

Julian had assured her it would be a simple, private affair. Liar. First of all, Kafir was to officiate, and nothing was ever simple with Kafir. Secondly, when she arrived at the private beach, on the private island in Biscayne, she found not just Julian, Kafir, Shelly and the babies as planned, but her entire family seated primly in chairs on the sand. Cara, dressed in a white lacy sundress with a circle of flowers in her hair, made a beeline to Julian. He, of course, stood there grinning, also dressed in white, hair shoulder length with an impeccable beard.

"You, you, you......" she stammered in her anger and frustration.

"Yes? Me?"

"You said this was going to be small and private. Just between us."

"It is just us, with your family. You want me to send them away?" he whispered.

Kafir watched the exchange, this could take a while, so he broke in, "Let us begin," he boomed. "Dearly beloved, we are gathered here today to witness the commitment of these two individuals to each other."

Cara eyed Kafir, then Julian, who promptly got down on one knee. She was taken aback. Nothing was going as planned, maybe she should have written something as Julian had suggested instead of thinking she could just come up with something on the fly.

Julian took her hand, "Cara, I know you haven't written your vows because you don't think you love me, but I know better. So I'm here before you and your family to pledge myself to you. I, Julian Aristo Starr, take you Cara Lynne Freidman, as my life partner." There were gasps and a general rumbling from the audience, but Julian continued, "I'm not going to promise to change, but I will promise to grow. I will make mistakes and unsavory choices, but I ask in advance that you forgive me and promise never to forsake me. We are blessed to have each other and our babies and I promise to love and cherish you now, and forever until death do us part."

He slipped triple bands of diamonds, eternity rings, on her finger, kissed it and looked at her. Cara was speechless. The eternity bands made her lightheaded – three eternities?? Still, she thought she saw something in his eyes. It was all the things she ever wanted from a man, love, devotion, possessiveness, passion, companionship and protection. She had finally admitted to herself, a while ago, that she probably loved him, but she wasn't certain she had the strength or the amount of love it would take to stay with him for a lifetime.

"I, I, ohm, I"......Cara stuttered.

Julian helped her out. "You accept," he said blatantly. She nodded. Producing a platinum silver intertwined ring, he handed it to her and helped her put it on his finger.

Kafir shouted, "L'Chaim."

Julian took her in his arms and kissed her. It was soft and sweet, yet had the intensity to press all his words into her. Cara was breathless when they parted, and felt perhaps she had lost a bit of her soul in the exchange. Julian grinned, he had gotten everything he wanted, and believed he had planted a little of his soul into her too.

Life continued to be a whirlwind. Julian lived in his house with Cara in hers. Music remained his number one mistress, but Cara thought she and their family came in a pretty close second. She continued to do everything herself, caring for the boys, shopping, cooking, cleaning, while Julian continued to offer her servants and kick in as much as he could. Shelly became less of a part-time nanny and more of a full time teacher. She had started speaking to the boys in multiple languages since they were born: French, Spanish, and Italian. Cara spoke a little Spanish from high school but was shocked to discover Julian was fluent in French. He had been narrating breakfast in French for Aiden and Quinton when she had suddenly arrived. Actually she had been standing in the hall eavesdropping.

"You speak French," she accused.

"Oui. I've whispered many things in your ears late at night. Why are you surprised?"

"I assumed you were just making that stuff up?" she admitted.

"Well. You know what they say about people who assume?"

"No, what do they say?"

He pulled her to him and let out a string of French softly into her neck line. She had no idea what he was saying, but it felt divine. He released her, pointing her towards the door, "This is boy time." She would have complained, but she was too weak in the knees.

For the boys' first and second birthdays, Julian planned an African trip. Invoking the spirit of adventure and Cara's love of treehouses, they trekked across the Serengeti, Tanzania and Kenya staying only in tree top facilities. The landscape was breathtaking, the night skies resplendent.

To celebrate the first anniversary of their commitment, Cara and Julian went to the Northwest Territory to see the aurora borealis. The magnitude and magnificence of the lights led everyone to tears and drove them into each other's arms. The spirituality of the experience, as well as, the body contact became an esoteric intimacy that made them feel literally like one. They clung to each other. Later in bed, still entangled in each other's arms, Cara realized something inside her had changed. All her defenses and walls were down. She snuggled close and whispered the words Julian had been waiting for her to say, "I love you."

Soon after Quinton and Aiden turned two and three, Cara noticed an almost indiscernible change in Julian. He still came to spend time with the boys, but not as often. Cara took it for the toddlers they had become. Instead of the dotting babies that adored him, they had developed personalities of their own that included words like 'no', 'uh-uh', 'I don't wanna,' as well as, spaghetti legs, indiscriminate crying and of course, the exchange of pulling, pushing and hitting. She just figured his aloofness was connected to the terrible 'T's'. Julian, never one for a lot of noise or commotion, seemed justified in his avoidance. He still visited her once the house was quiet. Since he never indicated where or when he was going and when he would return, his absenteeism at first went unnoticed, then became just part of the new norm. If he was on tour, working on contract negotiations, doing benefits or private venues, it was not unheard of for him to be gone for weeks. If that was the case, Julian usually skyped the kids. He was deeply devoted to his babies. In the meantime, Cara had things to do too. Besides caring for the kids, the house, and keeping up with the pre-school schedule, she had re-opened her studio and was busy submitting sketches and ideas to any and all solicitations. For rest and relaxation when Julian was not around, she had reconnected with her book club and met monthly to discuss predetermined reads.

Julian's shift away was barely noticed. He continued providing all financial support and anticipated all their wishes and desires. Cara, caring for two boys under four, did not have a lot of energy or time for much else. She chalked up the changes to family growing pains. It wasn't until Cara made a dedicated seduction attempt that failed that she started to suspect something else. While Julian had been playing with the boys, she had hurried to shower, make-up, fluff her hair and don French lingerie. After the boys were in bed, Julian had reacted as if she were in a snow suit. He never wavered in speech, eye contact and/or body language. His total affect was one of disinterest. She felt an immediate ache around her heart. She suspected he was seeing someone else.

Cara probably would have been more devastated except this was part of Julian's standard behavior, not the disassociation, but the distancing. She had known his penchant for other women and had still signed on, so whose problem was it really? Cara deigned to carry on and hoped it would be a short lived alliance. In the meantime, she had plenty to do and as usual was very self-entertaining. She stopped reaching out to him and instead waited patiently for his return.

At the end of summer, her book club readied for its final meeting of the year. Usually they rotated restaurants, coffee shops and peoples' houses. The concluding event was always an extravaganza. This year everybody was dressing as a character from the last book and gathering at a juke joint. Cara decided she would be the floozy and was decked in red from head to stilettos. She had created her own costume and it fit her like a glove, the slit riding high on her right leg, with a pill hat flaunting red netting and a feather. She took an Uber to the festivities, finding almost all the women preferred to be the floozy too, creating a wide variety of colors and attitudes. They all had a good laugh and took turns sashaying through the door. The men arrived in zoot suites. They all gathered around the table and book conversation was replaced with cocktails and appetizers. The D.J. starting spinning some blues, apparently to go along with the theme and couples began to form on the floor.

Cara was still reeling from the freedom and fun of the occasion, conversing with other members about their style choices when she heard someone ask her to dance. She didn't even turn or pause in her conversation, throwing a 'no' over her shoulder. She felt a vicious grab and jerk of her wrist. Turning she looked straight into Julian's angry eyes. Cara copped an immediate attitude too. She hadn't heard or seen him in weeks. Apparently, he didn't like it when someone else played his games. She had a randy retort on her lips when she noticed her friends were riled enough to make Julian's security team begin to close ranks. Cara knew this could have a bad ending, so she bit back her words, assured everyone she wanted to dance and exited the booth. Once on the dance floor a safe distance away from her companions, Cara let loose. "What the hell is the matter with you?" she hissed.

"Me?" he sneered, "I'm not the one dressed like a whore."

Cara took a deep breathe, "Julian, in case you haven't noticed we're all dressed like characters from a book."

"Oh, I know that, but I also know yours is the tightest and the raunchiest one in the bunch."

How did he know what they were reading? And better yet, who was he to make judgements about her? She attempted to pull away, which just made him squeeze tighter.

"Since you want to look the part, I think you should act it out too."

And there, in front of her friends, to her horror, he began to grind on her. Embarrassed and frustrated, she gave up trying to talk to him and began pushing against him with all her might. Julian laughed maliciously. He was still laughing when he suddenly let her go, her frantic efforts only helping to propel her stumbling backwards to the floor.

He turned to his nearest security, "Pick up that stupid bitch," and walked out.

Cara was in shock. Her friends were in open revolt. Brian lifted her from under her arms to her feet. She had lost one shoe and her hat.

"I suggest you calm your friends or someone is going to get hurt."

Cara hobbled over to her group. Biting back tears and avoiding eye contact, she did her best, "There's been a misunderstanding. I have to go. It'll be okay. I'll call you tomorrow." With that being the extent of her bravery, she picked up her purse and jacket, took off her other shoe and was escorted away by security. Entering the limo she found Julian sitting in the fore seat. She angrily took the back.

They drove away in silence, Julian pensively stroking his upper lip and mustache as he stared at her. As angry as she was, Cara was no fool. Her current confines were too small and he was wound way too tight for a confrontation. She remained sullenly silent too.

"Take off those clothes," he suddenly demanded.

"The hell I will," she snorted.

"You know I don't like to ask twice."

"Like I could give a flying fuck what......"

Before she could finish Julian was upon her. He must have been studying a strategic point because he grabbed her dress at the slit, ripping it up the bodice to the neckline without touching her. He jerked the dress free, leaving Cara in her lacy red underwear. He casually returned to his seat, open the window and flicked her outfit into the street, returning to his pensive stare.

Cara fidgeted in her undergarments, garter and stockings.

"I'm still waiting," he bristled dryly.

Cara sighed. There was a time that that threat would have brought exhilaration and satisfaction. Apparently that time was over. She finished undressing and handed over the remainder of her clothing which he promptly relegated to the street too. They finished the ride in silence. Upon reaching her front door, Julian ordered her out.

"I don't have anything to cover with," she resisted.

He threw open the door, "Nobody wants to see your fat ass," he jeered.

So she stepped out and walked to the door. She wanted to feel like Lady Godiva, but actually she felt like Thumbelina. Small. Very, very small indeed.

CHAPTER 19

Cara did not sleep much that night. There was something terribly wrong and it was more than just an extra woman. In all their time together, Julian had never treated her so disrespectfully. She tried to figure out what it was, but with minimal information, the distance and Julian's standard silence, she did not have much to go on. Maybe he was tired of their life. Just because he had been excited about being a father, didn't mean he wanted to stick around and be a dad. Maybe he was missing Aristo and that lifestyle, or maybe he was just tired of her. Whatever it was, Cara knew one thing for certain, she deserved better than that. She needed to do something, but what and how, she had no idea.

The following day Julian showed up as if nothing had happened. He picked up the boys and breezed back through the tunnel to his studio. He called later to ask her to come and help him bring them home. He rebuffed any and all questions, any references to the previous night and any acknowledgement that anything was wrong. To prove his point, after the boys were down, he attempted to get busy. Cara brushed off the attention. Julian pushed her aside, turning to leave.

"That's ok. It's your loss," he huffed. "You'll be sorry."

"I'm already sorry," she retorted.

Julian stopped mid-stride. For a minute Cara thought there was going to be verbal confrontation, but apparently that would have taken too much effort. He continued walking without even turning around.

Life went on. Cara had multiple, multiples of everything- appointments, preschool, well baby checks, soccer, t-ball, etc. In between pick-ups and drop offs they stopped for labs. She pulled a lab sheet from the bottom of her purse for herself. She had about five in there, since she had a tendency to be delinquent with self-care. Might as well kill three birds with one stone. The following week the boys passed with a clean bill of health, while she found out she was expecting.

Cara could not believe she was pregnant again. She knew that another baby would not save, rectify or redeem her relationship with Julian. The best she could hope for was to continue to look normal while engineering an escape plan. She could not have this baby and so she made alternative arrangements. This was a private matter, between herself, her God and her sanity. Cara found a clinic, made an appointment and called an Uber. Arriving to the office, she filled out her forms, looked at all the other women lining the walls and waited. When her fictitious name was finally called, she went in, disrobed and climbed on the table.

Three hours later Cara emerged, she felt exhausted. She rode silently in her Uber home. As she approached the gate, she was waved away. The guard advised she no longer had access to the compound. Cara felt her heart skip a beat. Then the guard got nasty, advising the police would be called if she did not leave.

Cara lost it. She advanced on the gate seized the bars and went crazy. She began hollering to Julian that she could not be cast out like that. Looping her arms through the bars, she dialed Shelly. Julian answered.

"She can't help you. No one can. What God has put asunder cannot be repaired."

"Julian, what are you talking about? Let me in."

"Where have you been, Cara?"

And then she knew, that he knew exactly where she'd been. She felt her heart race into double time with a pounding beat. She became diaphoretic and lightheaded.

"Julian, we need to talk."

"I think that time is over," then to someone in the background he yelled, "go get that bitch off my gate."

A limo pulled up behind her. Brian disembarked, his arms spread wide.

"Cara, please, let's not do this," he smoothed.

"If you, or that sick motherfucker in there, think I'm leaving my babies without a fight, you have another thought coming," she growled locking her arms together and screaming to the top of her lungs.

Brian calmly came behind her, placed his hands over her shoulders and gave a hard squeeze just below her clavicle. Cara felt her hands and arms tingle then immediately lose strength. He lifted her around the waist and carried her howling to the car. As he placed her in the vehicle, she suddenly slumped over. After several attempts to revive her, he called their private EMS, then apprehensively, he called Julian. Multiple people had already been served their severance that day. Brian preferred not to be one of them. All hell had been loosed when Cara's outing had gone unmonitored and un-intercepted. By the time Julian deigned himself to respond to the call, the ambulance was on the way to the hospital.

"This better be good," Julian hissed tersely.

Brian took a breath, "The ambulance is on the way to the hospital with Cara. She's unconscious. They were unable to rouse her."

The silence was deadly.

"Come get me."

The ride to the hospital seemed excruciatingly long and excessively fast. Julian bolted from the car and sprinted into the facility. By the time Brian parked the car and made it into the ED, Julian was surrounded by security as he demanded to see

Leandra Simone

Cara. The ED physician came out and the compromise was they would be escorted to a private family room where they would wait or they would be put out. In the family room, Julian paced like a caged tiger, muttering to himself and at one point punching the wall. Three hours into their confinement the doctor appeared, took Julian aside and quietly explained their findings. He was allowed out of the room and directed to the observation unit. He had just made entrance to the unit when a loud ruckus erupted. Julian immediately recognized Cara's voice and bounded toward the room. There were multiple staff attempting to comfort and subdue her as Julian elbowed his way in. As soon as Cara saw him, her thrashing and wailing increased ten-fold. She screamed out he had stolen her babies and was now there to finish her off. She had to be sedated. Brian arrived at the same time as the hospital security. It took all of them to remove Julian from the room.

Cara felt herself rising through a fog. It was like pulling herself through mud. When her eyes finally fluttered open, she had no idea where she was, but it looked medical. Then she remembered the baby. She sat up and grabbed her abdomen.

"It's still there," came a soft low voice from the corner. Tracking to the sound, she found Julian slumped in a chair, intensely gazing at her.

Cara groaned and turned her back to him. The absolute last person she wanted to see now was him. He called her name several times, but she refused to turn or respond. The silence grew and she began to drift back into her haze when she was jousted back into wakefulness by the weight of a body lying next to her. Julian did not touch her, but she could smell him, feel his heat. He started talking, actually whispering into the back of her neck. For the life of her, she did not understand a word he was uttering nor did she care. He was a master of words and manipulation. She focused on the tone and timbre of his voice. He sounded almost like he used to and again she drifted off, only this time it was in the warmth of his sound.

When Cara awakened again she was facing Julian and her hand was on his chest. She immediately began to pull it away, but he stopped her placing his hand over hers, pressing it over his heart.

"I shouldn't have done any of it," he admitted softly.

"What?" she croaked.

"Any of it."

Cara knew he was referring to his distancing, her book club humiliation and her lock out of the compound.

"There have been some complications, but I should never have taken it out on you. For a minute today, I thought I had lost you and I realized none of that shit matters." He stopped. Waiting.

"Something between us changed. I wasn't sure about another baby. I was afraid."

"But you didn't do it."

Cara merely shrugged.

Julian reached his other hand behind her head and pulled her to him, gently kissing her forehead. He remained there holding her tightly. Soon Cara was lulled back to sleep in the warmth, strength and security of his arms.

Following her discharge from the hospital, Julian moved in twenty-four/seven with Cara and their kids. It was the first time they had consistently been in each other's company. Cara soon began to appreciate their previous living arrangement. Julian was manic with his music. He could stop at any moment and begin writing on whatever was available or run out to locate an instrument. He had left Quinton and Aiden in the tub alone and she admonished him. When she returned, she found lyrics written on the bathroom wall in Crayola soap. Even though they had finally gotten back to great sex and the boys adored him, Cara decided Julian was best in metered doses. Aiden and Quinton continued their music time with their dad in his studio and nightly bedtime stories were added to the routine. Julian seemed to bloom in this new found family environment and Cara came to the belief that whatever was wrong had been righted and all was well. Eventually everything went back to normal. Julian returned to his house with regular visits to hers.

Just prior to the completion of her second trimester, Julian insisted they take a Lamaze refresher course. They had their same instructor, which they tormented as much as possible. After that, Julian became more distracted and his visits tapered down. For the first time, he actually accounted for the change, explaining he had upcoming concert venues to secure, arrange and prepare for.

One day, Cara decided to work in the garden. When she had initially moved to the compound, she had mentioned to Julian she wanted one. She had awaken the following day to find a landscaping team ripping up grass, building beds and fencing the area with a white picket timber.

Today they were weeding. Each boy had a bed and although there were plenty of trucks and shovels, there also appeared to still be plenty of weeds. Cara laughed and kept working. When Shelly came out, she asked where the boys were. Cara looked up to find them gone. She and Shelly split up to find them. Shelly took the house, while she took the yard. Sleuthing through the bushes around the house, she thought she caught sight of a motion in the opposite direction, heading up the hill toward Julian's. Doubling back and shielding her eyes she caught sight of her two boys hightailing up the hill. She hoped Julian was not home.

Cara yelled to Shelly from the door and started up the ridge to reclaim her babies. As she neared, she could hear them giggling and as soon as they saw her it became a game of chase. She struggled to keep up, but they topped the summit and disappeared from sight. She should have brought a switch. As she staggered up the slope, she could hear music and people talking. Holy God, there was a party going on. Now, she really tried to accelerate. Reaching the top, she was short of breath, sweaty and panicked.

Thirty to forty people were milling around a pool and some the most exquisite landscaping she had ever seen. Apparently this section had been omitted from her tour. There were white flowers strewn on the grounds, as well as, strung from trees and light fixtures. They were so abundant it created a fairy-land atmosphere that included the guests of beautiful people dressed impeccably in coordinated colors. Cara might have stayed transfixed on the landscaping, textiles and fashion, had not someone shrieked. She turned to find Aiden and Quinton covered in chocolate and icing, cupcakes in both hands, approaching a lady dressed all in white. Rushing forward she apprehended both boys by their shoulders and squeezed them into a halt. The lady in white was clearly furious.

"Who are you people and how did you get into my reception?" she exclaimed.

Aiden, never one to not have the last word, responded, "We're looking for my daddy."

The woman's eyebrows rose dramatically. "Your daddy most certainly is not here," she sneered.

Cara starting counting. Okay, everybody was a little dirty from the gardening, but these were still children, and there was no need to be rude to little kids. She managed to bite back a re-tort and the desire to shove the woman in the pool. Instead, she apologized profusely and headed the boys back to the ridge. The woman would not relent.

"You better be glad my husband hasn't seen this," she jeered at their backs, "or security would be here to toss you out."

Cara let go of the boys and rounded on her. "I don't know who the hell you think you are, but nobody is tossing us out, as you insinuate, like trash."

Apparently this was just what her opponent desired, an altercation.

"For your information, my husband is the owner of this compound, and he'll do anything I say."

"The owner?" Cara felt her heart quicken.

"Yes, Aristo. We've been married and this is our reception."

Cara felt a sharp pain in her chest. Then she took a careful look at the bride. She was young, very young. If she was twenty, then Cara was five. She was very beautiful, diminutive, fragile, exotic, most likely obedient, subservient and appreciative. She was everything Cara was not. This was his very own baby doll.

Cara exhaled. Apparently, she had been holding her breath. She looked around the venue, finding Aristo. He too was dressed in all white, clean shaven and completely made up. They locked eyes. He gave her a very unperceived shake of his head. Cara felt a veil of red descend upon her. She had a sudden diaphoretic surge, as well as, a rapid heart rate. She turned and headed down the hill behind her boys with the girl still throwing insults at them.

Cara made it halfway down the hill before the first Braxton-Hicks hit. Grabbing her lower abdomen, her aggressive stomping came to a sudden halt. After a few deep breaths, it receded and she continued her descent. The second one knocked her to her knees. Aristo, watching from on high, phoned security to assist. Cara was still on her knees, deep breathing, when they arrived, helped her up and into the golf cart. They scooped up Aiden, Quinton and Shelly, as well, on their way back down to the house.

Shelly cleaned up the boys while she tried to pooh-pooh Cara into laying down. Cara was having none of it. Having recuperated from her informal contractions, her vision had gone from red to magenta. She was suffering from a jumble of racing thoughts, but she pushed it aside to focus on Plan B.

Throughout everything Julian and Cara had been through, she

continued to have a smidgen of doubt/fear in the back of her mind. In order to quell it, she had created Plan B. The plan was basically an escape strategy. She had always toyed with the idea, but after her disciplinarian lock-out, she solidified everything. Shelly, of course, was an integral part. Since Cara believed the house was wired for visual and sound, all efforts to prepare for a quick exit had to be covert. Every time she or Shelly washed clothes, a few choice pieces were left bagged and sealed under the dirty clothes liner. Everybody had enough clean clothes to pack into the backpacks hidden in Shelly's closet. Alternative phones, laptops, as well as, bank accounts had also been secured and maintained. Shelly was still attempting to get Cara to rest, when Cara said the words – Plan B.

Shelly inhaled sharply.

"I'll explain later."

Without further ado, Shelly grabbed the backpacks, they stuffed their cache within, put the boys in the car and backed out. When they approached the front gate they were waved away.

"We have orders that none of you are permitted to leave today."

"Okay," Cara smiled sweetly. She backed up, turned around, heading for home. As soon as the guard turned his back, she made a U turn and accelerated toward the gate. Shelly grabbed her arm. Just as she neared the closed exit, the entrance gate opened for more guests. Cara careened to that side taking out the front driver light and fender of the oncoming car, overriding the median and just missing the guard. On the sharp turn onto the street, Shelly threw out all their old cell phones, laptops and tablets creating a crescendo of sound as they drove away, the boys clapping in their seats.

Time was of essence. Shelly made the call. They pulled into the nearest strip mall, abandoned the car and got into their just arrived Uber, which took them directly to the airport. Within two hours of finding out her supposed significant other had a

Leandra Simone

baby bride, Cara, Shelly and the boys were on a non-stop flight to Frisco.

No one wanted to tell Aristo. By process of elimination, pleads and payments, Brian was designated the task. Aristo took the news of Cara's escape with his babies well. He was intensely silent, giving Brian a visual dismissal, just before he snapped his champagne flute with his bare hand. He had underestimated Cara, again. So be it. Let the games begin.

CHAPTER 20

Four people lost their jobs the day following the reception. Two of them were guards, an unfortunate assistant and a very verbal publicist. Although Aristo sustained a large cut to the inside of his hand, he refused any and all medical attention, including that of his wife's. He had excused himself from sharing a bed with his blushing bride and settled himself behind the locked doors of his personal studio. As expected, she gave a small pout but acquiesced under the promise of extended shopping. He had already been forced to put her on a budget.

Aristo sat in silence, his hand throbbing, his heart aching. His babies were gone. He had played a dangerous game and lost. It was such a fluke that Aiden and Quinton would come looking for him, with their mother in tow, on the day of his delayed reception. What were the chances?? The wedding had occurred prior to Cara learning she was pregnant. None of it had been planned, it all just happened. His bride had been a background dancer. That had given him plenty of opportunity to wine and dine her. It had started, as all his dalliances did. A beautiful woman, a look, a touch, an inference, a suggestion, an act. He never consider it an affront to Cara. She was aware of his predisposition and accepted it. That was one of the things he loved about her. Not that she let him do as he liked, but she was accepting of his faults, as well as, his gifts and strengths. He knew she did not like it. When he drifted and returned, her lips were tight lines, there was a reddish tint about her and he thought her heard her cursing under her breath. Still, after a few days of codling and coaxing, she let him back into her heart, her arms and eventually, her bed.

He had slipped up with his dancer. He had taken it beyond the bedroom into the open. His reputation was built on being accompanied by beautiful women. Since he and Cara had been together he had let that notoriety slip. He had been having so much fun with his new roles as a consistent lover and a dedicated father, that he hadn't noticed his loss of stature. His publicist had brought an article to his attention that was again questioning his sexual persuasion, since a growing number of his public appearances lacked either a female escort or his infamous female entourage. A knee jerk reaction was to take his dancer to a high profile fashion show. They were immediately tagged an item and he merely continued to feed the fantasy. The flip of that, however, was that the dancer bought the hype. She was young, impressionable and idolizing. She really knew how to pump his ego. So in the end, he came to the conclusion he could keep her and Cara too. After all, neither needed to know about the other.

Initially, the wifey position had not been a part of the plan. He had merely intended to keep this particular piece on the side, but his damsel was so naïve and trusting, he saw no reason to crush her dreams. He had a partner and babies and while it wasn't stagnant, he had become complacent. It was an exciting thought that he could have them both. So impulsively, after an event in Paris, he had asked his mademoiselle to be his wife. They had wed immediately and the repercussions had soon followed.

Julian noticed belatedly, that his new bride preferred Aristo. That required a constant vigilance of being his alter ego. Julian morphed into Aristo anytime he was in public, but at home he preferred to relax and just be himself. No more. His baby doll required the clean shaven, man-scaped version, replete with complete makeup. He wasn't sure if it was about him, or about her dressing up. He also found her to be excessively needy. Calling to find out where he was, when he'd return and what their plans were. He had to put the kibosh on all calls, forbidding her to call him directly and diverted all phone contact through his assistants. She adapted to their lavish lifestyle like a fish to water, turning into a demanding diva overnight. The day she accumulated a $50,000 shopping spree was the day he cut her cards. No amount of tears moved him. Julian considered all this to be a part of her on-going transition. She was still so malleable, and so he continued to work with her patiently.

Down the hill, Cara was in open revolt. She sensed the difference in him almost instantly and would not relent in attempting to understand the reason for the change. He began avoiding her, seeing the boys then vacating the premises. His previous dames would have been waiting serenely for his eventual return, but not Cara – she was too damn self-sufficient. So, it was with a high degree of irritation that he received a call advising she had left the compound wearing a racy red dress. He had had to abandon his wife in the middle of a planned evening, causing her to throw a tantrum, which only increased his aggravation. When he had caught up with Cara, she received the brunt of his frustration and anger. He hardly regretted it. Actually, it had felt good to bring her down a few notches. Ripping her clothes had also given him the release of a lot of his repressed emotions. He had believed things had come to a head and all the situations would settle down. It was a short lived idea.

Cara's visit to the abortion clinic blew his mind. He had ordered her locked out and would probably have thrown out all her stuff. Her sudden unresponsiveness brought him back to reality. He had imaged her being locked out, begging to be allowed back in. He had never considered her demise and a life without her. For a moment, he thought she had perhaps bled out from a complication. He realized she was an integral part of his heart and soul, the mother of his children and his counter balance. It was fun to have someone to walk the red carpet but it was more important for him to keep his family. He had promptly shipped his wife out on a 'get-away' and attempted to repair his relationship with Cara.

Once he and Cara were relatively back on track, Julian return to finagling his former finance. He knew now his marital situation was already heading for extinction. Still, he felt he owed his wife a few things: at least one year of marriage, a wedding reception (which he promised) and a healthy settlement.

They had already been married six months and the promised wedding reception had been in full swing when the shit hit the fan. His poor baby was so dense, she had asked why the gardener's children had been looking for their father at their party. Aristo had assured her they were just little children, probably following the music and excitement and it had nothing to do with their dad. She had bought that hook line and sinker. He only had to keep her happy with clothes, trips and trinkets.

Cara, on the other hand, had bolted and taken his babies with her. He missed all of them already. Julian realized most of her actions were direct consequences to his behavior. He would have loved to take the blame but he felt better projecting it onto her. The more he thought about it, the more determined he became. This time it wasn't just about the chase. He was looking forward to her complete subjugation, because this time would be the last time she would ever leave.

CHAPTER 21

Cara's ultimate destination was the northern shores of Kauai. There was an overnight layover in Honolulu and a few incognito days in Lihue. She eventually called her sister, Erica, who lived on a homestead in Hanalei. Erica invited them up and while Cara initially resisted the invitation, she relented, thinking Aiden and Quinton would have more fun running in fields then in their hotel room. Renting a car, they made the drive to Erica's. Cara had more plans and provisions on her current escape. Although she had separate 'secret' accounts, she doubted that anything could be secreted away from Julian for too long. To extend their freedom, she conducted all their transactions in cash. She realized she could not do this indefinitely, but she had squirreled away enough reserve that she approximated they could go about a month. Staying with her sister might expand that timeframe.

Kauai is a beautiful island and the drive was magnificent. Aiden and Quinton slept through most of it. Upon arrival at Erica's, everyone was in prime form. Her sister's youngest two, were just a year older that Aiden and Quinton and acted like they had been delivered new playthings. They immediately claimed her boys as they disembarked from the car and disappeared into the foliage. Erica's older girls, newly developed pre-adolescents, decided they would oversee this rambunctious group, and followed. Cara, Shelly and Erica were left pulling bags from the car.

Cara, who had already fallen in love with Hawaii, looked up at the house. It was white with a porch that wrapped around its entire parameter. She loved it too, even if on closer inspection, it looked as if it was in need of some repair. Erica led the way, depositing her and Shelly into wicker rockers on the veranda before proceeding into the house with their bags. Cara had no problem relinquishing her stuff and just relaxing.

Erica reappeared with snacks and drinks and the conversation began. Cara was really not in the mood to discuss her abrupt departure, but felt she owed her sister something, so she revived her initial lies. Julian's wife had returned and he couldn't decide which to keep. Cara had helped him, she had removed herself from the situation. It was a plain and simple tale and she could tell it without tears or anger. Her days away had already begun to dissipate her emotions. The island itself seemed to be sucking the sadness from her soul. She was alive, well and free. Granted, she was due to deliver in three months, she had all her life and her babies' lives before her.

She was feeling omnipotent, but a lot of that probably had to do with pulling one over on Julian. Leaving him in the dust with his baby bride. Cara felt resilient, invincible and hopeful.

Erica listened to her woeful tale, harrumphed and advised she deserved better. Apparently, the case was closed. Cara felt she could have and do anything. She wanted to live on the water. Erica hesitated.

"What?" Cara questioned.

"Those are a little pricey," her sister advised.

"I have a little set aside. It doesn't have to be spectacular, a beach shack will do."

"I think Nahoa may know a realtor. I'll ask, when he gets home."

But Nahoa did not come home that night or the next, and while Cara had no right to judge or question anybody, she wondered if everything was okay. Eventually Nahoa returned and he did indeed know someone. The realtor arrived the following day to take Cara on a whirlwind tour of beach houses.

Cara promptly fell in love with a beach front compound on Tunnels lagoon. There was a main residence, several guest cottages, a studio, a pool house and multiple out-buildings. She made an offer immediately since it was in foreclosure and the previous buyer had fallen through. She would have to cash out the CDs she used to stash Julian's gift from years ago. Along with some more reserved funding, she believed she could own her dream home outright. Julian had always been generous with financial support. He had opened both checking and savings accounts to cover the children's and household needs. He initially deposited $5000 a month when she first returned then increased it to $10,000 per month after Quinton's birth. Since the babies were lavished with clothes and shoes by both Julian and Kafir, there was little to purchase other than groceries. Everything on the compound was handled through Julian's accounts including Shelly's salary. That had been the one point of contention. Could she afford Shelly's salary? But Shelly had demurred to living in the islands as a compromise. Long story short, she had access to the funds needed to make this house happen. Cara closed on the house that same week and had the keys in hand by the following weekend. She and Shelly were ready to abandon her sister's place, so they spent their first night on recently purchased air mattresses the same day the keys arrived. Aiden and Quinton were less excited until they saw the water. Once on the beach, it became a daily ritual. Breakfast, beach, lunch, nap, beach, dinner, beach.

Cara walked the lagoon each evening. It was a time to be alone in the sound and surf. She felt the beauty and the peacefulness of the island encasing her. It sucked all the anger, sadness and humiliation away until all that was left was the promise of a new bright beginning.

The baby came exactly on the due date. Cara had preregistered at the Wilcox Medical Center. On the day her labor began, her sister was at home with sick kids, forcing Shelly to stay home with Aiden and Quinton. She had not bothered to buy a car, relying on walking and biking as main sources of transport-ation. Since the facility was at least thirty miles away, she called an Uber, whose number was on a flyer she'd found in the mail. The driver took one look at her standing in driveway, put her and her bag in the back seat and got to the hospital in half the time. She tipped him handsomely for his precision driving, his hair-raising turns and his non-stop conversation.

Sitting in her delivery suite alone, her contractions coming ten minutes apart, Cara lost all her bravado. All the positivity she had cloaked herself in fell away. She was a single woman about to give birth to baby number three. She wallowed in self-pity, abandoning all Lamaze practices. Instead, she began moaning, groaning and flaying in the bed from side to side.

"I don't hear any breathing going on in here."

Cara stopped mid-groan. It wasn't possible, but turning she found Julian leaning casually in the doorway.

"How did you find me?" she hissed.

"Title search," he shrugged. "Sounds like a nice place. Maybe one day you'll invite me over."

"And maybe one day people in hell will get ice water."

"Tsk, tsk. You were just moaning about being alone. Now, I'm here. Let's get started."

Had she been talking out loud??? Or was he still doing that mind reading thing??

She would have given him some additional choice words had not a contraction snuck up on her. She stopped in mid-rebuttal to cry out.

"You're wasting time," he accused as he crossed the room, straightened her out and started coaching.

Cara, caught off guard, starting breathing, but she still refused to let him touch her. Of course, that changed as her contractions intensified.

Julian was flawless. He submitted to being pushed, pulled,

yelled at, cursed out and berated. Nonetheless, he continued rubbing her lower back, switching out cool towels on her head and providing endless cups of ice chips. By the time they entered the delivery room, Cara's anger had been spent, Julian looked calm as ever in his scrubs and their baby girl was delivered with one final push. Cara thought she was in an emotional void, but as soon as they laid the baby on her chest, she began to cry. These were the first tears since her climatic departure from the compound and the more she tried to stop, the more they seemed to fall. In the end, the doctor administered a calming agent and she drifted into a foggy haze.

Cara resurfaced, and found Julian sitting at the bedside talking to the baby. Marcella, eyes open, watched him. When he began singing, she smiled. Cara began to cry again. Julian looked up. He sat on the side of the bed, scooching Cara over and made himself comfortable in the bed. Holding the baby in his right arm, he placed his left arm around Cara and pulled her to him. The whole sensation brought out a muffled wail from Cara. Julian did not try to comfort her, instead he held her and kept on singing to the baby.

After what seemed like hours, Cara was finally devoid of tears. She snuffled, found tissue on the side table and blew her nose. When she spoke, her voice came out as a croak.

"Why, Julian?"

"I needed someone to be seen with."

And there it was. As simple as that. Not something necessarily new or different, just something presentable to the public. Something that reflected Aristo's style, grace and standards.

Cara felt ambiguous about the explanation. She wasn't sure if it was because she was exhausted, or it was irrelevant, or she didn't care. She had a new life.

Julian continued to sing to the baby. Soon, she and Marcella drifted back to sleep. Sometime during the night Cara dreamed she and Julian were sleeping together, an entanglement of limbs and warmth. She awoke to find she was indeed laying in Julian's arms, her head on his chest. She tensed at the reality of the situation, but he held her tightly.

"Cara, you know you will eventually have to come home."

She remained silent, it was useless. He would say and do as he wanted, but so would she.

"You have one year, until Marcella's first birthday, to come home. Don't make me come to get you."

Cara remained limp and quiet, but her thoughts were livid. A year was a long time. Her mind began churning new options as she drifted back to sleep. When she woke up again, he was gone. She didn't need to open her eyes to know. She could feel the absence of his intensity. She finally lifted her lids to find her room crammed with bouquets and balloons. Looking down she also discovered her commitment bands, the ones she'd left on the kitchen counter at the compound, were back on her finger.

Cara did not feel up for company, so she called an Uber to go home. She advised she needed a car with a baby seat. Low and behold, upon exiting the hospital, her Uber was waiting with her previous driver.

"Aloha," he smiled.

Cara smiled too, "You again? Are you the only Uber on the island?"

"Maybe. I'm Kris Kelekelio."

CHAPTER 22

It took a while for Cara to get over Julian's surprise visit. She had been so angry by his betrayal, then so proud of her departure that she had not considered missing him. His gratuitous visit opened up a new hole in her heart and a grieving for what had been lost. In the evening, after all her babies were in bed, she continued to walk the lagoon, sometimes making multiple laps until she had driven his residual demons away. It became her silent therapy, the releasing of her angst into the sand and the surf, taking in the tranquility. Within months she had lost the baby weight and several extra pounds. Julian had insisted upon natural hair, 'no chemicals in your body', which had also led to natural contraceptives which had also led to more babies. Cara took that massive puff ball of hair and had it locked. The mini tresses fell past her shoulders. She began to feel like a new woman.

Sitting on the beach one day, watching Aiden and Quinton run in and out with the waves, while Marcella, thankfully slept, Cara noticed two little girls playing in the sand. It wasn't what they were doing that caught her attention, but the fact that there did not seem to be anybody with them. They could not have been much older that her boys, and heaven only knew you could not take your eyes off of them. Cara kept her eyes on all of them. Eventually, the boys' forays into the waves took them closer and closer to the girls' construction site. She watched their initial survey of each other, the castle and the equipment, overheard Aiden's suggestions then some of a girl's gentle rebuff and then the general consensus they would play together. They worked together for hours, until Quinton came over for a snack. Cara sent him back with enough for everybody. Thinking back, she could not recall if the girls had already been there when they arrived or had appeared later during that morning. What she was sure of was that no one had appeared to check on them in the hours since she first noticed them.

Dusk and dinnertime were approaching when she packed up everything and called the boys over to go. The little girls came over, too, silently watching as her boys gathered their things as instructed. Cara looked at them. "Where are your parents?" she asked.

"The larger one spoke up, "We don't have a mom and our dad is surfing."

Cara looked out at the waves.

"Not here," she added, "at Lumaha'i"

That was several beaches over. There really was no one watching over them.

"He leaves us here because it's safer," added the smaller child.

Of course it was. People living along the lagoon in Ha'ena were friendly, considerate and fairly prosperous. Cara had only made it in the area with a foreclosure. All would be concerned over unsupervised children near the water. Still, she couldn't just leave them there.

"Would you like to come have dinner with us," she inquired.

The smaller girl answered 'yes' at once, but the larger one hesitated.

"Our daddy doesn't want us talking to strangers and if we go with you he won't be able to find us."

"Ok," Cara reassured them, "I'm Aiden and Quinton's mother. You know them, you've been playing together all day. Now you know me."

The girls looked at each other as the boys cheered for their assent.

"We can leave a message and a map for your father to follow. We don't live far, just there," she said pointing to the back of their house.

The girls conferred. "Ok," they chimed together.

"I'm Kalea and this is my sister, Leilani."

"How old are you?" Cara inquired.

"I'm seven and my sister is five."

"You are not," shrieked Leilani, "you're only six."

"I'm six and a half and that's closer to seven," Kalea insisted.

"That most certainly is," Cara interjected subjectively. "Let's get started before it gets too dark."

The boys were super excited that their new friends would be coming home with them and the little girls seemed relieved they would not be left alone. The concept of creating a visual trail for their father to follow turned into a frantic game of run, search, seize and deposit. In no time, they had created a map of shells, rocks, seaweed and garbage to show any seeing eyed person, where to locate Kalea and Leilani. The excitement continued once inside. Cara made no attempt at making dinner, she called out for pizza, then had everyone showered and in p.j.'s by the time it arrived. Shelly could not believe Cara had collected two more children and gave her a serious frown. Still she stayed with them and the pizza while Cara breast fed Marcella, then put her down. Everybody wanted to stay up all night, but an hour into an animated flick all the children were down for the count. Shelly helped her carry the boys to their room and the girls to the guest room, after which time she said good-night.

Cara got her book, opened a bottle of wine and prepared to meet the man who left his children on the beach. An hour later she was awakened by loud knocking on the back glass door. She jumped up immediately, someone was going to wake everybody up. She slide open the door to find the back of a tall, athletic man, with wet hair dripping down his bare shoulders. He turned to face her, anger apparent on his face.

"Who the hell do you think you are taking my children?" he yelled, making to walk through the door.

Cara blocked him. "Who the fuck do you think you are leaving them on the beach alone for hours and hours. No supervision, no food, no water. I suppose they would still be sitting there in the dark, waiting. What time is it 10? 11? And you have the audacity to yell at me?"

"Listen, just give me my kids."

"I'm not giving you shit."

"Do you want me to call the police?"

"Please do, and call Child Protective Services too while you're at it. I think everybody will be interested in this story. Especially me, when you get to the part of how I got them and how you found them."

Some of his hot air deflated. "Ok, I'm sorry. I should have started with how much I appreciated you taking care of them. Just get them and we'll be gone."

"They're sleeping and I'm not waking them up. You can wait until they get up or you can come back tomorrow."

"I'm not leaving my babies with a total stranger."

"You're right. It's better to leave them alone on a beach – good night," and with that she slammed and locked the door.

He began a double fisted bang. Cara held up the phone with 911 on speed dial. He did not complete the second bang. She turned leaving him scowling through the glass.

Cara awoke at six a.m. to feed and change Marcella. The house was still quiet, so they both went back to sleep. An hour later, she was jolted awake by the sound of all hell breaking loose. She ran towards the sound of the mayhem to find Shelly fighting off the man with a broom, who was defending himself with a pot top while he continued to stir a cooking pot. The girls were running in circles shouting 'Daddy, Daddy', while Aiden and Quinton fenced with a mop and a dust pan. Cara would have laughed but the pot caught fire sending all activities in hyper-drive. The girls started chanting 'fire, fire,' while the boys made siren noises. The feuding adults teamed together to put the fire out.

Cara shouted from the doorway, "Good morning to you all."

Kalea and Leilani ran to her, each grabbing a hand and pulled her into the fray in the kitchen.

"This is our Daddy," they beamed together, flushed with joy.

"I am Peleke Opunui, Aloha Kaua." He bowed, swooped up her hand and kissed her palm.

Shelly threw her broom on the floor and marched out. Aiden and Quinton began kissing Leilani and Kalea hands' and somewhere in the background, Marcella began to cry. Cara jerked her hand away, wiping her palm on her pants, excused herself and doubled back for the baby. She encountered Shelly in the hallway.

"That man is nothing but trouble, put him out," she hotly whispered.

"What about the girls?"

"They've lived this long without you and they've survived," Shelly hissed.

"Shelly, really??"

But she knew exactly what Shelly was worried about. Peleke was a perfect Hawaiian specimen. He was sun kissed brown with muscles in all the appropriate places and his hair, now dry, curled thickly upon his shoulders. He had the look and feel of every women's dream encased with every woman's nightmare. Still the house had a delicious smell of coffee, hot pastries and whatever else he had been cooking. That kiss had elicited a small jolt. Not a Julian jolt, but enough to give one pause. Shelly was right though, if Julian caught sight of him, there would be double...... Wait a minute, Julian was a happily married man.

Still, he had continued to deposit his monthly allotment, increasing it to $20,000 after Marcella's birth. Apparently girls were worth more than boys, or was it the usual $5,000 per child with an extra $5000 for pain and suffering. In any case, Cara had yet to find a job and while she bought the house outright, she still had utilities, groceries and household expenses, as well as, compensating Shelly, who continued to pooh-pooh the idea away. Having Peleke around could jeopardize everything, and for what, he was obviously very flaky. So to Shelly she said 'ok, ok', picked up Marcella and headed back to the kitchen to say good-bye to the girls and put him out. He was already gone. The kids reported he was going to allow Kalea and Leilani to stay for the day. Peleke had returned to the surf.

Cara was boiling. His audacity was beyond words. He had palmed his kids off on her without even asking. Obviously, he thought she cared. She didn't. She had enough on her plate without two more children, especially two that had nothing to do with her. She took a pastry, a cup of coffee and Marcella out to the patio. While she fed the baby, she thought of ways to return his girls. Although she was having an internal rant, the reality was she could not figure a way out. She could not abandon them on the beach, call CPS to engrain them in that system or call the police to report neglect. She couldn't bring herself to hurt Kalea or Leilani. It wasn't their fault their father was an ass. She was stuck. Right then, everyone came out of the house and headed for the pool. Shelly had everybody back in their swimming suits and together they all bounded for the shallows.

Shelly came over with a cup of coffee, "Where's daddy?"

"Gone."

"Damn."

Peleke showed up three days later, again late at night, only this time drunk. She and Shelly watched him over their glasses of wine. Cara didn't bother to open the door. She had installed child proof locks. They finished their wine, turned off the lights and went to bed.

The following morning, Cara greeted him with a bucket of ice water that she gladly tossed on him as he slept in a lounger. She followed that with a cup of coffee, which she handed to him. He took it like a man, merely sitting up and shaking the ice and water off.

"I suppose I deserved that," he grimaced.

"I think you deserve a lot worse," she countered,

"Maybe we could talk," he suggested.

"We don't have anything to discuss. Your girls are very sweet, but now it's time for you to take them with you, home, to another beach, maybe family or friends. I don't know. Just away from here."

He looked down, sullen, solemn then back up at her with puppy dog eyes. It was a practiced move. Cara recognized it immediately. Julian was a pro at it.

"Brother, I've seen that move too many times. You need to take it somewhere else. I'm not buying it."

Peleke grinned, dropping the pretense, "I know you're pissed. I know you've taken great care of my kids and I know you like them and can afford to continue to care for them."

"What? Just because I'm nice doesn't mean I'm your bitch. You need to get the hell out of my house right now," she demanded.

"Or what? You'll call the police? You could have done that days ago but you didn't and let me guess why, because you didn't want Leilani and Kalea to go into the foster care system."

"My being concerned for them doesn't mean I'm willing to be your pawn. Who in the hell do you think you are? Get out and take them with you," she scowled.

He rose, called his girls and they left, taking the path back to the beach. No one said thank you or bye. No one even looked back. To Cara that said a lot, she wasn't sure what, but a lot of something. She exhaled loudly and turned to find Aiden and Quinton standing sadly behind her.

"It was time for them to go home. Maybe we'll see them again on the beach." They brightened just enough to run off in a game of chase.

Of course, they didn't see Leilani or Kalea on the beach the following week or the week after that. At first, Cara tried telling herself they had never seen them before on their beach, so there must have been other beaches they frequented. Then the nightmares started. Several times a week Cara had bad dreams. Anything from Kalea and Leilani washing up on shore, to the police arresting Peleke and the girls being driven away in a police car, to a strange man luring them away to his shack. When they finally reappeared six weeks later, Cara was as ecstatic as Aiden and Quinton to see them.

Kalea and Leilani were already on the beach when they arrived. They were also wearing the same clothes she and Shelly had bought them on their last stay. The outfits looked slightly dingy and worn. Both girls had matted areas in the back of their hair. Cara felt horrible. They were not her responsibility but she had had an opportunity to make a difference in their lives. Peleke had been right, she could afford to care for them, but she had let her anger at him and his attitude drive them away. Obviously things were worse than they had been. She would not make that mistake again. With a knot in her throat, she and the boys hugged them. On a hunch, she offered snacks and the two of them devoured everything she had hauled to the beach. No matter, home was just a few steps away.

In between bites, Kalea disclosed their plight. After leaving Cara's house they had gone home. Their dad would leave them there whenever he went out. They ate whatever was there until all the food was gone. When they went next door for help, the lady called the police. Racing back home they found their father and told him what they had done. Hearing about the police, he had thrown what little they had in the car and took off before the authorities' arrival. Now they lived in their car. During the day, they stayed on different beaches, but were admonished not to speak to anyone. Their father came back every evening with food. Sometimes they would stay at their father's friends' houses but he never let them stay inside. He would lock them in the car and Kalea and Leilani would watch from the windows. There were women and men coming and going, getting louder and louder as the night wore on. Once a man had knocked on the window and their father had fought with him. After that, they left. Finally, they had returned to Cara's beach because Kalea and Leilani had asked to see Aiden and Quinton. Kalea assured Cara their father would pick them up later that same night. Cara was so overwhelmed by their saga, she merely nodded.

Their beach time was cut short by the lack of subsistence. When Shelly saw the returning crew, she ran out to hug the girls. Everyone went into the kitchen where they ate a smorgasbord of tacos, coleslaw, fried chicken, mac and cheese, salad, raw veggies with dip and of course, dessert. It seemed a perfect time for a movie and within minutes snores were elicited from every over-stuffed body.

Peleke showed up as promised that very night, but not before Shelly and Cara had bathed, detangled and re-outfitted both girls. By the time he arrived, they were both tucked tightly into bed with new gee-gees and stuffed animals at their sides. Cara and Shelly were by the pool when he arrived.

"Peace offering," he called, holding out several bottles of white wine. "All the way from the Big Island."

Shelly huffed, got up and went inside. She did, however, return with glasses and a bottle opener. Cara just stared.

Peleke had changed so drastically in so short a time, she was stunned. His beautiful muscles had evaporated to sinewy knots. His skin was sallow with multiple lesions scattered along his arms and face. When he inhaled deeply his chest seemed to rattle.

"It's not contagious. Well it is, but it's not something you have to worry about."

Cara realized she'd been staring and blinked. She wondered if her mouth had been open too. Peleke opened the wine, filled the glasses and took a seat. Shelly picked up hers and went inside.

"Maybe now we can talk," he started and did not wait for a response. "I know I look bad. I'm dying."

Cara took a huge swig of wine. Peleke started his tale.

Peleke was a pure blooded Hawaiian, through and through for multiple generations. He had been his father's pride and joy, his mother's golden child. He had several brothers and sisters, but for whatever reason they favored him. When he declared he wanted to become a professional surfer, they had supported him while his siblings had baulked at their partisanship.

He had made his parents proud by becoming a world champion surfer by the age of eighteen. Unfortunately, everything after that was years of sex, drugs and rock and roll. The final straw for his parents was when he fell in love with a white person. It was prohibited for them and he became an outcast. Even the births of his daughters and the fact that he had never married their mother could not erase his break with the Hawaiian traditions. No one in his family recognized him. Christina, the girls' mother, had been from the mainland. They met at a party and just kind of hung out. They moved in together when she discovered she was pregnant. None of this stopped his extra-curricular activities and by the time she gave birth to their second child, he discovered he had contracted a potentially fatal virus. Christina left him. Peleke had come home to find her gone, the babies sleeping in their cribs. No note. He hadn't bothered trying to locate her. If she had walked out like that, it was probably best that she was gone. He had started a medication regime and undertaken the care of his kids.

Peleke had initially done well. He loved his girls, they were the joy of his life but he grew tired of ingesting so many meds. He gradually began tapering himself off until he was medication free. He had been leaving his girls at different beaches for two reasons. One, for them to become more independent and get use to not having him around, and two, for them to find a potential parent, someone they liked, but also cared about them. He stopped and looked directly at Cara.

"Me?" she gulped.

He nodded.

"You don't even know me. How could you be prepared to hand over your children and just die?"

"I'm not just handing them over."

"It sounds like it to me."

"No, I want more than that. I want us to get married and for you to adopt them."

Cara stood up, refilled her glass to the brim, walked around the pool then returned to her seat. Obviously, she was destined to never have a normal relationship.

"Listen, I like your girls, but I've seen you, what two to three times. I have no idea who you are, what's true about your story or why you would even think I'd consider marrying you. You don't sound like the marrying type even if you are going to die. You sound like trouble with a capital 'T' and that's the very last thing I need. I can do trouble all by myself. Why would I need yours?"

"It's not that you need anything, obviously," he said, gesturing towards the house and pool.

"Don't be fooled by facades. Even if I would consider taking care of your girls, why can't I just adopt them?"

"There's more to it than that. My children are fifty percent Hawaiian. They are entitled to certain things. I need someone who will care for them without taking advantage of them. I don't know you, but I think I know the type of person you are. You could have left my children on the beach initially, but you didn't. You threatened me with holy hell and then when I cut out again you still didn't take them to the authorities."

"Wait, was that a test?"

"Kind of, and you passed with flying colors. I know you're probably afraid of marrying me, but I promise to die, and soon. You can accompany me to the doctor for certification of my condition. I have a homestead that should go to my girls, but they cannot receive it until they are eighteen. I don't want the family who denies my existence and theirs to suddenly step in. I need someone who will keep them and their inheritance safe. By marrying me I can designate you as my survivor."

"You live in your car. What is there to inherit?"

"My grandfather and his brothers had agricultural homesteads collectively, forming a large farm. Family members request their homesteads next to each other cooperatively increasing the farms size. My grandfather deeded his to me."

Now the picture became clearer. That land would be coveted.

"You still don't know me well enough to say I won't steal it."

"You can't, you're not Hawaiian. And you won't."

"Why not?"

"You're sitting on a million dollar beachfront property, you don't need it."

Cara became Mrs. Opunui two weeks later, after a series of doctor visits, mounds of paperwork and multiple trips to offices and court houses. Peleke moved into one of the guest cottages. He did not stay there often. He did not want his girls to get re-attached and he did not want them to witness his deterioration. He and Cara spoke often, mostly about his last will and testament. The girls, on the other hand, were excited, the boys not so much. They were concerned about their own dad. Cara assured them Julian would always be their father. It hurt just around the edges of her heart, that the marriage, she was so sure would raise a rampage, was met with only continued silence.

Exactly six weeks after their nuptials, Peleke's body washed up on a beach on the opposite side of the island. It was ruled an accidental drowning. She followed through with all of his wishes. He was cremated with no ceremony except the paddle-out. Two of his friends provided the canoe and power to take Cara past the lagoon to scatter his ashes. Upon returning to shore she completed her promise and in the privacy of a rock alcove formation, she sang and danced a farewell hula in his name. She had a strong, clear voice and she loved to dance. It was the least she could do. Peleke had not been a bad man, just a misguided one. Finishing, she placed her leis on the water and watched until they were taken out to sea. She had a sudden sense of someone watching, but when she turned she could find no one. She stayed there until sunset, wishing him a peaceful journey.

CHAPTER 23

Cara felt she had opened and closed multiple chapters of her life in quick succession, each with the acquisition of children. She was hoping all the excitement was over and she could just settle into raising all of them. It got off to a rocky start. Just as Peleke had predicted, his family showed up for Leilani and Kalea. It began with phone calls from his siblings, a letter from an attorney then finally his mother's unannounced appearance on her doorstep. Against her better judgement, being the only one home, Cara let her in. In the course of the conversation, Cara provided documentation proving she had legally married Peleke, adopted his children and been deemed the designated survivor for his homestead. His mother had ripped the papers in a fit of rage and thrown them at her with a laugh. Cara advised they were all copies. The woman lunged at her and as Cara ran out the back door, she ran right into the arms of her Uber driver, who promptly positioned himself in the middle of the fray. There was an exchange of several choice Hawaiian words before the irate woman departed.

When Cara's heart rate finally came down from an aerobic level, she turned to Kris, "Thank God you arrived when you did. But why are you here?"

Chris shrugged his shoulders. "I came to check up on you. I heard about you and Peleke, then his death. I wanted to make sure you were ok. See if there was anything you needed."

Cara stared at him. "How goes your Uber business?"

Now he smiled, "Not so good. You were my best customer, which is why I need you to be well."

Cara laughed, "How old are you?"

"Twenty-one."

She gave him the stink eyes.

"Eighteen."

"And all you do is Uber?"

"No, I'm a part-time student."

"Why just part time?"

"A dude has got to make a living."

More side eyes.

"Ok. I've been on my own since I was sixteen. Had a whole bunch of shitty jobs, McDonalds, landscaping, day labor. Between trying to find someplace to live and saving for a car, that's as much as I could do."

"Where do you live now?"

"In a tent on my friend's family homestead."

Cara had to stop herself in the middle of twenty questions. What was she doing? The answer came almost immediately. He had shown up and stepped in at a most inopportune time. Still, if he had not been there, Cara would probably have been found twisted into a pretzel stuffed under a couch. She liked him in a little brother kind of way. They could help each other out. Here was another Hawaiian he-man.

"Ok," Cara started, "I have a trial proposal for you. There are several structures on this compound. We find one for you to live in for free in exchange for your security assistance. In addition, I pay you fifty dollars a week. If it works out and we all get along, I hire you and increase it to one hundred dollars a week."

"Do I get a gun?"

"Absolutely not."

"Who do I need to get along with?"

"Everybody."

"Who's that?"

And right on cue, Shelly marched in from the beach with every-body in tow. Chris's eyes widened as child after child ran past with Marcella slowly toddling in the rears. Cara thought he was about to bolt, but he smiled.

"I won't be living in this house?" he questioned.

"No, we'll find you a place of your own."

"Whew," he sighed, "it's a deal."

Hearing the word deal, brought Shelly's eyebrows to life.

"We have much to discuss," Cara advised, "but right now, we have to find a place for our new security to live."

Kris was set loose on the property. While Cara fixed dinner and replayed the earlier 'situation' Kris had saved her from.

"Wow, you were lucky," Shelly concurred.

"Amen, sister."

"So do you think they'll come back?"

"I hope not."

"Do you think Kris can handle it?"

"I'm not sure, but at least we won't be alone."

Peleke's family did not return. Instead, the Opunui family dis-patched an attorney. Between Kris, Shelly, her sister, Erica and her husband, Nahoa, they found an attorney to fight their side. Eventually it was settled. While the children were minors the Opunui family would continue to work their land, sending an agreed percentage to a trust for each girl that they could access at eighteen. At the time both were at least twenty-one years of age, it would be up to them to decide what they wanted to do with their homestead.

With that settled, life slowly took on a 'normal' pattern. Kalea and Leilani started kindergarten and first grade, while Aiden and Quinton were enrolled in preschool. Marcella had such a fit that everybody got to leave but her, that the morning ritual soon included her riding along every morning, then doubling back for pick-up. After school, there was homework, work-sheets, dinner, playtime, baths, nightly reading, and studies then bedtime. Shelly continued everybody's' linguistic classes in French, Spanish and Italian. And to be fair, Hawaiian was added. Everybody was exhausted by the end of the day. Cara had toyed with the idea of resurrecting her costume career but time seemed a major factor. When the other kids were gone, she still had Marcella, and when she napped, it was time to clean and prep for the next go round.

To Cara's surprise, Julian never stopped her monthly allotments after she married Peleke. She wasn't sure if he knew but didn't care or if he didn't know and didn't care. She had money enough to care for everybody. She even started paying Shelly, although she was sure it was nowhere close to what Julian had been paying. Weekends were for fun, sun and excitement. There were hikes, star gazing, movie nights, treasure hunts and biking. Time settled in and passed quickly. Marcella's first birthday was fast approaching. Cara remembered Julian's warning, but since there had been so much silence, she wasn't sure it was still in effect. After all, in the time that had past, his baby bride could have conceived and delivered.

Marcella's birthday came and went, and so did another month, then another after that. Cara was so relieved that she sent tickets to all her siblings and their kids and spouses for a super celebration of Aiden, Quinton and Marcella's combined birth-days. Her mother and aunt declined, advising they would see everyone at Xmas. No one else said 'no'. Shelly thought she had lost her mind, "You don't even like your sisters."

"Yes, I do. I just appreciate them more at a distance. But you know we have a lot to celebrate. Freedom. Real freedom for the first time."

Cara's property was divided into zones. Tents in the center for the kids and adults in the surrounding buildings. Initially, the tents were assigned by families, keeping siblings together, but the kids had other ideas. Groups of girls and girls, boys and boys, teens and toddlers, geeks and gamers, glamour and style broke out along with lights, decorations and decorum. The adults just stood back and let the cards fall where they may. When the dust settled, everybody was situated somewhere and best of all, everybody was happy, except Marcella, who at one year of age was designated too young to sleep outside. That problem was rectified when the teen glam squad offered to take her into their tent. Her crib was brought out and jammed into their area. Kids outside, surrounded by adults inside. Between the main-house, the guest cottages, the pool house and the out buildings, all the adults found their perfect spots, including Fernando and Jenna, who opted to a pitch tent in an alcove on the edge of the beach.

The party was a raging success. There was plenty of everything, food, foolishness, noise, music, running, splashing and basic rowdiness. After the food, but before the cake, ice cream and presents, the festivities came to a lull. A few of the younger children, including Marcella, had succumbed to sleep. One minute they were in raging form and the next they were unconscious. Collected and put to bed, the pool area was now open to the teens and adults. Cara and her sisters had copped a line of lounge chairs, just out of splash range, and were decked in their bikinis. There was not a skinny one among them, but they were all 'bringing booty back'. Mai-tis in hand, they were sucking up the sun and just enjoying the moment.

A loud low wolf whistle came off the path just behind them. Cara jumped up and grabbed her sarong. She'd know that whistle anywhere. Julian.

CHAPTER 24

"What a luscious lineup of brown bodies," he quipped salaciously as he came around, stopping directly in front of her.

Cara avoided eye contact and held her sarong in front of her, trying to keep her heart from thundering out of her chest, while her sisters 'hi'd' him.

"Don't be shy," he murmured and snatched her sarong from her. "Nice," he crooned.

Cara could feel the heat of his intense inspection. She tried to cover herself with her arms.

"Ah, virginal," he smirked.

She could feel a blush rising, along with her temper. She took a different stance, putting her hands on her hips and looking him directly in the eyes. Her heart skipped a beat. "How's your wife?" she sneered.

"How's your husband?" he countered.

She lost it and swung her hand to slap him. Julian caught her wrist in mid swing and captured the second one that followed. He twisted them both behind her, not her back, but under each butt cheek, pushing her pelvis into his. Cara felt a wild electrical charge as soon as her body came into contact with his. She stood stock still. She could also feel his growing arousal.

"What? Nothing else smart to say?" he grinned.

She turned her head.

"Cat got your tongue?" he teased softly in her ear. "That's ok because mine is still here." Looking over her shoulder, he saw all her sisters staring. He licked her neck from shoulder to ear.

Cara shivered.

Julian laughed and released her, turned toward the pool, dropping his shirt along the way and entered the water in one smooth dive. Loud hoots, hollers and cat calls were immediately elicited. Cara, reluctantly, turned to face her sisters.

"Damn, you guys are still hot as hell," said Tina.

"I'm soaking wet," Erica chimed in.

"I think I came," added Patrice

"Shit, I think I'm pregnant," Jenna drawled.

"Shut up, you stupid bitches," Cara snarled as she stomped into the house via the side door, leaving their giggles behind her. She marched directly to her room and began jerking open and slamming drawers in search of something to wear. She took off her bikini top and replaced it with a tank top. Then thought better about going braless, not with Him around. She snatched off that top and whipped open yet another drawer, turning when she heard the door close.

There was Julian leaning against the wall. He was glistening wet with a towel tied very low. Her eyes were pulled to the lowest point, following the hair pattern up past his tight abs towards his chest. When her eyes met his, he threw the lock. Cara jumped, then realized she was topless. Both hands flew to her breast. Julian cocked an eyebrow and advanced with pure feline grace: long, slow movements. Cara had all the time in the world to get away but she was rooted mutely to the spot. When he reached for her, she said one word, "'No."

Julian smiled, "Ok," but he still pulled her into his arms and kissed her.

Cara felt herself becoming entangled with the sensations and emotions Julian was creating. When he pulled back, he said, "Say it again." She had no idea what he was talking about. Just like she couldn't figure out how her arms had become wrapped around his neck or when she had lost her bikini bottom and how had he lost his towel.

Cara took a deep breath. Julian used that opportunity to lower her to the bed and in one fluid movement entered her deeply. She gasped. She thought she heard him chuckle, but then he remained completely still. She waited for the next stroke, but nothing. So it was going to be like that. Well, two could play that game. No sooner had Cara had that thought, then she began to feel herself throbbing around his member. She squeezed her eyes shut tightly and concentrated on controlling her body. Whether from that or the other, she developed a fine moisture over her entire body. She stopped breathing,

"Say it, Cara," he whispered. What was it about men and their names? She pressed her lips together tightly. Now her throbbing was matched with his and someone had dialed the heat up past high. She whimpered.

"Cara."

She wasn't sure if it was the way that he said it, or the heat of his breath in her ear or the feel of him, or his weight pressing her down or their intermingled scents. Whatever it was, it pushed her over the edge.

"Julian," she groaned.

He pulled back and plunged deeply into her. She cried out and came in a cascade of colors, while he moaned and came to the sound of a roiling surf. Julian withdrew from her almost immediately, picked up his towel and headed to the door. Re-draping his towel, he turned.

"I missed you too," then he was gone.

Cara threw her arm across her eyes. What was wrong with her? She had spent the last year and a half convincing herself she was over Julian, then in less than an hour of showing up, he was ensconced between her legs. She was humiliated and could have laid there forever waiting for the planet to swallow her up, had she not heard the kids awakening. She jumped up out of her disarray, closed the door and got dressed. She did not have the stamina to face anyone so she bolted out the front door, walked three houses down and took a path back to the beach. She was going to walk this off or die trying.

Cara lost count of how many laps she did along the beach and lagoon. It was well after dark when she braved the path down the way from her house to peek around the foliage in search of a long black car. No such vehicle was in sight. She let out a long breath and slowly walked home. Her oldest sister accosted her, as soon as, she stepped in.

"Where have you been? You missed the presents, cake and ice cream," she scolded.

"I'm sure the kids barely missed me with all the excitement."

"Still, you should have been here," her sister continued.

Cara kept walking, reached her bedroom door, then threw the last word over her shoulder as she entered, "Who are you? My mother?" She promptly fell over a cluster of luggage by the door. Disentangling herself she stood up to find Julian propped on pillows in her bed, reading a magazine, wearing a low slung sheet and nothing else. She was outraged. She closed the door, a little too loudly, and marched over keeping a healthy distance. "Get out of my bed," she hissed.

Julian languidly turned a page, not bothering to look up. He had obviously heard her, she had practically shouted.

"Julian!" she demanded.

He looked up slowly. He was giving her those sexy big brown bedroom eyes, then he arched an eyebrow. "Make me," he smirked.

Cara was not about to tussle with this naked man. She backed towards the door, stumbled and fell over the luggage again. By the time she got up, Julian was consumed in a fit of laughter. She gave him the finger on the way out, to which he replied 'please,' then continued in his merriment.

Cara was tired, angry and frustrated. She walked straight into the kitchen, opened a bottle of wine and poured a water glass full. Walking outside, carrying both, she was dismayed to find her sisters in the exact spot she had left them. A chorus of questions erupted.

Cara held up both hands in surrender, "I will field no questions from the peanut gallery." Then she sat down to begin some significant drinking. When the boo's died down, she tried again, "Tell me about the party, what did I miss?"

The revelry of the retelling went far into the night. There was more wine and Mai-tis to egg the telling on. All the recounts were peppered with tales of Julian and his escapades and how all the children took to him. Cara ignored his components, instead enjoying everyone's attempts to reveal a new and different detail.

The following morning, Cara woke up in bed with a throbbing pain behind her right eye. While attempting to focus, she realized she was in her bed. She sat up, throwing the covers off and patting her body and extremities. Her clothes were still intact, she fell back on the pillows.

"Disappointed?" came the snide voice of Julian, leisurely propped on his elbow beside her. "You and the girls had quite a night, didn't you? Well, we have a lot to do today, so you better get yourself together. We're due in court this afternoon."

"Court?" Cara swallowed, hard.

"Remember, I gave you one year to come home. Now I'm here and we are due in family court at four forty-five. I suggest you get up and start getting ready. It looks like it may take you more than a minute."

Cara groaned and turned her face into her pillows. She felt her stomach clench and her world shift. Neither had anything to do with her hangover.

"I told you not to make me come get you," Julian jeered as he headed to the bathroom.

A hot shower, a little breakfast and three cups of coffee later, Cara was dressed and ready for her day in court. She wore a simple sleeveless A-line dress with a matching jacket. Julian was immaculate in a tan walking suit. The limo appeared and they rode silently the entire one hour trip, each looking out their respective windows. Once they arrived, they were escorted to court room twenty-two, where they waited outside. An attorney took Julian aside. Cara sat on a chair, alone. When their names were called, she flinched. Julian went in with his lawyer, while she dawdled behind. Separated into two tables before the bench, Cara tried to listen to the quiet exchange going on at the other table. There were notebooks, folders, laptops, briefcases and a variety of paraphernalia on the desk. Her table top was clear. She had not thought to bring a tablet and she doubted she had a pen. Julian refused to make eye contact and a cold chill of fear ran through her.

A voice announced the judge's eminent arrival, advising all to stand. A large Hawaiian, dressed in a black robe with an oversized square white collar took a seat behind the bench, gaveled for silence and began the proceedings.

Julian's representative immediately jumped to his feet, "If it pleases the court, I would like to start with my client's interests."

The judge assessed the man over his glasses, "Sir, this is an informal hearing in Family Court. Are you a part of this family?"

"Ah, no, but I represent....."

"Then your services will not be needed."

"I object."

"Bailiff," the judge ordered.

Julian dismissed him with a silent two finger wave. The attorney packed up everything but a relatively flat folder. Cara felt a ray of hope.

The judge addressed Cara, "Do you need to call and cancel your attorney, too?"

"I don't have one. I didn't know I'd been summoned until this morning."

The judge cut his eyes at Julian, "You have not been summoned by the court. This is a private review for custody that was requested by the father of your children."

Cara visibly exhaled.

"Make no mistake," the judge continued, "it is a legal proceeding. I will hear both sides and make a recommendation. Wherever custody is eventually filed, that court will receive a copy of my review.

Cara felt her new found hope withering fast.

"Now then, who will begin?"

Cara bolted to her feet, "I will. My name is Cara Lynne Friedman. I have three children with this man, ages five, four and one. I thought we were doing okay. He's a superstar, with a crazy lifestyle, but we were working through it. Then while I was pregnant with our youngest, I found out somewhere along the way he had gotten married. I took my children and left. I bought a house here, where we could have peace and tranquility." She sat down.

"Now you, sir."

"My name is Julian Aristo Starr. I recognize her three children as mine. They are my only children. When she took them, she took a giant piece of my heart. I did marry someone, but it's a façade. My stage reputation is to be a ladies' man. In the years that we've been together, I've let that reputation slide to the point it was being called into question. It is my music and my reputation that pays the bills, so I married one of my dancers. May I say, that I have a predisposition for women? Cara has always been aware of it. While we have been together, I have traveled with a female entourage and had several paramours."

The judge turned to Cara, "Is this true?"

Dumbfounded that Julian would say that in court, she could only nod.

"You need to speak for the court recorder."

"Yes," she said quietly.

Julian continued, "I knew Cara was upset about the marriage, but I continued to care for her and our children, depositing monthly allotments, buying the beach house of her dreams, bankrolling her staff salaries, utilities and any other needs. I have never stopped supporting them, even after she married Peleke Opunui."

"I object," Cara interrupted.

The judge held up his hand. "I'm sorry. Did you say she married Peleke Opunui?"

"Yes, your honor," Julian replied solemnly.

"Ms. Freidman, you seem to have a penchant for errant men. Peleke Opunui was infamous on this island and in less than one year you met and married him?"

"It was a marriage of convenience," she stammered out.

"Kind of like Mr. Starr's?"

"It was nothing like his," she insisted.

"From where I'm sitting, it sounds the same. Obviously, convenience has a very broad perspective for both of you."

Cara's stomach took a huge lurch and she had a very acidic taste in her mouth.

"You were objecting?" he questioned.

For a moment she couldn't remember what she had been objecting to, then she remembered. "The house," she said, "I found and bought that house on my own."

"I have a copy of the deed, your honor," Julian informed. He handed the papers to the bailiff, who handed them to the judge.

The judge reviewed the documents and passed them back to the bailiff who was instructed to hand them to Cara. It was, in fact, the deed to her house. "That's impossible," she muttered.

"Do you have a deed?" the judge inquired.

"No. The real estate agent said the owner had to sign something and I would receive it in the mail. It never came. I left several messages."

"Ms. Freidman, may I ask how you could afford a house on Hanena Bay?"

"The real estate agent told me it was a foreclosed property, a steal at two hundred fifty thousand dollars. It was tangled in a divorce."

"Did the real estate agent give you that price on viewing?"

"No, she said she had to get back to me."

"It seems you were blessed with a real estate agent that magically appeared and sold you a house for six figures in an area that has no homes listed under five million."

The acid in her mouth took a plunge to her stomach and began to rumble around. She had not been blessed, she had been manipulated. She cut her eyes at Julian, who continued to look forward at the judge.

"Now," said the judge, "about your staff and financial situation."

"Sir," she interrupted, "I don't have any staff."

"Well, the payroll listed by Mr. Starr, has a Shelly Stanton, listed as a personal assistant/tutor/nanny and a Kris Kelekelio, as a driver and security."

Cara was losing it. Obviously, Julian was prepared to say whatever it took to win. "Yes, yes, I know Shelly, she does work for me, but Kris was an Uber driver and a student that I took in for exchange of services."

"Ms. Freidman, there are no Uber services on this island."

"But there was a flyer on the door...." she started, then finally realized how deep the rouse was. Had everyone been involved? It seemed her entire support system was directly linked to Julian. Her sister and brother-in-law had been feeding her the contacts, Kris had just appeared, always at the right time, and Shelly just kept smiling and playing her part. She had felt so distant and free, when he had been involved all along. Cara was burning with indignation and humiliation at the depth of her deception.

"It appears," continued the judge, "that you have no visible means of income other than the monthly allotment Mr. Starr provides. Is that correct?"

She felt her stomach contents shifting around and upward.

"Mr. Starr, Ms. Freidman seems to be lost in thought, is there anything you'd like to add?"

"Yes, your honor. I have spoken to her adoptive daughters, as well as, my own children on a weekly basis and I have physically visited them monthly since our separation. The girls have agreed to have me as their father, since I'm also Aiden and Quinton's father."

So he had been visiting and skyping the kids. No wonder Marcella and the girls recognized and adored him. What else?? And then it occurred to her, she was living in his house and all his houses were wired for sight and sound. He had been watching everybody and everything the whole time. She thought about all the lewd things she had insinuated to him about Peleke being a better lover. The reason she could not create a rise in him was that he had already had a front row seat in that relationship. The rumbling in her stomach took a violent turn. When the judge asked Julian where he was staying, Cara already knew the answer and had a preemptive response. She yanked the trash can from under the table and vomited profusely. The light breakfast and multiple cups of coffee came up with all the bile and disgust she was feeling. Between heaves, Julian confirmed he was at her house, in her room, and in her bed. Finally, sitting back she inhaled deeply, wiping her mouth with the tissues the bailiff had provided.

"I'm hoping, considering this situation, that you are not pregnant," the judge admonished.

"It would be okay with me," Julian chimed in.

"Why is that Mr. Starr?

"Because it would also be mine."

The judge banged the gavel to issue a recess, Cara renewed her upchucking and Julian walked by tsking. "None of this would have been necessary if you had just brought your happy ass home."

It was pointless to get up from the table. First of all, Cara did not feel comfortable being too far away from her trash can. Secondly, she had nowhere to go and thirdly, she did not want to run into Julian. Instead she sat forward, laying her face directly on the cool glass covering her table. She even stretched her arms above her head because she was having a hard time catching her breath. The cooling sensation was welcomed after her torrent of emotions and the upheaval of her GI system. She knew she looked ridiculous and someone was going to have to clean all the smudges on the glass, but after everything that had happened and been said, that was the least of her worries.

She tried to keep her mind still, but it kept wandering round and round in a knot of duplicity. How could she have been so blind? Nahoa had found a high paying job within days of her arrival. All her referrals to people and services, had come through him or her sister. Their maimed house had undergone a radical transition, fresh paint, repairs, new shutters and appliances. Apparently thirty pieces of silver bought a lot these days. Shelly and Chris lived right under her nose and even they succumbed to the pressure. Or was it the money, or the promises, or the possible opportunities to come? Cara had a sharp pain in her right temple. Squeezing her eyes shut, she began to count backwards from one hundred.

The gavel echoed loudly. Cara awoke with a puddle of slob under her right cheek. She was beyond humiliation, so she cleaned her face and the table with a tissue as Julian and the judge looked on. The judge cleared his throat and began.

"Although this is an informal procedure, my recommendations will be written up and forwarded to whatever judge eventually hears this case. The brunt of this decision falls on both of you. Under nontraditional practices, you have decided to not only start a family, but to continue in a rather hedonistic lifestyle. That fact aside, there is only one of you that has any financial relevance to be able to provide a consistent, secure quality of life for your children. It is my recommendation that Mr. Starr be awarded full physical custody of all your children, while Ms. Freidman will have visitation rights that can be determined at the time of your formal hearing. Your attorneys can obtain a copy of this recommendation. You are both dismissed." One final gaveling and he was gone.

Although Cara thought she knew what the decision would probably be, she was nevertheless devastated. She heard a voice, as if from far off, calling her name. When she focused, she found Julian standing beside her.

"Shall we go?"

The self-satisfied smirk he wore should have angered her, but she was fresh out of feelings. She followed him to the car and entered in a numb state. Once inside, he straightened his clothes and continued his gloating.

"I think that went well."

There was really nothing to say, so Cara kicked off her shoes and laid down on the seat. Now what? Her mind raced in so many directions, she could not keep up. In the end, hot tears began leaking from her eyes into her ears, eventually puddling beneath her. Julian made a drink and studied her. He had told Cara if she made him come for her, she would be sorry. Right now, she was very, very sorry, indeed.

When Cara woke up, they were in the driveway of her house. She had no idea how long they had been there. Julian was still sitting there, observing her as if she were a specimen under glass. Sitting up, she found the back of her outfit soaked. Once she moved, he moved too, holding open the car door, then the house door. She headed straight to her room to change. She was wet, tangled, wrinkled and cramped. Grabbing a pair of shorts and a tank top she headed for the bathroom. It was then she recalled there was something different about the room. She doubled back without changing. Julian's luggage was gone. She felt a sudden stab of pain in her gut and a heavy pressure in her chest. She dropped her clothes and ran from room to room calling for her children, no response. She passed through the living room to the outside door, searching. Her sisters and their families looked as if nothing was amiss. Of course, why would they? They were all probably a part of this. She ran back through the house to the driveway. The limo was gone. Julian was gone and all of her children with him.

Cara had no idea how long she stood in the driveway. It might have been minutes or hours, it felt like days. She finally mustered the courage to go back into the house. Passing the kitchen she overheard her sisters arguing over who would get to stay in her beach house first and for how long. They were as stupid as she was, the house wasn't even hers. She didn't bother to comment. Instead, she went straight to her room and got the bat that she kept by her bedside. When she emerged, she came out hollering and swinging. People began scattering in all directions. At first, they thought she was just overreacting to the court's decision, which they all knew would favor Julian. But when she asked them where her children were and none of them could answer, they all became a little nervous and fidgety. When she started breaking stuff, people took action. They gathered their children, and they all left. Once they were gone, she went into the kitchen put all the alcoholic beverages on the counter and filled a water glass with ice. She'd lost everything.

Leandra Simone

To say it was time for some serious drinking, would have been an understatement.

CHAPTER 25

Julian was happier than he had been in a long time. He had his children back. He had not intended to leave Cara in the house after their court session, but the reaction she had to finding their children gone reminded him of the suffering he had endured when she left. Turnabout was fair play. He would let her stew in her own juices for a while to see how she liked it.

Julian had been frantic when Cara had initially bolted with his babies. He had taken out his anger and frustration on the immediate staff, all the guards at the gate had paid for her escape with their jobs. A few broken possessions, insulted feelings and a terrified bride later, he calmed down enough to gather himself. Unbeknownst to Cara, Julian had semi-regular contact with his brother-in-law's. The yurt experience had sealed their relationship. He barricaded himself in his studio and called all of them. Their immediate reaction was just what he'd hoped for, a male allegiance that swore to contact him at the first sign of her appearance. The days and hours before that happened had been heart wrenching. Isolated and alone, Julian had cried, raged and ranted, promising revenge that ranged from murder to outrageous mayhem that would only conclude with the return of his children. He had contacted 'his people' to put them onto her scent, then waited with malicious thoughts. Several days later he received a call from Nahoa. Cara and his sons were in Kauai. His initial desire had been to fly in, truss her and take his kids. Then he remembered she was pregnant. The description of her high speed car antics scared the bejesus out of him. His pursuit had to be cool and quiet, lest she catch wind and bolt again. Knowing where they were, calmed his spirit and settled his mind. Now, it was time for strategic planning. He had to set a steel trap into which she would willingly go and that would guarantee his success.

Nahoa was his first easy target. As usual money talked and bull-shit walked. Julian had plenty of money and was in no mood for bullshit. He put Nahoa on payroll with a mandate of daily reports. He wanted everything from his family's comings and goings, to personal interactions. When he received the report that Cara wanted to buy a house. Julian set-up a real estate agent to assist her but only take instructions and money from him. He fed that to Nahoa.

The details for her labor and delivery were easy enough since there were few hospitals on the island. Shelly had been a bit harder to win over. She had a personal allegiance to Cara. But the thirty percent increase to her already six figure salary along with the promise not to press kidnapping charges in her helping Cara take his babies, had convinced her. She became the link with his children, providing private weekly skyping sessions without which he probably would not have been able to endure their absence.

Once Cara's residence had been secured and he was satisfied with the safety of his children's situation, he could turn his attention directly on her. The baby was almost due and he had not missed any of his babies' births. He was not about to start now. The issue was his anger and him controlling it. That she had the audacity to leave him, take the kids and not so much as say boo about it, still sent him into a reverberating funk. He was not sure that he could see her without laying hands upon her. In the meantime, he salved and soothed his soul by watching his family on video feed. Cara's house, like all his houses were wired. His new found ritual was daily reviewing of the recordings. He watched Aiden and Quinton learning how to swim, building block structures and running rough and ready throughout the house. Cara, he watched with a grain of animosity and a strain around his heart. She appeared to be doing well without him. He had toyed with the idea of cutting her monthly financial allotment but cringed with the thought that his children would not be provided for at the level they deserved. So, he continued his payments and made arrangements for an increase with the birth of the new baby. The thought of the impending birth brought a profound level of sadness. He just knew it would be a girl and he would be missing her first months of life. That was Cara's fault.

Julian had yet to see her cry. Maybe she did it while away: walking, on errands, or wandering the beach. He suspected she didn't. She looked too contented with her new life. It was the destruction of that contentment that gave him the drive to keep going. Still, as he watched her struggling with her growing size and the impediments that went with it, he felt a softening around the edges of his anger. He made plans to be on the island in anticipation of her delivery.

Julian had long outgrown his wife. The last nail in her coffin, came the day Cara drove away. She had been clueless, detached and dispassionate as ever. She could not get over the disruption of her reception by 'common hooligans'. The fact that they were toddlers had done nothing to erase her ire. If she said it once, she'd said it a million times, finally driving Julian into his private living area, in which, he firmly remained. Every now and then, she'd send word that she wanted to see him, but for the most part she was content with his house, his money and his rare sexual encounters. She was way too easy, and not in a good way. Easily influenced, swayed, convinced or satisfied. If she had a clean, original thought, she had yet to share it with him. Julian was simply bored.

The day Cara went into labor, Julian beat her to the hospital. Her driver, a newly acquired employee, had texted him in advance. When he found her alone, moaning like a wild banshee, his heart soared. So, she was hurting, and from the sound of it, almost as badly as he was. He had jumped in, giving directions, reinforcing the breathing and providing repositioning, ice chips and back rubs. When his baby girl arrived, he cried too. She was everything he had ever dreamed of. Once cleaned, they laid her on Cara's chest and he had a hard time catching his breath. He had enfolded both in his arms, whispering 'I'm sorry' into her neckline. Cara's tears started and could not be stopped. He began to feel an ache around his heart that was dissipating his anger. He held her tightly. Eventually she fell asleep leaving him to hold their baby, Marcella. Her eyes were open and grayish, watching him with the intensity of a small animal. He began talking to her and at the sound of his voice, she smiled. So, she remembered him. His joy was bittersweet. They had just found each other, only to be separated again. Now he felt the stream of hot tears.

Before leaving, Julian had given Cara one year to return home. He had threatened her, but he knew she was not impressed. Cara never was. The chances of her willing return were nil to none, so it was his job to force her. He could easily take her to court and win custody of the children, but the truth was he wanted her too. He had the means and the money to make anything happen, and that was exactly what he was going to do.

Hearing of Cara's impending marriage to Peleke had just about pushed Julian to murder. Had Nahoa not called him with the low down, the hitman he hired would have ended his days before his early demise. Julian's visual of the residence, as well as, Nahoa's reassurances had gotten him through. He remained pissed until he witnessed Cara's final farewell hula after scattering the ashes. Much as he hated to admit it, he had a soft spot for her and all her craziness. He studied the process for adopting Kalea and Leilani. He wasn't about to complain, he had just doubled down on daughters.

The deadline date slip had been on purpose. He knew that with each passing day Cara grew more confident in her freedom. It was with utmost joy that he appeared in the middle of the birthday party. Although he had watched her from afar, he had been overwhelmed by her physical presence. He had forgotten all his staunch promises to make her beg. Instead, he had given her sisters a free tease and pounced on her the first opportunity he got. He was genuinely surprised by their reaction to each other. It was like they had never been apart. Things were as hot as ever and he had every intention of keeping it that way.

CHAPTER 26

Julian had not checked in on Cara for several days.   Frankly, he didn't have time.   He and all his children were doing the do.   They had gone on Jurassic Park helicopter tours, waterfall excursions and glass bottom boat adventures.   When he finally thought of Cara, after tucking everybody in tight, he was petrified by what he found.   Reviewing live footage of her house, it looked like a ghost town.   There was trash, broken debris, and empty tents with abandoned items, bottles and food cartons everywhere.   He was so stunned by the footage, he did not go back to review previous video, but merely scanned room after room that showed no movement or life.   He called his driver and raced over to the house.

Entering, there was no smell of death.   He would have liked to say that he did not know that smell, but his early days had taught him alot.   He called out to Cara, with no response, and so he began the search.   All the bedrooms were empty. The kitchen was a disaster of food, plates and flies.   He crossed the living room, filled with bottles and debris, to the outside.   In a way, that was worse.   Only days before it had been filled with children and happiness, now it was a ghost town of abandoned clothes, toys and empty dreams.   He sat at the end of the compound surveying the damage.   Where the hell was Cara?

Julian returned to the house.   He could not believe that she had bolted again.   Or had she?   Had he finally driven her over the edge?   The thought chilled him.   He became methodical.

Starting in her bedroom he searched her medicine cabinets, her clothes, and her drawers.   He was happy not to find a dildo.   He did find her commitment bands in a small bottle on the dresser.

He pocketed them. Nothing appeared to be missing. He went meticulously through each child's room. It would not have surprised him to find her in their closet or under their bed, but neither was true. Julian tapped down his panic and returned to the general living area. Scanning the family room, adjacent to the outdoor area, he believed he saw an aberrant item. Moving closer, he found a foot. Moving up the extremity he found the rest of Cara, under covers and pillows, surrounded by bottles, debris and food items, thankfully still breathing. She was dressed in her same court attire. He went into the kitchen and prepared.

Cara was floating on a cloud of 'nothing matters and I don't care', when the first bucket of ice water hit her on the back of her body and head. She reared up on the couch to her knees, only to be hit flush in the face and chest with another flash. She jumped to her feet sputtering.

Gaining her footing and clearing her eyes she found Julian perched on the arm of the couch with an empty ice bucket.

"So, you've come to gloat. Do it and be gone," she slurred. She was feeling very proud until he threw another round. "Damn you, Julian."

Julian was having fun. She was alive. He could do this all day.

She fell on her knees to floor, "Okay, I give. You win."

He threw more, he couldn't help himself. Cara leaned forward, her forehead on the floor. She held her hands up and started crying. So, this was how it was going to end.

Julian threw more water and ice on her deflated form. The last bucket hit her soul. He wasn't just here to gloat, he had come to drown her in ice water. It was an incomprehensible thought, but she had it just the same, and it pissed her off.

Cara stumbled off the floor, "I tried to lay here and get out the way, but you're such a stupid motherfucker, you couldn't appreciate it. Now, I'm gonna have to kick your ass."

Julian laughed and threw another pitcher of the same. Cara screamed, staggered up and chased him around the house. She lost him somewhere between the kids rooms and the den. Tiptoeing through those areas she was hit full frontal with another barrage of ice and water. She screamed again and charged forward. Julian caught her by the waist, pulled her into her bathroom and dunked her in a tub, full of more ice and water. He held her under and each time he allowed her to surface he'd say, "Are you ready?"

Finally, holding onto his wrists she submitted, "Yes, yes, yes."

He released her. She came up sputtering and fell by the side of the tub.

Cara struggled up. She felt chilled to the bone, waterlogged and very nauseated. As she cleared the tub, she stumbled to the toilet and threw up. When she came out, Julian was wearing a towel, just a towel. She had no idea what that meant, but she was sure it had nothing to do with sex. Passing a mirror, she confirmed that thought. She looked like shit. Her face was swollen, eyes red, hair tangled and her clothes were crumpled, stained and now, wet. Julian motioned her to the shower that was putting out a cloud of steam. She shuffled forward. She had every intention of getting in with her clothes on, but he blocked her way, undressed her, and pushed her in, entering behind her. Cara stood directly under the stream of hot water, feeling it run over her head, letting the heat do its magic. Julian dumped a load of shampoo on her head and began washing and finger combing her locks. When he was finished he threw them to the front, whipping her smack in the face. Next he began scrubbing her from head to toe with soap and a towel. Cara felt like an errant pet. It wasn't that he was rough but he wasn't gentle either. It was more like a diligent disinfecting project. When he was finished, Cara had lost her chill, felt a tingling of fresh scrubbed skin and a clearing of her brain cells. Julian wrapped her hair in a towel and wrung it tight like a vise. Now she also had a face lift.

In the bedroom, Cara found a pair of capris, a top and undergarments spread on the bed. She put them on, found matching sandals and to keep from looking so sad, put on eyeliner and some lipstick. Julian, redressed , was standing by the door.

"Let's go," he demanded.

She followed him through the house, where a cleaning crew were already busily at work, and out the front door. Brian was loading her bags in the car. Who had packed that? She looked at Julian but he continued silently beside her. They got in and the quiet rebuff persisted. Cara knew better than to ask any questions, so she just stared out the window.

An hour later, they arrived at a hotel. Again, Cara was not sure what it meant. Whatever it was, she was resigned to her fate. Exiting the car, Brian handed her the bags. Well, at least she knew she did not warrant her previous status. Carrying them, she followed Julian through the lobby, up the elevator and to a massive door. Now, she could also rule out murder, this place was too nice. He could have eliminated her in a dingy motel anywhere along the way. He opened the door and stepped aside.

A chorus of 'mommy' rang out and Cara was engulfed by several layers of little arms. Kisses and hugs were being hugely distributed when Shelly entered the room. Cara stopped in mid-squeeze to confront her. Julian jumped in.

"We'll put the kids to bed tonight, Shelly," he quickly instructed, restraining Cara by the shoulder. "Good night."

Shelly turned and walked out.

"Sooner or later she's going to have to deal with me and you won't be around forever," Cara grumbled.

"Won't I?"

Cara cut her eyes at him and went back to hugging and kissing her kids. Several hours later, after everyone told her all the fun things they had been doing with their father, what they had been eating and watching on TV, and eventually how much they had missed her, Julian announced it was time to go to bed. Before any discontentment could be voiced, he added a surprise was in store for any and all good children who went to bed quickly. There was a stampede to their bedrooms, a snatching off of clothes and jumping into pajamas, along with frantic teeth brushing. Julian and Cara kissed everyone goodnight and turned out the lights.

"We need to talk and you need to eat," Julian advised as he walked back through the suite, opened a door on the opposite side and went in.

Cara had little choice but to follow. She entered one of the most beautiful bedrooms she had ever seen, with probably one of the biggest beds on the planet. She stopped short.

"Um, where will I be sleeping?" she stammered.

Julian didn't bother to answer other than eyeing her and then the bed. She was having mixed emotions about that revelation when room service entered with a rolling table full of silver trays. Julian gently pressed her into a chair and lifted the lids. It was a wide array of sumptuous delights: fruit, salad, fish, scallops, cheese, crackers and local vegetables. Although Cara had not thought about being hungry, apparently she was. She gobbled a large amount of everything, then almost immediately felt extremely exhausted. She did not think she was up for the impending conversation.

"I'm sure you don't feel like talking," Julian started.

So, his mind reading skills were still intact. Too bad. Cara yawned, "I know we need to talk, but maybe it can wait until tomorrow?"

"No," he insisted, "tonight."

Cara sighed.

"You took my kids and I took them back. How did that make you feel?"

Up until then, she had avoided making eye contact with Julian, who was sitting directly across from her. Now, she looked him straight in the eyes. "Like shit," she growled.

"Multiple that by one year. So, I guess we can agree on not ever doing this again to each other. They are our children, Cara, not exclusively yours or mine, but ours."

Cara gulped. She could already see where this was going. "What about..?"

"Don't start with that," he interrupted. "This has nothing to do with anybody but us."

Cara knew that to be true. It hurt like hell that he had gotten married, but after she had gotten over her initial anger, she realized it was probably a temporary situation like all the others. The pain that it used to cause had been totally burned away by the searing squeeze her heart had experienced when she found her children gone. She was willing to do anything to make sure they were never separated again.

"So, what are you saying Julian?"

Instead of answering, he reached back, retrieved another covered silver tray, placed it on the table and pushed it towards her. Lifting the lid, she found a delicate white eyelet baby doll set with her eternity bands on top. Well, that pretty much said it all.

"I don't see you wearing my band," she countered.

Julian reached into his shirt and pulled out a chain with his ring hanging on it.

Cara exhaled loudly, "I don't see how this is going to work."

"Leave that to me," he quipped. "Now, it's time for bed."

She had been exhausted a minute ago, but suddenly she was not ready to retire. Before she could come up with an excuse, Julian cut in.

"Now, Cara. I have a call to make. I expect to find you where you're supposed to be when I get back." He walked out closing

213

the door behind him.

She ate one more strawberry, retrieved her bags, put on her rings and lingerie and got into the bed. Cara wondered who he was calling? His wife? She realized she didn't care. She was prepared to be the other woman, the sister wife, the mistress, Mata Hara or the man in the moon. By whatever means necessary, she was going to keep she and her kids together, and if that included Julian, so be it.

Julian returned a short time later. He actually didn't need to make a call, he was just giving Cara a minute. Apparently, that was all that she needed. He found her beautifully arranged, hair draped across the pillows snoring softly. He had intended to make love to her all night. The last time he had retrieved her, he had given her space and time. He had no intention of doing either this go round. He undressed and slipped into bed pulling her into his arms. She was wearing her bands. He kissed her fingers, her lips then her forehead. He had all the time in the world to make her his again.

CHAPTER 27

Several days later, Julian, Cara and their children were on Julian's plane headed back to the compound. The excitement level rivaled the intensity of Xmas. Ten minutes into the plane ride, Cara forgot all the apprehension that was beginning to fester. Julian had said not to think about it and she truly had no time for wasted thoughts. Their five children were hopping, jumping, turning, thumping, chasing, and touching everything within arms and legs reach. Cara had caught, scolded and subdued everyone at least once or twice only to have them slithered off to begin again. She was exhausted. Julian merely sat back watching the chaos with a smile of contentment. Just when she was about to lose it, Julian announced dinner. Every child froze as if they had never heard the word or maybe they were intrigued by the concept of eating on a plane in the sky. They quieted and awaited further instructions. Damn him, he could have done that hours ago.

With a wave of his fingers, people appeared with tables, chairs, linen, plates and utensils. Children were placed in seats and to their chiming delight kiddy cuisine was served: pizza, burgers, fries, corn dogs and for dessert, cookies and ice cream. Stuffed to the gills, eyelids began to flutter. Before Cara could make a move, more finger waving and the same people sprang into different action. Loungers were converted into beds, complete with sheets, pillows and cashmere covers. This new enticement worked like a charm. With heavy eyelids the little ones took themselves to bed. Shoes were tossed off, elbows jabbed into each other's sides in a bid for the window positioning, giggles, a yawn or two, then blessed silence. Julian was still sitting with steepled fingers. Had he moved, other than his fingers? His eyes took on a smoky look. Cara decided to get up and check on the kids. He blocked her way.

"What do you think of the mile high club?" He purred.

"If it's what I think it is, I will not be achieving membership status tonight."

Julian laughed, "You really know how to bust a brotha's wet dreams."

"If that's the kind of dreams you're having, then you and I must be on different planes. On my plane it's time for good night, sleep tight, sweet dreams." She attempted to push by him but he pulled her into his lap, nuzzling her neck.

"I'll give you a free pass tonight, but be warned, it's on our agenda." He released her and Cara scampered to a free lounger bed, jumped in and covered up. When she peeked back at Julian, he had his earphones on and sheets of paper scattered before him.

Being with Julian, and trying to believe they could make their relationship anything they wanted, became much harder under the reality of being back at his compound. Initially, there had been intense energy and excitement. Julian had been busy in her residence in their absence. He had created a room for Kalea and Leilani, and reconstructed and redecorated all the children's rooms. Aiden and Quinton's jungle, included an actual tree house with a bridge that went through the wall and into the clouds in Marcella's fairy world. She had a hobbit type house which included a cave that had a crawl through that led into the dungeon of Kalea and Leilani's princess castle. It was all amazing and allowed everyone access to each other without bothering with hallways. Consequently, no one was ever where they were supposed to be, and there were multiple hiding places. It was child's dream and a mother's nightmare. Julian could see no flaws with any of it. Cara thought her bedroom remained the same, with the exception of a new chest of drawers, which on closer inspection was found to already be filled with Julian's clothes. Which led to the discovery of her closet being re-arranged into his side/her side, and then to her horror, the finding of a guitar stand with multiple guitars standing in the corner. Before she could locate Julian and address any of her concerns, he came in, closed and locked the door.

"I feel like you're avoiding me," he accused, "What's wrong? I thought we were getting somewhere in Hawaii."

And they had been. They had spent their days going on family outings and activities and their nights getting reacquainted in highly romantic, provocative, steamy ways.

"I don't know," she murmured, "It feels like I'm back in the same place with the same old thing."

"It's not the same," he reassured her, taking her into his arms. "This time everything is going to be different."

Julian was correct about that. Besides the fact that he had moved in, they had five children, and all were under the age of seven. There was school registration, clothing shopping, and school supply lists. Julian insisted on everyone's presence and participation in completing all tasks. Children were running in stores, everyone was throwing things into the baskets, there was hunger, temper tantrums, tears and finally passed out bodies in car seats. Once school started, their days fell into a fairly regular schedule. Get up, get everybody ready for school, including Marcella who continued to insist she ride along to drop them off and pick them up, then homework, dinner, baths, reading, then bed. Shelly continued their language lessons somewhere in between it all. She and Cara had finally come to a truce.

To Cara's surprise, Julian remained a part of it all. He and Cara either did it together, or switched off depending on what was going on. He really seemed to live with them. He went to bed with her every night and was there every morning. He was still a late night worker, but Cara grew used to hearing him playing somewhere in the house. If he went elsewhere, he always made it back in time not to be missed. After several months despite all the chaos and drama, a contentment settled upon her and her peace spread out into her family. Maybe they could make it work.

Julian had made a ritual of cooking pancakes for the kids every Saturday morning. When that day arrived, everyone high-tailed it to the kitchen. It was an uproarious event no matter how many times it occurred. Pancakes with shapes, dramatic flipping and high aerial delivery were all part of the spectacle. Cara prayed for a Saturday sleep in, but as of yet that had not happened. On this particular Saturday, she moseyed in to find pancakes in mid-flight to plates. Of course, Aiden and Quinton had added catch to the festivities. She headed straight for the coffee pot. Julian intercepted her, bent her back and kissed her deeply to a chorus of cheers, claps and kissy sounds from the kids.

"Show off," she said pushing him away.

He swatted her butt with the spatula. Cara retrieved a cup of coffee then stood watching everyone's antics. Leilani and Kalea were tossing pieces of pancakes into the air as Aiden and Quinton tried to catch them with their mouths, in between trying to catch the ones their father was injecting into the air. There were pancakes on the floor, on the counter, and maybe one on the blade of the overhead fan. Marcella was content to serve herself from the array that had landed on the table within her reach. It was a quaint scene in most unorthodox manner. Cara was thoroughly enjoying it when Marcella let out a scream. Everyone looked up to find a young woman standing in the entry archway. She did not look happy.

"Why are you here? Who are these people?" she demanded looking around wildly.

Cara looked at Julian. His expression never changed, instead his eyes became cold and steely.

"Get out. You don't belong here," he hissed.

"Who are these people? And when are you coming home?" she persisted.

Quinton, always the helpful one, attempted to assist her, "He's my daddy."

The girl gasped and then shrieked, "What?? You've got me embedded with some year-long birth control while you're over here breeding like bunnies?"

What? This girl was under some chemically controlled sterilization while Julian had her in an archaic natural rhythm method. He had said multiple times that she would be the only mother of his children, but she had not believed him. She'd figured it was only a matter of time, given his track record, but now?

Just then, Aiden decided to help clarify. "We're not bunnies, we're Starr's," he announced.

Now the young woman took a good look at each and every child, finally focusing on Cara. Cara smiled. She wished she'd been wearing one of the sexy French lace outfits Julian insisting on buying, but that would have been inappropriate. Instead she was in shorts and a tank top, still she straightened up, arched her back and sucked in her stomach.

'You!" the woman screamed.

Cara could not wipe the smile off her face. A dozen clichés ran through her mind: revenge is best served cold, what goes around comes around, pay back is a bitch....

Julian on the other hand, was silently seething. He had remained relatively motionless, casually leaning on the counter. When he spoke again, the whole room came to attention.

"I'm not going to say it again," he sneered, his voice was hard and frigid.

Kalea and Leilani who had been twittering behind their hands, stopped and looked at each other. Quinton and Aiden both said 'uh-oh' at the same time and Marcella, who had lost interest in all of it, stopped eating. Although Julian had not taken a step, the girl flinched and took a step back. She finally gave an exasperated sigh, turned and stomped out. Cara was impressed. She would have broken everything in sight and then would have needed to be taken out by security. That probably explained why baby girl lived on the hill. She could follow directions.

Julian turned back to his audience, "Who wants more pancakes?"

A cheer went up and everything resumed like the interruption had only been a blip in the action. Cara let her breath and her stomach out, her smile vanished too. Julian still had a wife.

CHAPTER 28

Cara threw herself back into her costume designing. She pulled out her pencils, papers and swatches, called her old contacts, began sketching with a new mania and submitting proposals at will. She had politely invited Julian to move out after the 'visitation' and he had just as politely invited her to go to hell. Cara found the concept of out of sight, out of mind to be true. She had pretty much ruled the wife out, since Julian was living with her and the kids and it appeared she wasn't around anymore, but once she showed up Cara could not keep her out of her mind. He continued to live with them as if nothing had happened, and of course, there was no discussion on the matter. During the day she was standoffish to him, but no matter how much distance she put between them in bed, she always woke up tangle with his body. Julian kept the same contented expression and basically acted like he was just biding time for her to get over it.

Cara's first interview came several months after her enlightenment. She had submitted multiple sketches for multiple projects before receiving an invitation to present her portfolio in Los Angeles. Julian had offered to come with her, the use of his plane, keys to the beach house and the pull of any strings he could reach. She declined all the above, booking a first class seat on a commercial plane and a hotel room. The interview process took several days and in the interim all of the candidates got to know one another. Cara thought it was great. Adult conversation about fabric, notions, colors and pattern making were right up her alley. It was refreshing and a huge change from diapers, counting, hop-scotch and potty-training. Plus, she was free of the compound and the cloud that shrouded it.

Bailey, a beach boy if ever there was one, was submitting for the men's component of the project. He had a lax stance and attitude and always loosened his blond curls after his interview sessions. He had a killer smile and a well-groomed beard. All the other contestants had somewhere to be after their presentation time, except him and Cara, so they began to sort of hang out.

Cara could see nothing wrong with it. Sometimes it was drinks, or a pool game or even coffee and doughnuts. Once they went to the downtown garment area in search of textiles. He had a girlfriend, she had a significant other with a wife. What's good for the goose, is good for the gander.

On her final night, they had dinner. There was more conversation about the industry, accentuating trim and secret fabric turning techniques. She thought nothing of it when he walked her to her room. Unlocking the door, she turned to thank him for everything when he suddenly kissed her, gently nudging her into the room. Before she had the chance to rebuff him, all hell broke loose.

In the darkness, Cara felt a hand grab her wrist and whip her into the room. She could not believe they were getting mugged in her hotel room. Stumbling, she would have fallen had an arm not caught her around the waist. With her back to her captive she watched as the door closed and Bailey receive a vicious blow. Cold cocked he doubled over only to receive an upper cut to the chin. Cara attempted to scream for help only to have a hand clamp tightly over her mouth.

"You know I don't like other people messing with my stuff, especially my woman."

Julian.

Cara watched in horror as Bailey continued to be pummeled. When he fell and they started kicking him, she reached up and pulled Julian's hand down. Turning she sobbed into his neck, "Please."

"Enough," he ordered, "Let's go."

"My stuff..." she started.

"Packed," he snarled and led her over the body and out the door with a tight, slightly painful grip of her elbow.

Whoever said silence was golden, lied. Not only was it not golden, it was very tense. Julian felt like a spring coiled way too tight, while Cara, pissed as hell, attempted to fade into the upholstery of the car. Her heart sunk lower when they pulled up to his private plane. It was going to be a long night.

They boarded and took off almost immediately. The body guards, apparently exhausted from their workout, went to their section and closed the door. Cara took that as a bad sign. Julian continued his steely silence which was fine with her, at least he had not insisted she sit next to him. She chose a seat as far away as possible and out of his line of sight. The quiet took on an intensity of its own. The longer it went on the angrier and more uncomfortable Cara became. Who in the hell did he think he was? Unable to tolerate it any longer, she approached Julian, taking a seat directly across from him. When he looked up, she realized her mistake but was trapped under the gaze of his savage glare.

"I wasn't doing anything wrong," she began.

No response, just more angry eyes. She started to rise. The heat of his stare was scorching her, plus she felt a blush rising.

"That's not what it looked like, but if that's true, it's really too bad," he finally sneered, "cause that man got his ass whipped for nothing."

She was almost away when she felt Julian's grip on the back of her neck.

"You know, what's good for the goose, is not good for the gander or any one associated with her. They are likely to get sliced, diced and roasted. Now that we have that all cleared up, I think you should get out of those clothes," he hissed and began tearing her clothes away.

Cara was angry. At the sound of her blouse ripping she elbowed him in the ribs. He released her, but only for a minute. He caught her by her hair as she attempted to get away.

"Oh, so you wanna play rough?" he growled, "I was gonna try and be nice." He began winding her hair around his wrist, basically reeling her in.

Cara had little choice but to go with her hair, but she still had some rebuttals. "Nice? Since when do you play nice? You do whatever you want and the chips just fall where they may," she exclaimed. "I'm going to be just as bad as you, instead of pretending to be nice. I'm going to tell you all about me and Baily and all the things we did," she snarled.

Julian stopped, "Really? Tell me."

Cara had not expected that response, but being fast on her feet she divulged a series of wild sexual encounters occurring everywhere from a gas station bathroom, to under the beach pier. Julian was motionless and silent throughout her tale.

"Is that it?" he asked, releasing her hair and looking down at the floor.

Cara's courage was peaked now. The creation of such an elaborate tale had quailed some of her anger and his somber reaction gave her a sense of power and the feeling that now he knew how she felt about his escapades.

"Yes, that's it, unless you want to hear about some of the other people I met," she preened.

"No," he said shaking his head sadly, "That's enough."

Suddenly, he grabbed her around the waist and began dragging her across the plane. Cara would have thought he was going to toss her, but she knew that was impossible without getting sucked out himself. Instead, he pulled her into the bathroom, twisted one arm behind her back and began washing her mouth out with soap. She was initially shocked into inertia but then began struggling. By the time it was over, the front of her clothes were soaked, she had soap in her eyes and was blind with tears from the burning.

"Do you have anything else to report," Julian smirked releasing her.

Cara couldn't see anything, but that didn't stop her from swinging out towards the sound of his voice. She hit her hand on the wall. He laughed, covered her head and upper body with a massive towel and carried her out. He unceremoniously dumped her on the bed, gave her wet towels for her eyes and began taking off her clothes. She continued swinging and kicking out, but he snapped her with a wet towel each time until she stopped dejectedly.

When the burning finally stopped and her vision returned, she sat up to find Julian back in his seat. Wrapping a sheet around herself, she approached him again.

"Haven't you had enough?" he warned without looking up from his keyboard.

"How did you know I wasn't telling the truth?" she inquired.

"First of all, I know you and that's not the type of girl you are. Secondly, you were never out of my line of sight," and he looked up at her and winked.

"You sick son of a bitch," Cara said, taking another swing.

Julian laughed, caught her wrist, snatched off the sheet, carried her back to bed and introduced her to the Mile High Club.

Cara was sure Julian would require some space after the LA incident, but he did not. Not even when she mentioned Bailey or his possible injuries. Instead, he assured her Bailey was fine and advised it would be best not to have to do that again. Cara was surprised. Things were definitely different. He bounced right back into her house and her bed. They went back to their kiddy schedule, she went back to her studio and he returned to his music. In time everything settled back to what it used to be and they continued to be tangled up with each other every morning.

One night at the dinner table, Julian announced he would be leaving for a few days. The proclamation created a massive outrage. All the children verbalized their displeasure at once. Julian entertained all the madness, while Cara sat stunned. He never used to explain his comings and goings. Advising that he was going on a business matter, he promised upon his return they would all go on an adventure together. That possibility sent everyone into a feeding frenzy so they could finish their meals and begin researching where the adventure should be. Maps were spread on the floor in the family room – local, regional, national, world. Next came the books with world sites. Cara sat with Marcella, who insisted on turning every page of a Nat Geo travel log, while watching Julian and their kids. Everyone was in high spirits, laughing and tumbling over each other with suggestion after suggestion of where they should begin. Julian looked up suddenly and caught her looking at him. He arched an eyebrow then crawled over on all fours, scooping an arm behind her to pull her to his chest. Marcella tumbled down while Cara made a feeble attempt to brush him off, but he kissed her deeply to the applause of all the kids. By the time he released her, her toes were curled, her heart rate was elevated and she was moist in more than a few places. He smiled. In the middle of all that chaos, he still had an obvious effect on her. She blushed. He laughed and kissed her again. Later that night, after everybody had gone to bed, Julian finished what he started. He promised when he got back everything would be taken care of. It was cryptic talk and Cara could only hope for what it actually meant. The following morning she woke to find him gone.

The dynamics of the house changed with Julian's departure. The mood became somber and the children trudged mundanely through their daily schedule. The first few days, Cara employed all kinds of activities, surprises and outings to combat the blues, eventually pulling everyone out of their funk. She had finally settled into bed after a hot bath, turning the TV on as she nestled under the covers. Flipping through the channels she found a music award show in the midst of a live performance. Watching the finale of the song, she was shocked when the camera panned the audience. There in the first row was Julian with his baby bride draped all over him. Cara was outraged. By the time she found her phone and dialed, the program had cut to commercial.

Julian answered on the second ring. "Cara?"

"I can't believe you have the audacity to tell me you're handling things, then have your ass with that bitch in the first row of an award show," she huffed.

He said one word, "Rerun." Then hung up.

Cara sputtered. Had he hung up on her? What had he said – rerun? He must think she was stupid. She grabbed the remote and clicked info. Sure enough the program was live two years ago. She felt herself flush. Her phone chimed. It was a text from Julian:

Be careful, your jealously is starting to impress me and leak through your sharp edges. Possessiveness will get you everywhere with me and everything.

THANKS

LOL

CHAPTER 29

The first sound of breaking glass was integrated into Cara's dream. The second crash brought her to a sitting position with a racing heart rate. She jumped out of bed pulling on sweats and a t-shirt, ran down the hall and rousted her children. She was hurrying the parade of sleeping heads and carrying Marcella when she ran into Shelly. They had maintained a working relationship but never recovered their friendship after the Hawaii fiasco. Now all was forgotten and forgiven. They embraced each other tightly.

"I can't believe you came," Cara said, leading the parade into her room. The only room, besides Julian's studio, with locks on it.

"Where else would I be? What's going on?" Shelly whispered.

"I don't know…" And then they heard a woman scream.

"Oh shit," Cara muttered. "Lock the door. Hide the kids. Whatever happens, don't let her in."

"Who?"

"Julian's wife."

Shelly paled.

Cara grabbed the bat she kept hidden by the head of her bed. She had no idea what was going to happen, but one thing she knew for sure, that bitch was not coming up those stairs. She was moving stealthily down the steps, when she stopped, mesmerized by the amount of damage to the windows and room. The visual of the woman beating the hell out of everything in sight with a sledge hammer gave her palpitations. Obviously, she had come prepared. Cara had a sudden sense of dread. The woman looked up, saw her and screamed, "You." She was about to turn and run back upstairs when there was a roaring crash, as the front door caved in, followed by several large men on the run, followed by several loud pops. Two men accosted the intruder while Brian came up and met her on the stairs.

"Cara?" Brian reached out, supporting her at the waist.

She could barely hear him above the thundering of her heart, but when he touched her arm she felt a hot burning pain. Looking down she saw a blooming red spot on her sleeve. She tried to look up at Brian, but her vision was obscured by something dripping in her eyes. Cara gripped him tightly and attempted to say something, but felt her knees going out from under her and the room going dark.

The doctor having bypassed a large man stationed at the door, entered the hospital room only to view one of the oddest scenes he had ever encountered. The woman in the bed with a bandage on her head and a sling on her left arm was staring intently at a man seated at the foot of her bed, who was staring back. The air was full of tense silent recrimination. He cleared his throat. No one broke their focus. Obviously, this was a stalemate. He would have loved to know the story, but it was almost always the same – no one knew anything. In this case, the woman reported a break-in with an unidentified shooter who got away. No foreseeable reason why, but he knew better, obviously somebody knew something. The doctor started again, talking to the wall just above the woman's head.

"I have only good news. All your wounds are superficial and if you have any scars they will be small. The fetal heart tones of the babies are fine, so they too are doing well."

They both blinked.

"Twins," he grinned, "about twelve weeks gestation."

The woman suddenly let out a startling howl. The man's face unfolded into a wide grin, he jumped up, shook the doctor's hand profusely and thanked him while propelling him to the door.

The doctor was relieved to be out of the room until he was accosted by the big man stationed there who laid a hand on his shoulder and presented him with a clipboard of legal documents outlining the consequences of a breach of privacy. Outraged, the doctor was about to launch into a lecture on patient confidentiality and HIPPA, when the man tightened his grip. Instead he signed everything, reassured him there would be no breach and went in search of an analgesic. The last he saw of the couple as the door was closing, was the man climbing into bed with the woman attempting to hug her as she was whacking him with a bed pan.

Cara was discharged the following day. Julian sat, too close, with his arm around her, on the ride home.

"She's gone. It's over," he whispered tightly.

Cara did not bother to ask who or how. She was just glad she was still alive to tell the tale. She exhaled softly. She wondered if Julian had even contacted her family, no one had called. She guessed a best kept secret was one you held close to the vest. Suddenly, she noticed they were going the opposite direction of the compound.

"Where are we going?" she inquired.

"It's a surprise. We depart in about two hours. The kids are rip roaring ready to go."

"What? Can't you see I'm injured? I'm not in the mood for travel. I haven't packed."

"Superficial scratches. You and the babies are just fine," he smiled, "Besides your things have already been packed."

Cara sulked. Scratches made by bullets. She didn't feel so fine. At least, she hadn't seen it coming. She had only heard a sound and woke up in the hospital. If she had seen a gun aimed directly at her, she would probably be traumatized for life. She was glad she missed that part, still, she did not feel up for a trip.

Julian picked up on her mood immediately. "It you don't want to go, then you'll have to explain it to the kids," he chided.

"Why me?"

"Because they planned it especially for you, to make you feel better and take you to a happy place."

"A trip where?"

"It's still a surprise," Julian grinned.

Cara exhaled loudly.

They pulled up in front of a hotel. Cara looked at Julian, he merely shrugged. All the children ran out, jumped into the car, cheered, encircled and squeezed her. Cara was glad she had been medicated prior to leaving the hospital. They all announced loudly, that it was time to go. Julian shushed them, and organized them all in the car. Shelly appeared with lots of bags. Once that was all jammed into the limo and everyone was wedged together, they drove off. No one would give her a clue as to where or how they were traveling. It was to her great surprise when they pulled up to the train station.

Cara and Julian had previously discussed their travel bucket list and this was one of hers – having a trip with a sleeping car. The surprise didn't end there. Upon entering the station, she was greeted by her sisters, their children and husbands. More hugs and kisses by all. Julian interrupted everything to lead them through the terminal. He was greeted halfway through, by a distinguished man in a black suit that took up the charge. They were escorted the rest of the way through the terminal, along the boarding area and almost to the end of a very long train. Three cars before the end, the man stopped and invited her sisters and their crews to board. Once finished, the gentleman went to the next car, which appeared to be a dining car. Shelly and Brian were dropped off there. Julian finished the honors, leading the way to the last car. He stood aside smiling. The kids jumped on and the squealing began.

"What have you done?" she asked.

"What do you think?" he coaxed.

"I have no idea."

"Then get on."

Cara clumsily climbed up the steps with Julian's assistance. She gasped. It was not a sleeping car, it was a private car with sleeping arrangements. The kids were currently getting comfortable on couches and chairs, turning things on, opening things up and literally eating everything in sight. Past the sitting area was a small fully equipped kitchen with a counter and stools. Cara was overwhelmed. They were only in the middle of the car. Further down to the right she found the sleeping area, girls and boys rooms fully decorated. Apparently, the extra room with its own private bath was theirs. She started to enter, Julian held her back.

He pointed in, "Shelly's." Cara frowned. "She's helping Brian get situated." Now she raised her eyebrows. "You know nothing John Snow," he said.

Julian led her to a stair case at the back of the car. Their actions caught the attention of the wild bunch. Soon, Cara was at the head of a very chaotic parade. Thank God, Julian was providing support and a buffer from behind, otherwise she would have been stampeded for her slow progress. Julian silenced the disgruntled group by raising his hand, it lasted all of five seconds. Finally he gave up, wrapping his arms around Cara's waist, he carried her up the last few stairs, stepping aside as the parade stormed by. While waiting for everyone to file past, Cara noticed the roof was Plexiglas. Following the line of the ceiling, it appeared the entire top of the car was the same. Just over Julian's shoulder she could see the children bouncing from the couches to the lounge chairs that lined the observation deck. Cara wanted to stop and enjoy the view but Julian pulled her forward negating her actions with an 'uh-uh'. They advanced to a door, Julian reached around opened it, then backed her in.

Cara turned and gasped again. It was a master suite that included a king size bed, sitting area, work studio – already complete with instruments and a private bath, replete with a large claw footed tub. Julian was leaning on the door watching her.

"Oh, Julian," was all she got to say before there was a series of knocks on the door. As soon as he removed his weight, the door was thrown open and an energized brigade of excitement took over. All of their living space was thoroughly investigated, touched, manipulated and basically mauled. Julian held up his hand, this time the silence held. Cara wished she could learn that trick. He announced everyone had to go back down and let their mother rest. In the excitement Cara had forgotten she was injured. Now it all came back to dampen her spirits. There were hugs and kisses, then a rambunctious departure of their crew. Julian looked at her.

"I was too slow in taking care of things. It'll never happen again. It's going to be ok," he soothed.

He gently pushed her down on the bed, removed her shoes and placed a light coverlet on her. "Rest," he urged, giving her a wicked wink. Cara was sound asleep by the time he shut the door.

Cara woke up aching, nauseated and hot, way too hot. It took a minute for her to remember where she was, then she had just enough time to stumble into the bathroom and throw-up. Julian found her there, draped over the toilet in a foul mood.

"Well, I guess you're not up for dinner," he quipped.

He had all the suaveness of a snake and to accentuate that thought, Cara threw up again.

He held up his hands, "Enough said."

Julian came behind her, lifted her from under the arms and took her back to bed. He also brought the trash can and placed it by her side.

"I'm going to go to the dining car to let everybody know you won't be down for dinner. I'll bring us up something to eat."

"Don't bother. Can't you see I'm sick?"

"Ok, you're not feeling well, but you don't know what it is. When was the last time you've eaten? Maybe you need to eat something. You had medication at the hospital. You're being shaken on a train and you're pregnant."

He didn't need to add that last point. Cara groaned and turned her face into the pillows. Julian left the room. He returned a short time later with crackers and a 7-Up, refusing to leave until she had consumed all of it. To Cara's surprise it stayed down. He gave her an 'I told you so smirk' and went downstairs. Cara fell back to sleep.

Julian returned later that evening, after dinner and visiting his brother-in-law's. The children were all asleep. He came up the front staircase with a porter who was carrying a tray of food, expecting to find Cara still asleep. Instead, he found her gone. Searching he found her in the observation deck, wrapped in a blanket, looking up at the stars. He did not have to read her mind to see where this was going.

"How many times do we have to talk about this?" he started.

"Talk about what?" she inquired sweetly, not breaking her gaze from the sky.

"Don't play with me, I am not in the mood," he threatened, "and I'm getting tired of this conversation."

That did the trick.

Cara snapped her eyes to him and fisted her blanket, "You're getting tired!" she jeered.

"Yes, I am," he said calmly. "It's not just about you and me. Did you stop and think of the kids? They weren't injured, but they went through the same experience. They were jerked out of their beds in the middle of the night, heard all that commotion and then had to be scurried away from the scene. They should be first. All of them are handling this remarkably well, but all you can do is think of yourself and bring up the same old shit. This trip is as much for their recovery as it is for yours. I'm getting tired of telling you to let me take care of things, believe in me and love me. When do you think you'll get there?"

Cara was so taken aback by his speech, she lost a lot of her discontentment and anger. Truth be told, she had not thought of her children, other than they were safe. Now, she felt remiss, but she was not about to tell Julian that. She didn't know what to say, so she huffed, "This is all your fault."

Wrong answer.

Julian marched over grabbed her by the blanket and began shaking it. He was hell bent on shaking her out of it, while she had just as much intent to hang on. It turned into a battle for the cover, neither giving in. Soon the tussle went to the floor with both combatants rolling this way and that. The commotion came to an abrupt halt when both became so entangled that neither could make much of a move. Laying on their backs, both breathing heavily, they stared silently at the stars. For some unexplained reason the outer corner of Cara's eyes began to leak tears. Julian untangled himself and placed his head on top of the mound of covers over her abdomen.

"For God's sake Cara," he whispered, "Why can't you- just- love-me? It's just about us, regardless of my actions. You and me, nobody else. If you could just concentrate on that instead of everything else."

She was about to mention her injuries interfering with her concentration, but he beat her to the punch.

"Don't say it," he insisted.

Damn him and his mind reading. Her eyes were creating puddles in the folds of the quilt. Julian reached up and wiped them away. He could not possibly see them in the darkness and she had not made a sound. She exhaled a deep breath.

"Please," he pleaded softly burying his face in her neck.

She exhaled again. It always came back to this, she did not have much choice. She was still stuck with him.

"I know you wanted a knight in white," he added. "I wear a lot of colors, but white is not often one of them. You got me, and you're right, you are stuck with me."

Damn him, damn, damn, damn.

"I want it all, just like you. Only in my case, I also want it from you. Give it up and just love me. If I can't be your knight, than love me as your knave, your pawn, your prince."

Another deep breath and silence.

Julian had her and he knew it. He would have made love to her right there to seal the deal but there was no door. Instead, he rolled over, pulling her to his chest. Cara breathed him in. She felt stupid. There was just something about him she could not resist, his energy, his warmth, his essence.....

"Just let go," he purred.

Cara closed her eyes. This was going to be the end of her, but maybe she had known that all along, which was why she internally still tried to resist him. It just wasn't fair.

"It's not fair. Its life," he interjected.

"Julian?"

"Yes?"

"Can I have a single thought without you in it?"

"Never."

He pulled her up, took her to bed and sealed the deal, pushing all her fears and doubts aside.

Later that night, eating apple slices and sipping champagne, Cara attempted to get some answers out of Julian.

"And my sisters and their families are here because....?"

"I thought you'd like it," he projected.

"You thought I'd like it?" she protested, "You know me and my sisters. What part of that did you think needed to be together?? Enlighten me."

He huffed, but stopped in mid-peel of the next apple and looked her directly in the eyes.

"Your nieces and nephews are my children's first cousins. They will associate with each other for the rest of their lives. What good does it do to raise mine on one level of experiences while their closest relatives are on another?"

Cara sat up, letting the sheet fall from her bare chest. "You're providing the same opportunities for them as for our kids?" she paraphrased astonished.

"Yes," he murmured, resuming his peeling.

Cara was overwhelmed. His reticence, generosity and magnanimousness under the canopy of moonlight left her speechless. That was ok, because that was how Julian liked her best. To his surprise, she laid her hand over his, took the apple from him and kissed him. It was something he had waited for a long time. Not the approach or the kiss but her intimate approval of him. He'd done something good, outside the box, and she was perhaps finally believing in him.

Their first group vacation covered every cavern, canyon, cave and national park, as well as, every river, trail, monument and historical site west of the Mississippi. It took several weeks. There was hiking, kayaking, biking, walking, climbing, zip lining, horseback riding, you name it and they were all there. To Cara's surprise, Julian did not abandon the adventure or miss one activity. He did, however, supplement it with luxe tent camping, spa treatments and all the other amenities he felt he could not do without. A good time was had by all and everybody behaved themselves, relatively.

Their group vacations, from one end of the world to the other, became legendary. The Hawaiian compound became one of their homes away from home. Julian, true to his word, included all her worthless relatives and while it had initially been for the kids, it seemed that the exposure was as beneficial for the adults. Her sisters and their spouses changed. They sought out better jobs, went back to school, started businesses, and re-grew their relationships. It was as if everyone's dreams and imaginations had been rekindled, let loose, or catapulted into the stratosphere.

CHAPTER 30

Cara and Julian's life together took on an acceleration of its own and it seemed to revolve around their kids, his career and concerts and occasionally her designs.

The year the twins, Giselle and Giovanni, were born by C-section was the same time Julian decided to take their birth control matters into his own hands. After seeing the low transverse incision below Cara's abdomen, he made an appointment and had things permanently fixed. By the time she had recovered and was over her post-delivery sex band, so was he. It gave their sex a whole new freedom, although that was the least of their needs or concerns.

The year Selle and Gio turned three, was the same year Quinton, who had just turned seven, came up with a profound question. While ensconced around the dining table, Julian at the head, with Cara at the other end, boys on one side, and girls on the other, sans TV and in mid–discussion of everybody's day, came the inquiry.

"Dad, are you Aristo?" asked Quinton.

Julian was as calm as ever. Cara stopped breathing. Silence descended on the room.

"What do you know about Aristo?" Julian inquired.

The room broke into an uproar. Everyone knew something about Aristo except Selle and Gio.

"He wears make-up and high heels," Aiden offered.

"He's a womanizer," accused Leilani.

"He's gay," added Kalea.

"Where did you get all this information?" Julian asked, sitting back in his chair and steepling his fingers.

"At school," came the reply in unison.

"What if I am Aristo?" Julian countered.

The room fell into silence again. Marcella began to cry. Her family was nothing if not dramatic. Cara took Marcella's hand. "Baby, why are you crying?"

"If Daddy is Aristo, does that mean he's not our daddy?" she whined.

There was a gasped intake of air all around the table. Clearly this was a novel idea. Cara looked at Julian, shrugged and raised her eyebrows. Julian stood, slamming his palms on the table, drawing everyone's attention.

"Regardless of who I am or what people say about me, I will always be your father," he explained.

"Does that mean you are Aristo?" Quinton persisted.

"Yes," Julian sighed, "I am Aristo Julian Starr and you are all my little stars."

"Why don't we live in the big house?" Kalea asked.

"Are we a secret?" Aiden inserted.

"Do you wear make-up and high heels?" Leilani backtracked.

Julian lowered himself into his seat and looked at Cara. She was not helping at all. She continued to shrug and shake her head, although he got the distinct impression she thought this was funny.

"You are a secret," he finally confirmed, "It's to keep you safe."

Suddenly, there was a tearful outbreak with multiple squeaks.

"Someone is going to try to steal us?"

"Hide us?"

"Kill us?"

There was so much woe around the table, Cara could not keep

up with who it was coming from. Julian tightened his lips, closed his eyes and pressed his index fingers to his temples. Suddenly, Cara found it hilarious. She covered her face with a napkin and laughed. Julian's eyes flew open and he frowned. The harder he frowned the funnier it became and the louder the children wailed. In the end, Cara was also in tears.

Julian jumped up and raised his hands, at least that gesture still worked, the room came to a quiet hush.

"Let's go over to the big house," he announced.

That proclamation was followed by a whoop, chairs scrapping, booster seats bouncing and feet running in all directions. Cara's humor disappeared. She still avoided that house at all cost.

"I'll go upstairs and get sweaters," she suggested.

Julian caught her elbow and veered her on, "We'll take the tunnel." More cheers from the peanut gallery.

Fears and tears forgotten, the rowdy ramble hopped, skipped, jumped, raced and twirled its way through the cavern. Upon exiting at the other end, the expedition turned into a party. The elevator was a huge instigator. An elevator in a house was just too much. By the time everyone piled out on the first floor, the initial inquisition had been forgotten. Julian plied his offspring with dessert. Cara was surprised. She had been unaware that he was a cookie, candy, ice cream and cake sort of guy. Before she could form the question, Julian answered it.

"I'm always prepared for company," he interjected.

"I'm sure you are," she replied snidely.

Goodies in hand, the tour began. Cara had not been in the 'big house' for so long, she had forgotten the magnitude of its size, and that was not counting the business complex component. Starting at the ground level they went through living rooms, libraries, theaters and indoor courts and pools, bedrooms with outrageous bathrooms and several party areas equipped with massive speakers and lights. Cara was proud to say that their children left their mark on most of it: handprints, spills, scratched surfaces, chipped vases, overturned art work, displaced pillows and a mired of smudges. Still, she was overwhelmed and had a sinking feeling that she would never be able to squeeze her littles ones back into her house now that they had been exposed to Oz. She looked up to catch Julian studying her. A slow wicked smile blossomed on his lips as he slid to her side.

"You're right. They're excited enough to stay here regardless of who I am," he cooed.

If she could just learn that Jedi mind trick to block his reception of her thoughts.

"Won't happen," he laughed and kissed her cheek. "I've been waiting for this for a while."

"This doesn't mean they want to give up their rooms and stay here," she insisted.

"Ok," he whispered to her and shrugged, "It's time to go home."

A high outcry commenced. Children dropped to the floor, others began to wail and some hid in plain sight.

"Ok, ok, ok. How about a movie instead?"

Immediate recovery transpired. People got to their feet, quieted down and resumed safe and sane personalities. Julian gave her dancing eyebrows and led his troops back to the theater. Cara would have been impressed but she had developed a sour stomach. They had a theater room in her house, but it was gaged for normal size people. Julian's theater appeared to have been sized for giants. The screen was actually the size for a movie theater and the seating was a series of couches, oversized loungers, but mostly round daybeds, all covered with pillows of all shapes, sizes, colors and textures. Her mind went directly to the obscene, it looked like a giant orgy room. Before Cara could object, Julian gave a hand signal and their children dispersed into the room. There was jostling and jumping, pillows were flying everywhere with giggling and laughing throughout the room. Cara gave up and was sitting on the edge of one of the oversized loungers when Julian returned (when had he left?), followed by several personnel carrying linen, pillows and covers, as well as, a serving cart full of snacks. Again she was about to protest, when he held up his hand. Everyone stopped in mid action.

"No snacks until everyone is ready for bed and you're in it."

"But we don't have our jejes," whined Marcella.

"Who says?" questioned Julian. And like the magic man that he was, he produced another cart with an array of oriental silk children's pajamas. Cara would have baulked, but she was beyond that now. She merely stared as he grinned and assisted everybody with their beds, directing the older kids to the bathrooms at the side of the room while dressing the little ones. When everyone was finally nestled into place, snacks at their sides, a series of animated films, all currently at the movies, began.

Sometime after the lights went out, Cara watched Julian make his way over to her lounger carrying a tissue wrapped package.

"I've been saving this for you," he whispered, tearing open the paper. A beautiful fuchsia lace set with matching robe fell out. She gasped and was immediately shushed by the audience.

"You could have given this to me anytime," she squinted at him in the darkness.

"I could have, but I was waiting for you to wear it here," he purred.

Finally, she understood. Julian had been dreaming, planning, and preparing for this. But for how long?

He grinned his full sexy smile, "Put it on," he coaxed in a husky voice.

"The kids," she stuttered.

He snorted. The audience shushed them again. Cara got up and stumbled to the bathroom in the dark. She guessed they were generic and not men/women, so she entered the first one. It was beautiful, like everything else in the house, antique fixtures, large bowl sinks, toiletries, a sitting area and a toilet and a bidet, of course. She changed slowly, doubting and second guessing the whole afternoon. The lingerie was not as inappropriate as she thought. The lace trim covered all the right spots plus she had the robe, which she knotted tightly. By the time she returned, Julian had made up a round bed in the back and changed into his pajamas. He was perched on pillows with popcorn watching the movie. He threw back the covers when he saw her. She hesitated.

"Get in woman, this is not about you, this is about my babies."

Cara was so relieved, she forgot to be insulted. Instead she climbed in, nestled against him and promptly fell asleep.

Cara awoke the following morning in the state of utter confusion. She did not recognize where she was or what had happened to her pajamas. Then she remembered, Julian. Sometime during the night, after all the snacks were finished, the movies were over and everyone was fast asleep, he had awakened her and convinced her to go upstairs with him to see something. She objected, not wanting to leave their children in a strange new place but he insisted he had that covered and literally dragged her upstairs to his room. As groggy as she was, she recognized that this section had not been on her original tour. This was his bedroom. She froze. Did he bring his other women here?

"Never," he said, "this is my space. Over there," and he pointed to a door that led to another set of rooms, clearly female in decorum, but completely vacant. This felt totally inappropriate. She was ready to go back with the kids and was nearing the door when Julian called her over to some equipment he was fiddling with. Cara was too tired for anything more and was about to tell him that, when the wall at the foot of his immense bed lit up into a series of screens. Several displayed various channels, news, sports, movies, cable and music videos and then with a tap, the interior of the theater, showing all their babies quietly sleeping. She was just getting focused on that when he clicked something else and the images turned into the interior of her entire house.

She turned on him, "I knew it. You dog," she fumed.

He grinned deliriously, turning towards her slowly, "You're right. I am a dog. Woof," and he pounced on her.

Well, at least that explained what happened to her pajamas. Suddenly, there was loud screaming from downstairs. Throwing on her robe, Cara ran barefooted towards the sound. Locating the commotion in the kitchen, she found all her children gathered at the table demanding pancakes that were flying through the air, served by, none other than, Aristo, in full make-up and high heels. It was pointless to be surprised. The kids were obviously loving it. So, the dysfunction of their lives expanded.

Upon further inspection of the second floor, Cara found that Julian had already established and decorated rooms for each child. When she cut her eyes at him, he merely shrugged and said he believed it would eventually happen. Again, it made her wonder. He had never said a word. How long had he been waiting, longing for this? Julian established a routine. It was one for all and all for one. Where ever someone went, the group had to follow. It started out that if Julian was working on something, a new album, concert, project, they would be staying at his house, but somewhere along the line the drifting back and forth decreased and staying over increased until they were all just living there. Cara tried to object, she missed her studio. Julian, ever resourceful, fixed that too. The set of rooms off his were revamped into her studio and closets. There was no need for a bed, she would be sharing his. The only vague sense of restriction was when Aristo was having an event at the compound. In that case, all kids were prohibited from being in the area and re-

routed to Cara's. Since Julian never explained anything to anybody, there was never a question as to why he had children's
rooms in his house.

CHAPTER 31

That same year, both Julian and Cara were nominated for film awards. Julian for best song in an animated children's film, and Cara for best costumes for a film remake of a previously animated classic tale. Julian took it all in stride while Cara was a nervous wreck. She was shocked to the core since the original project she had worked on had been shelved for several years. She had been unaware of any activity until the film premiered and she received a check in the mail. Cara was willing to watch the proceedings from home but Julian would not hear of it. He thought everyone should attend. Cara vetoed that idea. She thought their children were way too young, their secret was way too new and too big to be out in public in such a huge venue, but Julian insisted, so per protocol, Julian got his way.

They actually flew into Los Angeles, a week early, taking up residence at Julian's beach house. Cara had given up on trying to keep track of the number of residences he had. It was far enough north of LA to be sequestered between other high profile stars, rendering the beach to private access only. Venturing out clandestinely, they took in the California experience – Disneyland, water parks, the missions and even the TMZ tour bus.

The evening of the ceremony, Julian left early for the sound check since he would be performing his nominated song. Cara was left to catch, clean and dress their crew. Having completed that task, she was about to turn the attention on herself when there was a knock at the door. In came hair, make-up and clothing specialists. She was prompted, plucked, preened, pulled and prodded into an exquisite dress that Kafir had made just for her. She appreciated the genius of the dress. Besides looking divine in it, the supporting under structure was actually built into the garment. By the time she was stuffed and laced into her gown, she felt like pure perfection. The rustic gold set off her skin tone and hugged her in all the right places while her hair, a configuration of locks were held together magically with a few decorative golden pins. Her makeup was flawless.

The kids oohed and aahed over her, as well as, themselves and could not wait to go. Cara attempted to go over and reinforce the rules for the engagement, but it became obvious no one was listening. She gave it up and instead worked on taming the butterflies ricocheting throughout her stomach and chest. Brian, of course, was their security along with Kris Kelekelio, who had unofficially been adopted by their family. Shelly was stunning in a beautiful blue gown. She received the verbal appreciation of all the kids, as well as, hugs all around. Then, it was time to go.

Cara felt she had worked herself into a frenzy for nothing when she discovered non-A-listers never got anywhere near the red carpet or any carpet for that matter. They were guided through a side door to seats that were on the main floor, but far from the stage. There was an extreme possibility that her family would only encounter their father while he was on the stage performing. The safety of the situation almost relieved her. At least she could take a few deep breaths and that was enough to calm the flutters in her interior. Shelly and Brian were near but not on their row, and Kris had somehow made it back stage. She put the oldest children on the aisle, with Marcella and the twins on the other side of her. Things went really well with almost everybody falling asleep within the first hour. With all the troops ad ease, Cara began to enjoy the ceremony. The stars were glowing. Their gowns were dazzling and the entire atmosphere was festive. Apparently she got carried away because during the performance of another nominated song, she looked up to find Marcella three seats down, dancing in the space between her sisters and brothers near the aisle. Cara hissed and waved to get her attention but Marcella danced on. That performance complete, Julian was the next to perform. He appeared in a subdued navy blue suit with an acoustic guitar, sitting on a stool at center stage and he was Julian, not Aristo. Cara stopped cold. She thought he was gorgeous. His hair fell to his shoulders and his beard was perfectly groomed. She sighed. Julian strummed the initial bars softly, then gained momentum, sound and frenzy as he began to belt out the lyrics. Cara looked back to Marcella, she was gone, skipping blithely down the aisle. She fell back in her seat with a rush exhalation, only to find Selle and Gio making their way across other people's feet to the other aisle. Cara closed her eyes. When she opened them it was to find her remaining children in a comatose state. They all looked like cats that had swallowed then choked on their canaries. Marcella and the twins had made it to the stage and were happily dancing on both sides of Julian. As Cara tried to count backwards from one hundred with measured breaths, she found her saving grace. Not in the breathing exercises, but in the fact that all the other attendees had also lost control of their children too. Everybody five and under were either on the stage dancing or were on their way there. Julian, the consummate performer, never blinked. He added some extra bars and some new verses for his extremely interactive audience. Completing his song, he placed his guitar on the stool, had all his additional performers hold hands and everybody bowed. The crowd broke into thunderous applause as he signaled for everyone to return to their seat. Selle and Gio skipped off, but Marcella had to hug him one last time, he gave her the hand, which quickly sent her on her way. He then shrugged it off to the audience, like how could they not adore me? He picked up his guitar and left the stage only to be called back three categories later, as the winner for best song. Thanking all his small ardent fans, Julian blew kisses to all the children, focusing particularly on his, as they all shimmered with delight.

Several performances and awards later best costume was announced. Cara thought she heard her name but dismissed it as a hallucination until Aiden reached over and pinched her. She came out of the haze to find all her children grinning at her saying she had won. She stood. Seeing no one else moving toward the stage, she approached. It was like traveling in a dream, none of her movements felt real. She made it up the stairs and to the podium, where the presenter handed her the award. Before she could say a word, the music began, she smiled, held it up and said thank you. She could see her children cheering in their seats. Following the presenters off stage, she continued her floating, until an arm reached out from the heavy velvet curtains and pulled her in. Julian. He immediately began smothering her with kisses while his hands roamed over every inch of her dress. Flushed and exhilarated, Cara absorbed all his personal attention.

"Promise me you'll let me peel you outta that dress," he whispered.

"Hmmm," she sighed.

Just as suddenly, he shoved her out of the folds. She would have continued to float away, but a hand extended out and whacked her on the butt. She yelped, bursting her transcendental state. The presenters turned to give her a distasteful glance.

"Caught my hem in my heel," she mumbled, hoping no one noticed her raging blush.

Immediately following the ceremony, Cara and the kids were ushered to a waiting limo and whisked away. Julian was nowhere to be seen. She would have been content to return to the beach house, but Kafir had insisted the kids needed to attend an after party to have the entire experience. So, they were racing to his private event, to get in and out before the real partying began. Upon entrance to an extravaganza that resembled the inside of a pasha's domain: rugs, pillows, draped fabric from ceiling to floor, beds covered in cushions and food of every kind arrayed on every flat surface, Cara lost track of all her children as they scattered in seven different directions. By the time she located them, they were covered in crowns, silks, chocolate, glitter and a few other unidentifiable items. She was overwhelmed with the amount of mayhem that had occurred within so few minutes and the idea she would have to continue to try to contain them. Just as she started stuttering out orders, Kafir appeared, hugged all his god-children grandly and escorted them into a photo room. If the first room wasn't enough, here was a room that snapped photos in five second sequences then shot them on the wall for you to see. The children were immediately intrigued. They started out calmly but it soon turned into chaos. Cara was in the middle of the soiree, trying to stop the twins from strangling each other with Mardi Gras beads, insisting Leilani and Kalea stop dropping it like it was hot, deflecting Aiden and Quinton insistence that they should pose with giant joints and a handful of money, and comforting Marcella, who had been knocked down and was crying on the floor. Julian slipped in in the middle of the pandemonium. He took Cara in his arms, flicked some glitter off her face and grinned at her. For a moment all the madness stood still and they stared at each other. He drew her in slowly, then kissed her softly but deeply. She grinned back. There was a loud sound and several more children started to cry. The dream bubble burst. Julian held up his hand and the craziness dissolved into a series of sniffles, whimpers and mumbles. He escorted everyone back to their limo and sent them on their way, within minutes everyone was asleep. Cara would have been relieved except Julian forgot to get in, which meant she would be getting everybody out alone, when they got home. To her immense delight, Brian and Shelly were waiting at the door. The task divided by three was quickly surmounted. They all toasted each other over champagne, then her heaven sent assistants departed. Cara was left alone in the darkness with the sound of waves, still in her dress with her award and the bottle of champagne. She wandered into the bedroom and practiced several sexy poses before falling asleep propped on pillows, on top of the covers.

The first light of day woke her. Cara had a slight pain behind one eye, a dry mouth, the imprint of several bobby pins on her face and pinches in places she did not know had ever existed. She pulled herself out of bed and sulked to the coffeepot. First things first. She had spooned in the coffee and was adding the water when she noticed the sliding glass door was open, letting in a refreshing breeze. Cara knew she had locked it the night before so she began surveying the room. She found Julian lounging at the end of the kitchen table, shirt open, casually watching her over a glass of juice. She froze. A small insidious smile grew on his lips.

"I'm glad you're finally learning to follow directions," he said rising and advancing slowly towards her.

She frowned.

"The dress," he cooed, "you're still in it."

Oh right, that was one of the reasons for all her discomfort. She watched him. For as long as they had been together, she still could not get over the way he moved, so fluid, intense, measured. Had she brushed her teeth? She had not. Just as he gathered her into his arms, she clamped her hand over her mouth. He bit the back of her hand.

"Ow," she exclaimed shaking her hand, "I haven't brushed my teeth."

"That's ok, I haven't brushed mine either," he quipped pressing his lips to hers. He tasted like several stale things, so she guessed that was fair. When he broke for air, she got an up close and personal look at his scraggly beard and mussed hair. Aristo, he most definitely was not. Julian let her study him as he removed every pin from her hair, causing a cascade of locks to fall down her back. Next the zipper began its slow descent.

"Julian, no," Cara declared, "we have children and we're in the kitchen."

"I know what we have and I know where we are," he hummed.

Cara was about to protest further when has other hand hit her bare back and began to follow the zipper's downward trail. As her dress fell away she was further shocked by the sensation of her breast being pressed into the hair of his chest. When he found that spot on her neck, she just about swooned. Suddenly, they heard an argument advancing toward them in the hallway. Julian calmly stepped back and pulled up his pants, but Cara was highly flustered finding herself totally in the buff. He casually kicked her dress under the table as she scramble into a full apron in a frenzy. At least the front of her was covered. Selle and Gio shuffled forward in unison, rubbing their eyes and mumbling 'mommy'. When they saw Julian, they switched their cadence and demeanor. They cried out with joy and yelled 'daddy'. Julian scooped them up, kissing them gingerly on their cheeks.

"My bubalas," he said squeezing them tightly. They giggled.

"Daddy, we had a nightmare. Aiden said we weren't supposed to dance and a monster came and chased us off the stage."

"Oh no," he countered, "You both did a great job. I would never have been able to have a finish like that without you."

"Really?" a mono response.

"Really. Now it's time to go back to bed. It's way too early."

"But you and mommy are up," another dual response.

"That's because we have some adult stuff we have to do," he said giving Cara a raised eyebrow before carrying them back to bed.

Cara was busy attempting to fish her dress out from under the table when Julian returned to find her bare bottom in the air. He couldn't resist tweaking it, which caused her to rear up and hit the back of her head on the table. He tried to muffle his laugh but was unsuccessful. She came up spitting bullets. "Damn it, Julian," she hissed holding her head.

He hid his smile by taking her place under the table, retrieving her dress and handing it to her contritely. She snatched it away. He sat back on his hunches, studying her gravely.

"I don't think we've ever done it under a table," he mused.

"Well, you don't have to worry, cause that's not about to happen today," she fumed.

"I don't know," he continued undeterred, "there's something about that apron that intrigues me."

"That's because you're incorrigible," Cara said, making a quick move to distance herself from him and the table.

He caught her by the strings of the apron, pulling her back beside him.

"Take these for instance," he lectured rolling the strings around each of his wrists, "they could have multiple functions."

Right then they were working as a vice, trapping Cara in the apron and bringing her closer and closer to an ill-defined fate. He stopped when her waist was cinched and there was no more play in the strings. They sat chest to chest. His wrists restrained and her waist so tightly constrained she could barely breathe.

"Now, what?" She inquired.

Julian smiled, then leaned under the table, pulling her along. She knew better than to ask, and of course, there was only one thing to do under there.

CHAPTER 32

Their life together continued to fly by fast. Maybe children years were like dog years, they doubled down. In between tours, some of which Julian insisted they accompany him on, there was school and extracurricular activities. Kalea and Leilani had insisted on going to 'regular' school. Aiden and Quinton were all about the music, like father like sons, and would have abandoned the cause all together except for Julian's stipulation of no school, no stage or tour work. Marcella wanted to pursue acting and the twins were just trying to keep up with everyone else.

The year Aiden turned seventeen was the year the shit hit the fan. As usual, it occurred at the dinner table. The standard amount of chaos was taking place when Aiden asked the question.

"Why would a man need more than one woman?"

It sounded theoretical, but when Cara looked up she knew it was personal. Julian sat as stoic as ever, as if someone had just asked for the salt, but Cara could see in each of her children's eyes that everyone knew what she had not even suspected. Julian was seeing someone else. She pushed her chair back, excused herself and went back to her house. She didn't even bother to take the tunnel, but walked around the outside of the buildings, taking in as much fresh air as she could suck in, before going inside and throwing herself face down on her bed.

Marcella and the twins were the first to arrive. Marcella hugged her from one side while the twins doubled hugged her from the other. Everybody was crying.

"We're sorry, mom," Marcella whimpered.

"Are you and dad going to get a divorce?" and they all wailed at once.

How to begin that discussion? No need for a divorce, since they were never officially married. Geez, it just kept getting worse. Cara flipped over, they were breaking her back. Leilani and Kalea came next, taking the outer circumference, followed by Quinton at her feet. The crying continued but quietly, with sniffles, occasional hiccups and a few loud burps. Lastly Aiden arrived, "I'm sorry mom. I didn't mean to hurt you. Dad says if I have to ask such a question, I'm not ready for the answer."

That sounded just like Julian, he was still such an ass. Aiden, having nowhere to go, just threw himself across the pile of bodies on the bed. They all stayed there in subdued silent sadness until everyone fell asleep. Cara was the first to wake up, mostly because she was wet from being under a pile of damp kids. She disentangled herself from the fray and headed to the bathroom. She found Julian sitting in a chair in the dark staring at the bed. As she passed he grabbed her hand and kissed her palm.

"You know it doesn't mean anything," he murmured.

"It never does for you, Julian," she said as she pulled her hand away and kept walking. She hadn't even cried. She wasn't angry at him, he was exactly the same. She was mad at herself for forgetting who he was and what that meant and allowing herself to trust and believe in him for so long. Now she wasn't sure how she felt. Julian followed her into the shadows, encasing her in his arms, "You know me. You know how I feel about you and the kids and what we have. Don't believe the hype."

Cara didn't try to break his embrace, but she didn't believe him either, not anymore. Her kids had been hurt and she had been greatly embarrassed for them to find out about Julian's extra-curricular activity. She was ashamed of herself, because who else could she fault? Now, how was she going to explain this to their children? Especially her girls? As far as she was concerned, she was never going back to the big house. She didn't even want to ever see it again.

Julian had a whole other take on the situation. Aiden and Quinton were always on the back lot, in the studios, or anywhere the action was going on. They had walked in on a woman getting friendly with him. He had only been enjoying the attention. He had not pursued it or reinforced it by any means, although he probably would have polished her off if not for the interruption. He had dismissed her and taken it as an opportunity to teach his boys about the hazards of the music industry. He hadn't a clue from either of them that they would take it back to their mother. He had not explained anything beyond that incident. He was not of the nature to explain anything to anyone and he was not about to start with some knuckle-headed teenage boys. The truth of the matter was his reputation far-outreached the reality. He loved women, but that didn't mean he had to be physical with all of them. A lot were business associates and the implication of being seen with him was enough to drive their careers into accelerated motion. Others were just friends, people he shared music, conversations, ideas and projects with. He was willing to admit some were about the physical thing, but they were far and in between since he had been with Cara. He had kept those on a very, very, low down so as not to have happen what was currently happening. They hadn't been on this road in some time. Cara was hurt as hell, and he was going to have to do everything in his power to bring her back to him.

Their kids had a totally different perspective. They had only known their parents together. The thought of them apart was agonizing. They did not want to choose. Originally they shunned their father's residence, but after a while flitted back and forth uneasily until eventually they came and went as they did before. No one asked any questions. They had each other and the internet. All they needed now was a plan to get their parents back together.

That summer a family meeting was called by the kids. It took place in a neutral setting – the green area between the two houses. It was actually laid. There were tables stretched with chairs, flowers and twinkling lights. Cara was impressed. All of her children appeared to have a sense of flare. They announced during the service of the deme ta, that they would be going to Europe for the summer – alone. All of the older children had taken it upon themselves to test out of high school. They all presented their diplomas, passports and reservations, as well as, their acceptance to various schools of higher learning. Kalea and Leilani were going to the University of Hawaii. Aiden and Quinton had opted for a local community college so they could remain involved in the compound action. They would be moving into an apartment Julian just happened to own, and it incidentally happened to be her old place. Marcella had not tested out, but was accepted to a local performing arts high school. Cara's reaction to everything, was like, hell no. Julian's, was to let them go. His one condition to the Europe trip was that they had to have a chaperone. The only one they all agreed upon was Kris Kelekelio. Try as she might, she could not override Julian's decision. She was furious with him. She put her foot down on Selle and Gio, they were only twelve. On that he had agreed, although Marcella had weaseled in at fourteen.

Julian appeared at her house, in her room later that night.

"What did you think they'd do? Become?" he whispered leaning just inside the doorway. "They're world traveled, language fluent and trussed with cash. Did you think they'd stay your babies forever? Did you want to see them go to prom, decorate their dorm rooms in college, watch them get 9-5 jobs? That isn't who we raised."

Cara was miffed. What had she expected?? Their children were of the wild bohemian world they had created. Julian left her alone with her thoughts. Where was a good mind reader when you needed one?? Several days later she received multiple calls from her sisters. Apparently, their children were also going to Europe, and they felt like she did. She referred them to Julian.

No one called her again.

Selle and Gio sulked and bemoaned their situation until Kafir invited them to his and Cara's annual Textile Crawl. It was something Kafir did fairly often, but he had gotten Cara involved shortly after her return from Hawaii, while she was still trying to 'readjust'. It had given her an opportunity to step back from that fiasco and catch a breath. It was a great adventure. Scouring the world in search of unique fabrics, textiles, trims, notions and bric-a-brac. What started as a one-time deal, became their annual passion. Besides the searching, part of the fun was trying to evade Julian. It was supposed to be only Kafir and Cara, but every year Julian caught up with them in some obscure market, no matter how secretive their plans. Since Kafir made all the arrangements, Cara had suggested that maybe he was included in Julian's spy network. Kafir had been outraged, and threatened to kick Julian's ass if he ever detected any surveillance. She liked the idea, but was disappointed that so far that hadn't happened.

Cara was disillusioned. Having the twins along would change the whole scope of the trip. She attempted to dissuade him, but Kafir demurred, insisting the exposure would be great for them. Giselle and Giovanni were ecstatic on the crawl. They were all over the place, in and out of markets and bins and baskets. Truth be told, they probably found things Kafir and Cara would have missed. They were that diligent in their search of everything. Kafir was enchanted with the twins. He used them for live drape models, bounced ideas off of them and captivated them with his outlandish statements. Cara felt a little like the third wheel.

A couple of days near the end of their two week excursion, Julian was still a no show. As much as Cara acted like his appearance was an intrusion, she enjoyed his uninvited attention and company. Of course, she would never admit that, but none the less, his shunning of the event dampened her spirits. Gio and Selle were all over it. They texted all their siblings in an attempt to locate their father.

To Everybody: Has anyone heard from Dad?

Aiden: Last time I talked to him, he was headed to LA on some contract negotiation.

Kalea: Doesn't he show up on the Crawl?

Selle: Yes, almost over and he's not here.

Gio: Mom in a funk.

Leilani: Oh no. Was hoping an exotic hook up would do the trick.

Quinton: Just call him.

Marcella: That won't work, too obvious.

Everyone: Keep us posted

They were at a restaurant in Istanbul, sitting on piles of pillows on the floor, waiting for their food to arrive when Julian appeared. He was dressed in traditional middle-eastern garb, a white shirt with gold embroidery around the neckline, chest and sleeves, white pants. He had a full beard and his hair was straightened, feathered and just past his shoulders. Gio and Selle thought he looked like a black Jesus. They hugged him tightly and dragged him to the pillows. Kafir welcomed him. Cara remained in stunned silence. She had wanted him there, but had no idea how to act toward him in front of the others. Julian took care of that. He hugged his kids, shook hands with Kafir, then seated himself next to Cara. Taking her into his arms, he kissed her directly on the mouth. Kafir gave off a huge 'ho ho', while the kids' faces stretched into enormous smiles. When he released her Cara was sputtering, but she still couldn't find the words, so he kissed her again. The next time he released her, she held up her hand and said 'ok.' Julian smiled, the food came, Kafir announced 'let's eat' and everybody dug in.

Much later that night, after several stops at bars, dens and dives that did not forbid children, which were a lot, after the music, dance, hookahs and drinks, they all returned to their hotel. Julian, who had stayed close to Cara's side the entire evening, entered too. Cara shared a suite with the twins, who immediately went to their room. They closed the door, then put their ears on it. They could hear their father's voice. It sounded soothing, and then the volume decreased to whispering. Selle ran and got a glass. There was just silence. Gio and Selle looked at each other, put their ears back to the door, but still nothing. The silence was killing them both. They cracked the door to peek. Their mom and dad were locked in an embrace, kissing, but at the sound of the door, their mother pushed their father away, went into her room and closed the door. Their father looked at them shrugged, then left. When Selle and Gio relayed the story they got mixed messages.

Selle/Gio: We don't understand. They looked happy.

Aiden: Why didn't you stay in your room?

Kalea: Mom's conflicted.

Quinton: We almost had it.

Marcella: You should have kept your nosy butts out of it.

Leilani: She's just being mom.

The following morning, Cara found everybody already seated for breakfast, a vacant seat between Kafir and Julian. All of them looked like they were up to something. She did not need a mind reader to see that. She lowered herself slowly into her chair. Julian did not try to accost her in any way, a sure sign to guilt.

"What's up?" she questioned, to the eyeballs bouncing all around her.

Kafir cleared his throat, "I already know what you are going to say, they are too young, but I would like to offer Gio and Selle an opportunity to walk the runway in my fall show."

Highly expecting looks from the twins, all focused on her.

"What does your father say?" she muttered not looking his way.

A giant exhalation of air, "He says it's ok with him, but it's up to you," a mono response.

Cara turned toward Julian. He smiled, "I'm trying to get you back in my house. There's no way in hell I'm going to release your last babies without your permission." He leaned in close, his breath hot in her ear, "But we could discuss it further in private."

She pushed him back. It was a trap, pure and simple. Kafir wanted them. The twins were dying to go. Julian, of course, recognized the opportunity, but deferred it to her. The villain would be the person who said 'no'. While she was ruminating, Kafir added the restrictions and stipulations.

"Their father has some concerns. He does not want his underage children posing in any provocative shots. No female on female, male on male, male on female shoots. Shelly and Brian are to accompany them at all times and they can only do runway and photo shoots at non-school times."

The twin's eyes swung from Kafir, back to Cara. She took a deep breath. That just about covered any and all of her objections, but still, they were her last babies.

Julian picked up on her thoughts immediately, he took her hand and kissed it, "Believe in what we've given them and let them go," he whispered in her ear.

Cara said 'yes', then immediately had to excuse herself. She had something irritating her contacts. When she came out of the ladies room after bawling her eyes out, Julian was right there.

"I'm proud of you," he said taking her into his arms.

Cara sniffled, her head on his chest, "They're all gone, all my babies."

"You still have me," Julian suggested.

"Yeah right, me and half a million other people. You don't need me," she mumbled.

"You're wrong. I actually belong only to you. It might have taken me some time, but I have also always needed you too." He lifted her chin and kissed her deeply. She sighed and leaned into him, then the twins came around the corner and she pushed him away.

Julian smiled, shrugged and went back to join Kafir.

"Conflicted," Gio and Selle said in harmony.

CHAPTER 33

The remainder of that summer Cara tried to reinvent herself. She found she resided in a huge empty house. Marcella was bound and determined to do her own thing. She was often up and gone by the time Cara arose. She would have worried if not for Julian's network. Enough said. Her babies started their daily runs to Kafir's, which eventually morphed into stay-overs, which eventually morphed into we'll be home after the show.

Her anger at Julian continued to dissipate as she recognized she slept fitfully without him. She was pressed to admit any need of him and yet over the years her body had acclimated to his comings and goings. She wanted things to be how they used to be, but how to do that when her children knew their dirty little secret. She liked to think she was bohemian, but apparently she wasn't quite there yet, and she wanted her children to never be there. So, she sat alone.

Once Cara returned to her house, she found she had lost her drive. Not to be a costume designer, but to travel and submit proposals. On an evening out with friends, she had a chance encounter with a member of a children's theater. One thing led to another and one week later, she was the costume designer for their company. The caveat of the deal was that she would also teach costume design to the children. She was ecstatic. Several days after having coffee with the administrator of the theater, he was injured in a car crash. Cara was livid. She called Julian.

"It didn't do it," he said, "come home," and hung up.

Cara was afraid for a while. She loved everything about the job, but she didn't want anyone injured because of her. Still, she wasn't ready to submit. She continued living in her house and Julian continued living in his.

That fall, the twins having turned thirteen, left with Kafir, one week before his fashion show in Paris. It would be transpiring in the Hall of Mirrors at the Palace Versailles. Her older children assured her they had made all the arrangements for her and themselves. Their father would be ensconced in his chateau outside the city and not near their location. They further advised that he would be in Kafir's VIP section and she would have no face to face contact with him. Aiden and Quinton picked her up at the Charles de Gaulle Airport. Something about them seemed older. Was it the way they were dressed, or their stance and attitudes, or their speech patterns? She couldn't put her finger on it, but their trip had aged them. She did not want to think of what experiences could be attributed to their change. Never the less, they both hugged and kissed her like her old little boys, then chatted excitedly about their accommodations and the festivities.

They had a magnificent suite at Trianon Palace Versailles. It was humongous, with four bedrooms, each with its own private bath. Cara, of course, was designated the master bedroom. A beautiful silk robe was spread on her bed waiting her arrival. There was a balcony overlooking the actual Palace of Versailles, baskets of fruit, champagne and vases of flowers everywhere. She would have loved a bath and a nap but with her European travelers all there, she was regaled with stories, pictures and the re-telling of all their adventures.

The day of the show Marcella, Kalea and Leilani spent the day shopping, while Aiden and Quinton contented themselves with movies and video games. Cara spent most of her day in the tub. Everyone eventually regrouped, got dressed and proceeded to the show. There was high tension and expectation in the air. Cara felt all of it in the pit of her stomach. She and the kids were seated in the front row near the foot of the runway. The room was a cacophony of whose who: actors, athletes, musicians and reality stars, all milling around until the lights flickered, indicating the show was about to begin. As people took their seats, just before the lights died completely, Cara caught sight of Aristo sitting in the front row center with an exotic figure draped all over him. She inhaled sharply and as the darkness descended he looked up, caught her eyeing him and gave her a nefarious wink. Cara felt like a load of bricks had been dumped in her gastric track, each one hitting her heart on the way down to her stomach.

The candelabras came up creating a soft romantic light reflected majestically in the mirrors. That alone created a sense of awe. Then the music began, and the runway came to life. Cara kept her eyes glued to the entrance, watching each model as they traipsed along but only to a certain point. There would be no more eye contact if she could help it. That was until Giselle appeared in an oversized sleeveless black and white ostrich feathered floor length coat. She advanced slowly in impossibly high heeled boots, throwing back the hood almost immediately. Halfway down the runway, she stopped, opened the coat and released Giovanni from beneath it. He stood and stalked forward in an open vest with leather pants. The crowd went wild. Somewhere along the walk way they engaged each other and when they stepped apart, he was in the coat and she was in the vest. Everyone applauded as they made their trek back to the curtain. She heard her children cheering loudly. Was that appropriate? Who cared? Cara felt herself grinning insanely and as they walked back she forgot to divert her line of view and wound up looking directly at Aristo who was grinning just as wildly. They made eye contact and continued smiling deliriously at each other. To hell with it. This was not about him or her, it was about their babies. Gio and Selle made three to four more passes in different outfits, each more outrageous than the last. At one point Selle walked Gio out on all fours, collared with a leash. Cara was stunned by his seductive feline movements. She recognized them immediately, like father like son. This time when their eyes met, Julian gave her a lascivious wink. Cara returned to her avoidance tactics.

At the end of the show, Kafir emerged with a twin draped on each side. The crowd jumped to its feet with a standing ovation. When Cara had the view and the nerve to look, she found Aristo's seat empty. Just as well. That was a confrontation she would not be sorry to miss. The whirlwind of the show besieged her and she was swept up by her kids and whisked behind stage. The madness was even more frenzied. There were photographers. Models in states of just off stage to semi-nude, celebrities, journalist, and other fashion designers all toasting, talking and photo-opting everywhere. Soon she and her children had champagne and were standing with Kafir, who was still wearing her twins. Kisses were exchanged by all and they were pressed into a group photo. For a brief moment, Cara wished Julian was there with them celebrating their babies' exhilarating moment with Kafir, as the deity in the center. And just before the flash went off he was, his arm around her waist, his body squeezed to hers. All the children were on him, even Gio and Selle left Kafir. Kafir bellowed his over the top laugh, pushed in among the hugs and slapped Aristo on the back. Perfect, Cara thought, then she left the group in search of more champagne. She was just turning away from more congratulations as the mother of this 'phenomenal new find', glass in hand, when someone accosted her elbow. She had to stop or risk losing her just obtained refreshment. Cara turned. It was Julian.

"We need to talk," he said.

"Julian, I have no idea what we need to talk about, but I'm almost certain whatever it is, now is not the time. Besides, where is your...." Cara paused to search for the right word.

"Arm candy," he finished.

"Arm candy," she repeated. "How quaint."

"Cara," his volume dropped, his voice took on a deep husky note and his grip tightened. "Don't start."

Just then his candy advanced out of the crowd, bee-lined over to them, re-draped herself on Aristo and turned a dismissive stare on her. Cara jerked her arm free and walked away.

The feverish tempo of the evening continued. Her children, at some point, suggested she go back to the hotel. Obviously, they were trying to ditch her and given her encounter with their father and the amount of alcohol she had consumed, she thought it was a pretty good idea too. Back in the suite, she soaked in a long hot bath drinking two giant pitchers of water. Once dry and rehydrated, Cara put on her beautiful silk robe. It was navy with pink blossoms scattered on the back stretching over and down one arm and encircling the hem. She loved the feel of it and saw no purpose of putting anything between it and her skin. The suite was excessively quiet and having nothing else to do, she opened the sliding glass door to the balcony, letting in all the frenzied excitement that continued below. Not in the least bit tired, she lit candles on the balcony, found more champagne, retrieved another pitcher of water and seated herself outside to absorb the final sensations of the night.

Julian was peeved. He had ditched his date almost immediately after leaving the event. She had been way to presumptive and obvious. She had approached him and Cara without permission and had done everything except hand him her panties. Not only had he had his assistant give her walking papers, he also cancelled all her access to any other event, closed out her hotel bill and provided her a morning ticket back to the states. He had brightened when he ran into his kids at an after party, only to discover their mother was not with them. Leave it to Cara to be a party pooper. He did not get a chance to question them about the misinformation they had provided about their mother, since they all seemed to disappear at once. Since his private plane had landed just prior to the event and he had come directly to the show from the airport. He decided he needed to go home, freshen up, change clothes and decide what he would do next.

Julian welcomed the stillness of his space. He didn't bother with the lights, since he knew these rooms by heart. Following his usual pattern, he made a stroll through the place stopping short when he saw a flicker of light on his bedroom balcony. He approached slowly. To his surprise, he found a pair of feet propped up on the balcony, attached to legs completely uncovered except for a robe tucked between. The precarious owner of all this, was none other than, Cara, who nonchalantly continued sipping champagne. Perfect.

Julian quietly went into the bathroom, disrobed, washed his face, freed and ruffled his hair and exited wearing a loosely wrapped towel, champagne flute in hand.

"I hope you saved some for me," he said leaning on the balcony door.

Cara choked on the sip she was taking, jerked her feet down, attempted to stop coughing and cover herself at the same time. Julian stepped out, poured a glass of water and handed it to her. She continued to try and catch her breath, but the surprise had been so great that her inhaled gasp had sent champagne not just down the wrong pipe, but up her nose and out her eyeballs as well. When she was finally able to draw in enough breath that she thought she might survive, she was still unable to make a sound.

"Surprise!" Julian grinned.

Still unable to speak, just barely able to breathe, she wondered what the sentencing in France was for murder or mayhem, then why was Julian there and why was he wearing a towel? Julian watched the play of thoughts across her face and the blush that developed when she got to the towel. His smile deepened.

Finally Cara was able to croak out a single word, "Why?"

"Why am I here?" Julian asked helpfully.

Cara gave an almost unperceivable nod.

"I was going to ask you the same thing," he replied smiling

widely.

Cara gave him ugly eyes. He laughed.

"Ok, ok," he continued, "this is my suite."

She jumped up and croaked out another word, "No!"

"Yes." Julian motioned for her to follow and since she was finally on her feet, she did. He approached a wall, put his foot on a piece of molding and stepped aside as the wall drew apart. There inside, Cara saw a walk in closet filled with men's clothing, a wall of shoes with elevated heels and an island covered in jewelry and shades. She sat down heavily on the foot of the bed.

"But the kids said they'd made all the arrangements," she muttered miserably.

"They did," he piped in, "they asked me for a key and I gave it to them."

Then Julian did something he hardly ever did, he roared with laughter. At the time, he had thought nothing about giving them a key, but now looking at Cara shocked shitless, he knew that both of them had been hoodwinked and bamboozled. Frankly, he was enjoying it. No one ever got anything over on him, and here, his own children had gotten the best of him and he hadn't had a clue.

Cara took his laughter as an affront. She hopped off the bed in a surge of energy, "I'm outta here," she hissed.

"Really?" Julian inquired, leaning lazily in the doorway, "And where might you be going? This city and every other city nearby are booked tight for fashion week. You might as well relax and enjoy it."

"Relax," she practically shouted.

"Yes," he soothed, "Relax. It's not me. Your kids connived this. So, I think we could use this opportunity to talk."

"Talk," Cara repeated robotically.

"Yes, talk. Unless you have something else on your mind," he said huskily.

Cara suddenly remembered she was in a robe and he was in a towel. She tightened the belt which just accentuated the nothingness she was wearing beneath it.

"Nice," he drawled.

"Julian," she growled angrily.

"Ok, just talk. Come on." He took her elbow and steered her back to the balcony.

"Wait, why are you wearing a towel?"

"Because you're wearing my robe."

Cara's mouth flew open, then she snapped it shut. Julian laughed. Wait until she caught up with her kids. While attempting to situate herself and the robe, which kept slipping off or open, Julian retrieved an ice bucket, several bottles of champagne and fresh flutes. She eyed him suspiciously.

"Don't look at me," he grinned, "you're the one that lit the candles."

She grimaced.

Julian did exactly what he said they'd do – talk. He started with the twins, their impact on the show, their visual imagery, then the fashion show with its textiles and combination of layering and last of all, about the people who were there. Somewhere along the way she got lost in his words. She forgot she was on the balcony with little on next to a man wearing less, both sipping champagne and reliving the moments of their children's lives, issues, and chicaneries. Hours later, it was hilarious that both of them had been fooled. Through the laughter and tears, Julian finally said what he wanted.

"It's time for you to come home."

Cara stopped in mid mirth. "What? What are you talking about? I am home."

"No, my home," he insisted and all the humor had left his face.

"Wait a minute. You show up with arm candy and you think I'm gonna consider moving back in with you? That's ridiculous!" Cara huffed.

"You don't see her here, do you?" he whispered, "I told you before, do not be fooled by the visuals."

"I don't know who you think you are, but whoever it is, I'm not interested."

"Are you sure?" he cooed and his hand came down just above her knee and slid up her thigh.

Cara yelped and attempted to halt the progress of his hand. In her struggles, her robe began falling open. She was angry, but she was also getting hot and not in an exertional type of way. It was more like her internal butterflies had turned into dragons and were scorching her insides. How long had it been? Obviously too long, if a hand on the thigh could elicit such a reaction. She heard Julian purr, pull her chair next to him, then felt his other hand slip inside the top of her robe, skimming along her ribs and brushing the underside of her breast. His face was on her neck.

"Julian, please," she pleaded.

"Please, what?" he hummed.

What, indeed.

Cara woke in a tangle of sheets. She didn't have a hangover, thank God, but her mouth felt like she had been through the Sahara and her body felt like she'd been brutally massaged. She sat up slowly catching a whiff of coffee and the sound of running water. Treading lightly into the bathroom, she was immediately scooped into the shower. Her protestation of wet hair and near-by kids fell on deaf ears as Julian soaped, smoothed and sexed her up. She escaped, just barely, before round two. Retrieving her robe from the balcony, she kicked Julian's towel, swigged some champagne and went in search of coffee.

Exiting the bedroom, she found all of her children in various forms of dress, from robes and pajamas, to perhaps what they had had on the previous evening. She received a half-hearted 'hi' from the room. Everybody immediately looked behind her, then went back to whatever they were doing. She figured they were tired and probably hung over, and continued to the coffee carafe on a cart ladened with food. Cara poured a cup of black French roast, took a deep whiff and a long slow sip. In the interim, Julian appeared in a long white terry cloth robe. The room went ballistic.

"Dad, you're here." The exclamation was resounding. That was followed by a lot of self-congratulations, high fives and 'job well done'.

Julian dropped on the couch beside her, "Apparently, there are people who wanted us back together," and he leaned over and licked her neck. Cara swatted at him, their children giggled and Julian smiled.

Later that morning, Julian left with things to do. All their children went to bed and Cara decided to take a walk. She was descending on the elevator when it stopped on a random floor. The doors opened, and there was Julian in the hallway handing yet another woman an envelope, at which point she pulled him near and kissed him on the lips. For Cara, it was like watching a horror movie in slow motion. Shocked, she stood motionless until the elevator bell dinged. Julian turned at the sound, saw her and ran towards her. Cara backed up until she hit the rear wall, still mute in her misery. The doors closed just before he reached them and the elevator continued its descent. The motion jarred her out of her suspension. She emerged angry, humiliated and energized. She asked the doorman for a cab to the airport but there was a wait. She took off down the street at a full run. After several blocks, she realized she had no destination or directions and sat down at the first outside table she encountered to rethink her life.

Julian called for his car on the elevator ride down. He crossed the lobby at a clipped pace, questioned the doorman about Cara's possible destination then took off towards the airport. The doorman shook his head. Had the rude American waited for him to complete his statement, he would have known that the woman ran down the street instead of taking a cab to the airport.

Cara was still sitting at the table enjoying a glass of wine and eating croissants when a limo pulled to the curb and a highly agitated Julian emerged from the car. His tightly controlled steps brought him table side, then to a chair. Tenseness radiated off of him and washed over her. She had no idea why he was so mad. She was the one offended and she had decided to let it go. When in France......

"What are you doing?" he questioned through tight lips.

"What does it look like?" she countered.

"Do you know I've just come from the airport?"

"Really? Picking up more candy?"

"Cara, I was there trying to stop you from leaving." He leaned forward, drew down his shades to peer over the lenses at her. "I was frantic, running through the airport like a madman."

Cara pulled her shades down as he did and looked at him. "You? Frantic? Now that's something I'd have to see to believe," and she pushed her glasses back in place using her middle finger.

They sat in silence. Stalemate.

"There were actually seven women here with me. A different one for each fashion show."

Cara was stunned. Not by the number of women but by the admission. Julian never explained anything. "I've sent them all away. What you saw was the last one being served her traveling papers." She was speechless. After the car had circled the block several times, Julian finally rose. "It's time to go," he said holding out his hand to her.

Cara stared at it. She couldn't sit at the table forever. She looked up at him and took it.

CHAPTER 34

They remained in France as a family for the rest of fashion week with his children filling in as his dates. It was a royal group, Julian dressed to the nines as Aristo, the now city wide infamous twins, a pair of exotic Polynesians, two gorgeous guys and an overly dramatic aspiring actress. Cara attended all the shows but she was several seats down given the number of children in attendance. It was fine with her, Aristo still gave her the heebie jeebies.

The flight back was uneventful. Julian and Cara returned alone. Gio and Selle remained with Kafir for some additional modeling gigs, they were exclusively his. Shelly and Brian stayed as well. Jenna and Fernando had shown up and weaseled into some activities, then the older kids took off with them. Everybody promised to be back where they were supposed to be by the time school started. Julian spent most of the flight trying to convince Cara to come home. She was loving the invitation but not feeling its implications. Upon return to the compound, Cara asked to be dropped off at her house.

"As you wish," Julian replied tightly.

Her suitcases were placed in the driveway and the car pulled away. The driver could have at least carried them to the door, but she supposed this was her punishment for not acquiescing to Julian's wishes. Cara placed her purse on the steps, then made several trips back and forth to get all her luggage to the door. It was a work-out and instead of dissipating her anger it only intensified it. By the time she finished, she was sweating and cursing up a blue streak. Opening up the front door, she let out a loud shriek. Her house had been completely gutted. It was empty.

Cara stomped herself all the way over to Julian's. She banged on the door. No answer. She yelled several obscene words. No answer. Finally she tried the door, it opened. Once in, she hollered his name from the entry way. Several of his assistants came out into the hallway. They took one look at her, turned around and went back from whence they came. Continuing her stomping rampage, she immediately went upstairs. His private studio was locked and he wasn't in his bedroom. In her old adjacent suite of rooms she found her studio recreated from her house, right down to the placement of her sketches on the wall. In her upstairs search, she never found her bedroom. That would probably be because she always shared his. Cara began to realize that ten thousand square feet was a lot to search, especially if someone did not want to be found. She went back to the studio and hammered on the door. She just knew he was hiding in there. Julian was in fact, in the kitchen enjoying a glass of juice and watching her on his laptop.

Cara really wanted to break something but didn't have the heart to destroy something beautiful just because she was pissed. She settled for displacing everything she could. She threw and kicked pillows, especially anything with his insignia. She tossed covers, disrupted frames, turned over vases and awards and everything else that was movable from the second floor to the first and all the way out the door. By the time she walked home, she was exhausted, until she found all her belongings were gone. Damn it. She got hot all over again.

Cara stomped back to the other house. This time the door was locked. She hammered, she hollered, she rang the bell like a mad man, all without results. Finally, she sat down on the front steps. In her initial angry march, she had left all her stuff on the porch of her house, including her purse. The grounds were secure. Now she found herself without her phone, money or cards. Apparently, when Julian was ready, he'd do something with her. Cara sat there simmering for an hour. Finally, Julian pulled up in one of his convertible sports car.

"Get in," he ordered.

"Where are you taking me?" she demanded.

"What difference does it make since you don't want to be here with me? Get in."

Cara hesitated. "No." She had been locked out the compound before. That was never going to happen again.

"I said, get in," he commanded.

"And I said no," she insisted.

Julian threw the car into park. For a minute, Cara thought he was going to get out and physically attempt to force her in. She could not see his eyes because of his shades. He heart clenched just a little. He muttered something under his breath, changed gears and drove away. Cara exhaled loudly. That was unpleasant, but it hadn't solved anything. She was still outside on the steps.

An hour later, she was still there, hopeless, hungry and soon to be in the dark. As the sun set the front lights came on. Cara wasn't sure if someone had been kind enough to do that for her or they were set on automatic. She didn't bother to move. The front door creaked open. Cara turned to find Julian donned in a silk robe standing in the doorway.

"Are you ready to come in?" he quipped.

Cara could not trust herself to answer, so she nodded her head.

"I can't hear you," he prodded.

"Yes," she said through gritted teeth.

"Ok then, come on," he cajoled.

She could hear the humor in his voice and her anger began to roil up again. She would try to hold it in, at least until she got inside.

"It will cost you a kiss to enter," he smirked as she drew near.

"Julian, if you think, after all this, I'm going to......."

He began closing the door.

"Ok. Ok. One kiss and you better believe that's all."

"That's all that I asked for, unless you have other ideas."

"Oh, I have other ideas and they all begin with 'M': malicious, mayhem, maul, murder."

Julian laughed.

Cara intended to just give him a quick peck on the cheek but as she leaned in he grabbed her and gave her full frontal contact with a deep French kiss.

"Tres bien," he said, as she snatched away.

Cara did not get a chance to tell Julian she would not sleep with him. He escorted her to her studio suite, advised she had a pull-out couch and left. She closed the door. There was no lock on it. Once she had finally calmed down and went in search of food, she found that Julian had actually incorporated most of her belongings into his house. Each time she found something, it gave her a pleasant sensation. She had not been displaced, she'd been absorbed.

Their children were ecstatic that she was back in the big house. All their stuff from her house had been jammed into their old rooms at his house, so they all had a fun time exchanging, tossing or reinventing their possessions. There was a lot of reminiscing. All the older children no longer lived in the house. Marcella spent most of her time between school auditions and extra classes. Selle and Gio, did return to school as agreed, but they piled on a lot of additional shoots that took them off and out almost every weekend.

Cara continued at her children's theatre, then came upon an opportunity to have a private showing of her work. Well, maybe not private. Anyway, she met some local artist at a charitable event. They were organizing a gallery showing of their work and invited her to participate. Each artist had their own set of rooms, it sounded fun. She did not tell Julian. She worked late into the night, pulling, redesigning and recoloring her sketches. She enlarged, overlapped and fused various renderings with fabric, textiles and trim. When she was finally pleased, she had them framed and called the gallery people for pick-up and delivery. It was a great diversionary activity. She had been at Julian's now for several weeks and only saw him in passing, even though they slept just one wall apart. She was beginning to feel like an acquired possession, and that did not feel good. Nonetheless, she carried on. After all, she had asked to stay.

The night of her gallery opening, all of her children made a surprise visit. Even Kafir swept in, bringing a slew of designers in his wake. The city as a whole responded, bringing in art critics, businessmen, yuppies, students and a wide swatch of the general public. The only person missing was Julian.

Cara smiled throughout the entire six hour event. Initially it was real, but as the time wore on and the realization that Julian wasn't coming sunk in, it lost its brightness and became tighter and tighter. At the end, sitting alone on a bench in the quiet, Cara still could not believe Julian had not come. She had slipped a personal invitation under his pillow. She was so stupid. Lost in those thoughts she heard the door open. She thought it was probably the cleaning crew, so she didn't bother to turn.

"That's not the look I would have expected for what I hear was a highly successful showing."

She turned. Julian. He was holding one of the largest bouquets she had ever seen. He approached and kissed her on both cheeks.

"Congratulations," he whispered, "Now, I want a private tour."

Holding hands they walked her exhibit. Julian asking questions about this and that, retracing steps, requesting more detail. They talked into the night then he kissed her cheeks again and left. She took her own car home, when she arrived, he was nowhere to be found. The show ran for two weeks and each night

Julian appeared after hours for a new review. She tried to divert him to the other artist, but he remained insistent that he wanted to just see her renderings. Julian always appeared with something: champagne, flowers, candlelight dinners, once with traveling musicians. Always they walked hand in hand and always he came up with new questions, a different perspective, a historical reference and a kiss good night. Cara was loving it. She waited in anticipation when they would return in the same car to the same room. It never happened.

On the last day of her show, Julian did not show at all. She waited and waited until she realized the fool for which she was. She exhaled, found her purse and headed for the door. A man in black was there upon her exit. He handed her a beautifully wrapped box and pointed her to a waiting limo. Julian loved drama. Once inside the car, she discovered it was empty. Opening the box, she found tons and tons of tissue paper and at the very bottom, a card with a hotel key inside.

The suite was divine. It was filled with flowers, appetizers, wine and another box that contained one of the most beautiful and delicate French lace lingerie sets Cara had ever seen. She rushed to the bathroom to find her packed suitcase waiting with a note, 'don't soak too long.' She laughed, jumped in, then out of the tub. Spritzed on perfume, donned the lingerie, then practiced poses and positioning. Three hours later, she had consumed most of the appetizers, polished off a bottle of wine and was attempting not to open another one. She failed.

Cara woke up on top of the covers with a fierce headache. There was no sign of Julian. She crawled out of the bed, walked slowly to the bathroom and into a cold shower. She had just pulled on a pair of jeans and a t-shirt and was reaching for the phone to order coffee when someone began pounding on the door. Besides causing great distress to her head, she wondered why that was even necessary and was about to give someone a big piece of her mind. When she opened the door her heart fell. It was Shelly and Brian. Her knees began to tremble.

"There's been an accident," Shelly whispered.

"The Twins?" she stuttered.

"No," Brian cut her off, "Julian."

It was a long ride to the hospital. Cara didn't hear anything clearly. She caught words like, motorcycle, severe injuries, ICU. Upon arrival to the floor, Cara stopped short. The waiting room was packed with some of the most beautiful, exotic women in every color and shade in various stages of mourning. She would probably have gotten no further had not Brian and Shelly each taken an arm and propelled her forward. In the private waiting area she found all of her children wailing down the house. She was hit with a barrage of questions.

"Mom, where have you been?"

"Why didn't you answer your phone?"

"When can we see dad?"

"What's going to happen?"

Brian disappeared and returned with the doctor. He took Cara into the hallway, explained that Julian had suffered a severe head injury, had been rushed to surgery and was currently intubated on a ventilator in ICU. He suggested she see him first, then usher their children in. She did not believe she was up to the task, but since she was the mother and significant other, it all fell to her. The doctor led her to the room, his body guards were outside the doorway. Cara took a deep breath and entered.

People on vents don't look like they do on TV, sleeping in peaceful serenity. Cara thought Julian looked dead. He was pale as a ghost. He had been shaved clean from head to toe, and had a giant dressing covering most his head. The only indication that he was still of this planet was the rise and fall of his chest, but the machine at his bedside was doing that. She approached him slowly, took his hand and leaned in close.

"Oh God, Julian," she whispered. She brought his hand to her lips and kissed it. "I don't know what the hell you think you're doing, but you're not getting out of this that easily. We've got a room full of distraught children, so you are going to have to pull yourself together." She realized when she finished, she had spoken in anger and the trembling that had started in her knees, racked her entire body. She sat down on the bed. She was still holding his hand.

Only two people were allowed by the bedside in ICU. Cara walked each child back, starting with Marcella, who volunteered to go first. There was no time for Cara to cry, she had to bolster up all her babies. Her heart hurt by the time she finished the rounds. No one was allowed to stay bedside, but no one would leave the hospital either. The private waiting room became their personal domicile, full of funky, damp, swollen eyed people. Two days later, Julian was extubated and moved to a private room. He still had not regained consciousness, but at least he was breathing on his own. The doctors gave vague explanations of expectations, diagnoses, and recovery timeframes. Everyone moved from the waiting room to Julian's bedside. Shelly and Brian became couriers of food, clothing, and encouragements. Their children talked to him all day, taking individual turns and creating stimulating activities, with intermittent clandestine crying spells. Cara had him all to herself every night and into the morning hours. She talked her entire shift, filling him in on everything from the kid's lives and their current mental states, to the weather, political situation, world events, and hospital gossip. It was during this time, three days after his extubation, she suddenly realized maybe Julian would not wake up.

A spiritual consultant had visited and advised that people will often hold on until they have been given permission to go by their loved ones. He had to be rescued by hospital security as Julian's staff were busy restraining Aiden, Quinton and Gio. That consultant did not return. Cara had not thought of that. She had always assumed that it was only a matter of time before he got up and told everybody where to go and what to do. He was way too stubborn, arrogant, controlling and determined not to get better. But now, in the darkness listening to a change in his breathing pattern, to the elongation of his exhalations with an extended pause before the next inhalation, it occurred to her that he might be trying to check out.

Cara had a sudden rush of fear, anxiety and anger. She started with a tirade on his self-centeredness that quickly disintegrated into a teary plead for him not to go. There in the darkness, with silent tears falling, she confessed to how she had resisted him, but admitted that she really did love him. She acknowledged that she seldom said it, but vowed to try to do better and be more demonstrative of her feelings. She would even attempt to follow directions, if only he would stay longer. Julian coughed. It was the first sound he had made since the accident. Cara peeled her wet face from his damp gown and sat up. His lips appeared to be moving. She would have been excited, had she not been previously rebuked by the nurses for reporting autonomic movement. Nothing had changed but the movement of his lips. His eyes remained closed, his extremities slack. She leaned forward, watching his mouth. It looked like words with no sound. She leaned closer, her ear just above his lips.

"Damn girl, a brotha gotta die and come back to make you admit how you feel," he croaked.

"Julian," Cara whispered and hugged him tightly. She pulled back, but he gripped her wrist.

"Marry me," he murmured. Cara hesitated. "Humph, nothing but empty promises."

"Ok, Julian, I'll marry you."

"One more thing, for God's sake, stop talking."

CHAPTER 35

Julian and Cara were married by the hospital chaplain. If their children were surprised by their lack of legality, no one gave a clue. They all smiled as witnesses, along with Kafir, Shelly, Brian and Kris. Julian refused further treatment. The doctors recommended inpatient rehabilitation. He declined everything but additional imaging that revealed his cranial injuries had resolved.

The following day, status post discharge, everyone was loaded into limos, taken directly to the airport and ushered into his private plane. Julian was the last to load, requiring the assistance of his body guards to make it up the steps. He fell into his seat, weak and winded and did not insist Cara sit by his side. In fact, he dropped an iron curtain of silence that everyone acknowledged and adhered to. It was going to be a long flight, Cara was okay with it. She had Julian back. She could catch up on some much needed sleep and she was in control. She was taking him to a quiet, beautiful, healing place: Hawaii.

If Julian was surprised by their destination or had any qualms about it, he never said a word. Upon their arrival to her Kauai compound, he secluded himself in one of the guest houses. Over the next several days he summoned his children to him one by one. The end result was he wanted all of them to go back to their lives. Slowly they all departed and Cara was left alone in the main house. She never received a summons.

Cara had one of the other guest houses set up as a rehab facility. It had all the state of the art equipment including a full-time occupational therapist, physical therapist and masseuse. There was also a nutritionist and chef standing by. Julian had so far refused to participate in any of it.

By the beginning of the second week, Cara lost her patience and her anger and resentment began to brew. She had been counseled on the death/dying/anger/grief process and had been trying to give Julian the benefit of the doubt, but to hell with all that. They literally had full-time staff sunning on the beach and picking their noses while getting paid for nothing. It was time for someone to do something.

Cara walked over to Julian's cottage and banged on the door. No response. She had been expecting that and came prepared. The mainland compound was Julian's establishment, but the Hawaiian compound was hers. She took out her keys and opened the door. Cara could not have been more surprised. The place was a pigsty. There were open containers, clothes and dishes everywhere. She found Julian lying in bed staring at the ceiling. He had apparently gone rogue or insane, because he was dressed only in a Polynesian sarong and had not attempted any personal care. Obviously he had not shaved since their arrival, his hair was matted in places and self-dreaded in others and he smelled.

Cara cleared her throat. No response. "Julian," she started.

He pulled up on his elbows and stared at her. "What are you doing here? Get the hell out," he demanded.

"I'm not going anywhere. You need to get the hell up and out," she replied.

"Who do you think you are? Who do you think you're talking to?"

"I know who I am. I'm the wife of a jacked up, sorry ass has been."

That did it. Julian starting throwing everything within arm's reach and there was a lot, but Cara gave back as much as she was served. Because she was a moving target, she took a few glancing blows but Julian took the brunt of the exchange. When he finally took a blow to his noggin he threw his legs to the floor and sat up. Cara took off out the door. She was standing on the grass a few feet away by the time Julian made it to the door. He was sporting a growing red knot just above the left eyebrow.

"I'm gonna whip your ass," he growled.

"Come and get it," she jeered.

He made to lunge, but stumbled and rolled down the stairs.

"Tsk, tsk," she continued nonplussed, "guess that wouldn't have happened if you'd gone to therapy." Cara heard a low steady growl. She was actually loving it, any response was better than none. She continued to verbally taunt him, although she did keep a healthy distance between them. She did not believe Julian could catch her, but she was well aware of his surprises. After an hour or so she grew tired and had run out of things to say. Julian had never moved, remaining face down in the grass. She knew he was hot in more ways than one. The intensity of his anger was scorching even at her distance, but she offered him no solace, no water, and no help.

"My, how the mighty have fallen," she cajoled. "I should get a photo of this," and she went into the house to find her phone. When she returned, Julian was gone. Now all the humor was over. She went back inside locked the doors and shut and locked all the ground floor windows. Maybe she'd gone too far. She began a tentative search of her house. She was still trying to get a handle on her heart rate and stomach contents when the phone rang. She was so wound up, she hit the back of her head on the doorframe of a closet she was checking. It was Kris. He was calling to say Julian was in the therapy house. She exhaled loudly. She had gone beyond poking the bear and for a minute she thought she was about to get bitten. If Julian returned to the man he had previously been, it would only be a matter of time before her comeuppance. If he didn't, then she had nothing to worry about.

Julian became an avid disciple of therapy. He worked out every day from dawn to dusk. Cara was not allowed anywhere near the sessions, but she could see his progress when she spied him going to and fro. He never came to the big house and basically they were still not speaking. She reinstated the nutritionist and chef who sent meals daily to the cottages, but whether Julian partook of any of it, she didn't know.

Weeks later, sitting in her kitchen eating fruit salad, Julian suddenly appeared. She had finally gotten over her fear of a sneak attack and had gone back to open windows and doors. He knocked softly.

"May I come in?" he questioned gruffly.

Cara was so shocked by his surprise visit, she merely nodded. She still could not get over his appearance. He had always been so impeccably groomed and now he continued to sport this wild look. His beard was almost to his chest, his hair was dreaded, and he continued wearing only sarongs. This one was slung low, very low on his hips. Cara tried to keep her eyes above the neckline. She kept her chair and her distance.

"I need to talk to you," he continued.

"Sure," she said, "Have a seat, have some fruit," and she pushed the fruit bowl, as well as, dishes and utensils toward him.

Julian stared down at the offerings and erupted. "Is that all you have to say to me?" he shouted and in one swing, he sent all the items flying. He didn't stop there, continuing up the table to where Cara was sitting, displacing centerpieces, flowers, decorative items, place mats, dishes and glasses until he stood before her with arms raised and with ragged breath. Cara had been so overwhelmed by the suddenness and voracity of his anger and attack that she hadn't moved. She merely closed her eyes and awaited the blow about to be delivered. It was slow in coming, so she opened one eye. He was gone.

Cara surveyed the damage, letting out a long slow breath. Not only had Julian cleaned the table, he had cleared the counter tops as well. She must have been in shock because she had missed that. Now she just looked at all her pretty things broken into shards on the floor. Well, none of this was going to clean itself, so she got up. It could have been worst, she could have been sporting a knot on her noggin. Cara returned with the broom, dust pan and large trash container. She found Julian on his knees making piles of the larger pieces. Neither of them said a word. Cara began sweeping as Julian picked up and deposited all the broken pieces around the room. When they were done, he sat down in a chair with his head in his hands. Cara left him there to retrieve something from her closet. Returning, she laid it on the table in front of him. When he finally looked, she heard him gasp. It was his guitar case, containing his first acoustic guitar. She had had Brian secret it away before their arrival. Now watching him open and caress the instrument, Cara turned away. It was like watching your significant other being intimate with someone else. She left the room.

Cara listened at night through open windows to Julian's struggle with the music. First the fingering, repetitive until perfect, then the phrasing then finally the melodies. It seemed the more the music came back to him, the more Julian came back to himself. Cara noticed that while the beard remained, it appeared to be groomed and his hair was now restrained in a ponytail or a knot. The sarong gave way to shorts and a shirt. She was ecstatic with his progress but not by the continued silence. To avoid the quiet, sadness and loneliness, Cara took to walking the beach again.

One day she walked from morning to dusk, there was no reason to hurry home. When she returned she found Julian by the pool wearing a sarong.

"Where have you been?" he inquired.

"Walking."

"All day?"

"Why not, I have nothing else to do."

He sighed. "Come with me." He got up and led her back to his cottage.

Cara had not been there since her turbulent encouragement session. She hesitated.

"Scared? You should be," he taunted, accosting her elbow and propelling her along.

"Julian, you do realize that I was just trying to help, right?" she stammered out.

"Yeah right, and you do know that I still owe you for that," he added.

Yikes, that didn't sound good and his grip on her elbow tightened. Cara knew that sooner or later that day was going to come back to haunt her. Julian never forgot anything. It had just been a matter of time. She exhaled loudly.

By the time they made it to his door her stomach was doing flips. He threw it open and stepped aside. Cara peeked inside, the floor was covered in flower pedals. There were candles everywhere and there was a table in the center of the room replete with exotic dishes, as well as, several buckets of champagne. Julian suddenly scooped her up and carried her over the threshold, kicking the door close along the way. When he put her down, she slide along the front of his body. That caused a giant intake of air, from both of them.

"I do believe we still need to consummate our marriage," he purred.

"I do believe you are right," she replied.

"Are you hungry?" He inquired

"Starved!" she exclaimed.

"For food," he smiled.

"Who's got time to eat?" she said wrapping her arms around his neck.

In a matter of minutes his sarong was gone and his hair was loose. Whatever she had been wearing was gone too. The sensation of their bare skin on each other, after such a long time, was about all that it took. In seconds they had both come. Round two and three were much more leisurely and in depth. Taking a break, they went to the table for nourishment. They looked at each other in the candle light and smiled.

"Wife, my sweet wife," Julian said between cracking crab legs, "that was very enjoyable, but I hope you haven't forgotten I still owe you an ass whipping."

Cara stopped in mid-bite. "Really? After all this, you still haven't learned forgiveness?"

"No," he replied, "and you still haven't learned submission."

Cara who had a hot retort on her lips, clamped her mouth shut.

"Nice," he taunted, "very nice."

She felt a hot blush rise to her neck and cheeks. She couldn't tell if it was from anger or anticipation.

"It's the anticipation," he laughed.

Later that night, after all the candles had burned down, she took her whipping with great enjoyment. The champagne was gone, they were both thoroughly exhausted, and they laid entangled in each other's arms.

"I love you," he whispered.

"I love you too," she agreed, "thanks for staying."

"Thanks for blocking my escape," he smiled.

Their lives settled into an off-beat rhythm. Julian remained in his house, going to therapy during the day and playing his music at night. In between, he shared meals at Cara's, as well as, sexual encounters. She would fall asleep in his arms only to awake and find him gone, guitar riffs drifting in on a breeze. Their children came on hints and whims. Every spare opening, vacation, holiday, or birthday found them back in the Kauai compound.

Weeks turned into months until Cara actually forgot why they were there. Julian appeared to have made a full recovery and had switched his therapists for a personal trainer working on strength and endurance. They spent time together, they spent time apart. Cara continued her walks, took up art classes, and did the cooking and shopping. Occasionally, Julian would give her a list of something he was in the mood for and so it wasn't odd that on this particular day he produced a list. Cara advised she'd pick it up after class and arrived back home just before dark.

Cara entered a silent and locked house. If she was out at dusk, Julian was usually waiting in her house, sometimes even starting dinner. Tonight her house was quiet. She walked through the rooms calling out. Her pace and heart rate increasing with every step. At the back door, she found the compound dark and void of sound. Cara threw open the doors and ran to Julian's. "No," she whispered, "no, no, no." It was empty, except for the Polynesian prints he used as sarongs, neatly folded at the foot of his bed. She knew better than to go to the exercise cottage, but she couldn't help herself. It too was devoid of all the equipment and gear. It had been reverted back to a guest cottage. Cara walked back home. She promised herself she would not cry. Julian had not asked for assistance in his recovery. She had taken that on herself, goading and torturing him into it. Still, a simple 'thank you' would have been nice, but to leave without good-bye was heart wrenching. What was the purpose of making her his wife? She threw all his requested items away, locked the back door and headed to her room. There on her pillow was a note.

It was time for me to go.

I still have much yet to do.
Love J.

So the whole premise that Julian Aristo Starr had changed was now debunked. He was the same asshole he'd always been. Cara tore the note and envelope into tiny pieces, then cried hot tears of humiliation, as she taped them all back together again and hid them in her bottom drawer.

CHAPTER 36

Cara felt she rebounded well. Ok, not that good. She quit all her classes and became a recluse, only walking the beaches. But, she did get a dog, a puppy from a box in front of a grocery store. After a few months, she and her mutt, Trixie, made friends with a new neighbor a few houses down. After several walks, they finally had dinner together. He had an auto accident with minor injuries a few days later. Cara did not believe it was a coincidence. That relationship withered on the vine.

Her children came and went and no one asked about their father, so she figured they were in direct contact with him. She and Julian had had such a questionable relationship that she figured it was over. They had been greatly held together by their children and now that almost everybody was out and about doing their own thing, she saw it as a sign of the times. Cara did not believe her designation as 'wife' would bode any better for her than it had for any of the previous recipients. She felt it was just a matter of time before the papers arrived. She was not that old and still had a bunch of life to live. What to do?

Cara called Leilani and Kalea. They were native to the islands. One was studying its history and political science and the other was consumed with environmental science. Within no time they had set up a non-profit afterschool and weekend program with art, music, textiles, and history. The program also offered meal subsidies, free health screenings and organic gardening. Sources let her know, Julian liked the idea too. Cara felt she'd found a new fulfillment in life. Excessive funding from an anonymous donor made it all come true. She still preferred not to think of Julian. She'd known from the beginning that he would never be totally hers, and yet she had become gravely entangled with the piece she had. She was having a hard time letting go.

One day Cara returned home from her pattern making instructions at the center, to find all her children had descended in mass. Her quiet household had a barking dog, multiple voices in varying volumes and food on every surface. The energy level was invigorating.

"Mom, you have to come," chimed Gio and Selle, "we'll be presenting at an award ceremony. It's our biggest gig yet. Please mom, please."

While Cara was contemplating that, she was bombarded by the remaining group.

"Oh yeah. When was the last time you were off this island?" questioned Aiden.

"Sounds like fun, let's all do it," declared Marcella

"Mom, don't say no, we can take the dog," added Quinton.

Cara was overwhelmed. Actually, she was delighted. Sure, why not? A hooray went up that was so loud all the dogs in the neighborhood began barking. After all the hoopla, Cara realized she had nothing to wear. Not to worry, Kafir called her a few days later.

"Gio and Selle said you'd be attending their affair. I would love to make you a gown."

"Kafir," she wooed, "you're the only man who dresses me." Although, secretly in her mind, she always suspected Julian had had a hand in it too. Well, not any more.

Cara loved her island home and had come to terms that she might become either a cloistered wife or a divorcee there. So, it was hard to leave the safety and security of her sanctum. When she had agreed to go to the ceremony, she had been caught up in the energy and excitement of her children. Now, sedating her dog and boarding a six hour commercial flight alone, she was having second thoughts. The kids had gotten access to the beach house. Upon arrival, she and Trixie found solace in the sand. Minutes later, child upon child arrived and took everything up another level.

Kafir arrived the following day for a fitting of her gown. It was grayish lavender, off the shoulder with rouging and sequin that flowed from the bodice to the floor. It fit her like a glove and emboldened her with a confidence and beauty she had not felt in a while.

Cara kissed Kafir. "Thank you," she whispered. She thought she heard him say 'it's not from me,' but he appeared confused when she questioned him.

The night of the ceremony was chaos. The twins had luckily gone early for rehearsal, hair and make-up. Cara gave up. There were too many, it was too loud, it was too much. It probably had to do with the laid back island lifestyle she had been living. She was tucked into a chair with a glass of champagne for the final touches to her hair and make-up. Her waist length locks were contrived into an audacious bun and she was inserted into her dress and placed into a car alongside her still raving offspring. Cara soon realized she did not miss mainland living.

Arriving at the venue, everyone was quickly escorted to their seats. In all the mayhem, no one had divulged what type of ceremony they were attending. Now holding a program, she discovered what type it was – music awards. For a moment she felt her gut clench. She looked at her children to the right, who suddenly had a great interest in the ceiling, then to Kafir on her left, who was engaged in an intense conversation with the person sitting next to him who looked like he wasn't listening. She developed a very uneasy feeling. Then the lights went down.

It was like a live concert with performances of rock and roll, rhythm and blues, and pop classics interwoven with new style rock, rap, fusion and electronic. Cara was enjoying herself immensely when Aiden and Quinton said they had to go, they would be performing. Cara was stunned and elated, a double surprise. During intermission, Kalea, Leilani and Marcella disappeared on a bathroom break, never to return. She was having too much fun to be concerned. She and Kafir had drinks and were just getting back to their seats when the lights started to flicker.

The first chord of the first song set Cara on edge. She would have fled had not Kafir's grip on her wrist, restrained her. The shadow at the top of the extended staircase on stage struck a pose. The crowd went wild. Cara's stomach seized. It was Aristo.

He pimped walk down the staircase with a cane, then threw if off and donned his guitar. Everyone was on their feet, except maybe Cara, who was trying to figure out where the gene of deception in her children had come from. She listened and eventually, she had to look. He was everything he had previously been, a consummate performer, perfectionist, fashionista and rouge all rolled into one. He played to the audience, to the women, to the heavens above. Cara didn't fault him for it. He was everything he had always been and in a way she was happy he was back on his game, because she had seen him without it. Somewhere along the line, she noticed Aiden and Quinton as back up musicians. Her heart soared, she knew what music meant to them, like father, like sons. She smiled.

At the end of the performance the applause went on forever. Clearly, they thought Aristo had been lost. He graciously bowed and blew kisses until swept off the stage.

"And now, presenting the lifetime achievement award to Aristo Julian Starr, his children."

The crowd fell to a hush. Cara's heart stopped. There on stage came all of their children. Gio and Selle holding the award and approaching the podium.

"We are happy to present the lifetime achievement award to Aristo Julian Starr, to the best dad and musician ever."

Julian came back on stage. Somehow he had washed off all the make-up, changed clothes, loosed his hair and donned a pair of glasses. Julian. Cara could not take her eyes off of him. The crowd went wild again. There were hugs and kisses exchanged on stage. He approached the mike and quieted the audience.

"I thank you all. As you can see I've been a little busy," and here he looked back at his kids, brushed his eyebrows and his goatee with his pinky finger and pulled a face. Aristo, pure Aristo.

"Still, I would not be here except by the grace of my God and the woman that literally talked me back from death, my wife, Cara." The crowd went silent. "Come to me, Cara," and he held out his hand.

If not for Kafir, Cara would probably have never left her seat.

"Cara," Kafir nudged her, "go to him." She rose trembling, as if in a dream and floated toward the stage. Assistants helped her up the stairs where Julian met her, wrapping his arm around her waist, he led her back to the podium.

He could feel her trembling, "It's ok. It's going to be okay," he whispered and kissed her.

That was when the dream ruptured into the overwhelming sound of the applause. He picked up the award, said thank you again and never letting go of her, ushered them all off stage. While the stage escorts went to the left, Julian took them right, to a back door exit, packing everyone into a waiting limo.

"Save that dress for me," he murmured into her ear, kissed her neck and pressed Cara into the car. The photo flashes started before they reached the street and continued until the limo out-raced everybody on the freeway.

They were whisked to the airport where multiple men wearing black were stationed at the gate. Security was extremely tight until everyone was safely ensconced on the plane. Their children were in high form. There was champagne, food, movies, games, tweeting, facebooking, and texting while waiting their father's arrival. Cara was both physically and emotionally exhausted. She fell asleep amid the revelry only to wake up hours later to find the plane a clear disaster. There were bodies, blankets, food and drinks scattered everywhere. Cara gingerly stepped over everyone and everything to make her way to the window. Still full security and no Julian. She looked down at a stack of newspapers and magazines piled on a table. Front pages of magazines already had a photo of their family with Julian holding her in one arm while raising the award with the other. She flipped through several covers. Cara took a deep breath. Now what?

"I like that one best," said a voice from behind her. She turned to find Julian leaning just inside the bathroom door, shirt open, dreads hanging loose. Cara approached him. He grabbed her by the waist and pulled her in.

"I see you've finally learned to follow direction. You're still wearing that dress," he whispered huskily as he pulled the pins from her hair, causing a cascade of locks, and began to slowly unzip her dress with one hand as the other traced its descent along the bare skin of her back. Cara felt the heat of his hands and his lips on her neck. She shivered. Then, she leaned back, closed and locked the door.

———————